For more information about David Jenkins
please visit his website at www.paxbritannica.co.uk

PAX BRITANNICA

DAVID JENKINS

VAULT

A Vault Paperback

New, revised edition

ISBN 978-0-9926436-4-5

Typeset in Garamond

Published by Vault
36 B Mornington Terrace
London NW1 7RS

PAX BRITANNICA

ONE

The monumental galleries of the British Museum are calm, ordered and climate-controlled. Despite the crowds that teem through their spaces, there is no discernible movement of air. The treasures themselves act as sentinels, unruffled and self-confident in their allotted place in the great historical schema. From the tiniest artefact to the mightiest sculpture, each object is allocated its position on a starting grid that still references the birth of Christ at its fulcrum.

In contrast to the measured calm of the public areas, the office accommodation of Dr Sterland Morris is a maelstrom of disorder. On this fine autumn morning the window of his office has been wedged wide open, in clear contravention of the museum's security guidelines. A free flow of cool air and traffic noise enters at will, guaranteeing to ruffle the voluminous paperwork adorning the shelves, as well as the feathers of any line manager unwise enough to enter unannounced. Morris, an informally attired, fifty-something academic, is sitting at his desk surrounded by piles of books and files. He's on the phone, his demeanour suggesting that he's not relishing making the call. In front of him lies a collection of old coins and objects, which he repositions as he waits to be connected. Finally, he is put through.

"How very good of you to answer. This is Dr Sterland Morris from The British Museum. I'm phoning in connection with the Burgh by Sands hoard. To whom am I speaking?"

"Hello, Dr Morris, very nice to speak to you. This is Robert Jamieson, coroner for North Eastern Cumbria. What news of the find? It's not often we attract the attention of the world's press up here. How are your investigations going?"

Jamieson's boyish enthusiasm and gentle Scottish brogue catch Morris off-guard. He's not in the habit of modifying his mode of address for anyone, but to his surprise he's about to make an exception in the coroner's case.

"Things are going pretty well, thank you, Mr Jamieson. We're making solid progress. The investigations, however, are revealing some unexpected results."

Morris pauses to consider his next step. He's aware that he's poorly-shod for the treacherous terrain that lies ahead but tip-toeing is not a gait that sits naturally with him. "I'd be obliged if we could discuss the findings before compiling a report for the inquest."

"Of course, Dr Morris – we can talk now if it suits you?"

"That would be very helpful."

"And I'd be grateful if you could shed further light on the find," Jamieson prompts. "Is the British Museum interested in acquiring objects from the hoard on behalf of the nation?"

"Yes, indeed. The general nature and content of the hoard fits well with our earliest expectations. Mid-third century Roman; a large cache of gold coins, indicating extreme wealth for the period, a wonderful array of gaming and gambling pieces, quite unique in their completeness, and a few random metal objects of indeterminate use as yet."

"But you say the results were unexpected?"

"Yes, in a way that's likely to pose a considerable problem."

"Whatever the difficulty, I'd have thought we could smooth it out. I've been reacquainting myself with the Home Office Circular on treasure inquests. It's been a while since I've dealt with an archaeological find that requires an inquest, but if the British Museum wants to acquire objects then it should be straightforward to declare the find treasure trove. What difficulties are you anticipating?"

"To put it bluntly, we've come across an anomaly that is causing us considerable concern."

"What sort of anomaly?"

"The metal brooch."

Morris pauses once more, picks up the object in question and examines it under the light from his desk lamp.

"I'm sorry to say that it doesn't fit within the timeframe that we've established for the rest of the hoard."

There's silence at the other end of the line as Jamieson absorbs the implications of what he's heard.

"Is this the eagle crest that the media have found so intriguing?"

"It is."

"And what's the problem with the dating of the brooch?"

"The problem is it's composed of anodised aluminium."

Again, there is a pause, this time longer.

"Correct me if I'm wrong, Dr Morris, but I'm assuming that this is not what you'd expect to be the case?"

"No, not unless the Romans manning Hadrian's Wall in the third century found a way of smelting bauxite that they kept secret from the rest of the world for sixteen hundred years."

Jamieson emits a confused groan. "You have me at a disadvantage, Dr Morris. I've always toiled under the illusion that aluminium is the earth's most widely distributed metal."

"It is, but not in the manifestation that you mean. The Roman army used aluminium salts as an astringent for dressing wounds, but that's about it. The fact is we have a problem that casts serious doubts on the probity of this entire hoard."

Morris's blunt assessment causes Jamieson to shift in his chair.

"Dr Morris, my apologies for appearing so dense, but couldn't we conduct further tests to date the object definitively? What about carbon dating?"

Jamieson is now beginning to flounder, He's grasping at straws, and it's not an experience he relishes at ten past nine on a Monday morning.

"No. Carbon-14 dating is definitely a non-starter. Metal doesn't contain carbon in its structure; only objects that were biological can be dated. Take my word for it, this brooch, badge or crest - call it what you will - is less than fifty years old."

"Fifty years old?"

"I'm afraid so."

"But how can this be?"

"We haven't got a clue at present."

"Then we have to entertain the possibility that the individual who hid this treasure is still alive? Is this the inference I should draw?"

There is a reverberating silence at the other end of the line. Morris is rarely lost for words but he is clearly struggling to define the exact nature of the problem.

Jamieson takes up the challenge once more, a hint of exasperation beginning to reveal itself.

"Dr Morris, I'm having great difficulty absorbing the implications of what you're telling me, and heaven knows what the press is going to make of this. What about the other objects? Do they all appear authentically Roman?"

"Oh yes, everything else is as it should be. One of the bone gaming dice has been carbon dated to the period 250 AD, give or take fifty years. The strangest feature is that the small remains of wool fibre of the garment to which the brooch appears to have been pinned at some point are also contemporaneous with the rest of the find. We're simply unable to account for this. All we can say with any certainty is that someone recently placed a late twentieth century metal object in with a genuine hoard of third century Roman gold coins and artefacts. And they did not dig up the find before doing so. Those objects appear to have remained *in situ* under the soil of Cumbria for eighteen hundred years."

"But you do realise that a coroner can't declare objects to be treasure if there's any prospect that the owner could be alive?"

"Indeed I do," Morris replies.

"And even if the person who placed the brooch isn't the owner of the Roman objects, he may still be able to claim a share of the valuation as the original finder of the hoard."

"So, you can see why we might have a problem at the inquest?"

"Lord, yes - things could get very complicated. This is the stuff of which coroner's nightmares are made. I'll seek advice from colleagues with greater experience of these matters."

"Yes, that might be a sensible place to start."

"Is there anything else I need to know before you compile your written report for the inquest?"

"Only this, I suppose. It's worth remembering that the brooch isn't a fake, as such. In other words, it's not purporting to be a Roman relic. One advantage of anodised aluminium is that it's intended to resist corrosion, but in this case its condition has deteriorated substantially, more than one might anticipate given its supposed recent provenance. This may have been done to prematurely age the object to try and fool the archaeologists, but that's pure conjecture."

"Can we identify the crest, at least? Is it an eagle? Wasn't that the classic symbol of Roman military power?"

"It's an eagle alright. But we think it's likely to be something other than a brooch; something more along the lines of a modern military cap badge, for example. It's been damaged or hacked at somewhat, so it's not complete. The best one can say is that it appears to share strong similarities with current British armed forces insignia. That would seem to be the most likely bet at the moment, but I must stress that this is still highly speculative guesswork on my part. The primary concern of the British Museum is to preserve our historical legacy by acquiring the Burgh by Sands hoard on behalf of the nation. These priorities are clearly provided for under the terms of The Treasure Act 1996; it's really up to the coroner's inquest to implement them justly and fully. And in that respect, the British Museum will do everything within its power to furnish you with appropriate archaeological and historical information to help you discharge your duties."

"I'm grateful for that, of course. But what do you think is going on here? Is it a hoax, a case of grave-robbing, or desecration? What's your professional view, off the record?"

"Off the record, I'd say it doesn't appear to be a case of grave-robbing, nor desecration. In fact, I'd say it's quite the opposite. It feels more like an act of atonement or respect, rather like the laying of a poppy wreath at a war memorial. But in all likelihood we'll never know."

"Oh, Lord, do you really think so?"

"Yes, the odds are we'll never uncover what's gone on here. But, as a historian, I'd urge you not to repeat that comment in ear-shot of my colleagues."

"Of course, Dr Morris, this is strictly between us two."

Morris chuckles at the coroner's well-meaning intensity. "That's good of you, Mr Jamieson. After all, when everything's said and done, no sphere of human cultural activity - no matter how unfathomable - is beyond the interpretive and curatorial reach of the British Museum. That's the official line."

He pauses for theatrical effect, knowing that he has the coroner's full attention. "At least, that's the line we've happily peddled for centuries. And it's always stood us in good stead, whether it's been to stone-wall Greek politicians or to mollify the British exchequer. So, chin up, Mr Jamieson, I have every confidence that the British Museum can devise an elegant solution to the inconsistencies that we're facing here, and in a way that guarantees to serve the interests of both the law of the land and our glorious national heritage."

TWO

DIRECTED LETTER - ADMINISTRATIVE SANCTION
To: (320904071, Lieutenant K.A. Sands, Army Air Corps):
Details of Deciding Headquarters
12th July 2013

Dear Lieutenant Sands

1. I am directed to inform you that in consequence of the following misconduct:
Failure to seek official clearance from a commanding officer before submitting a letter to a national newspaper, thereby expressing a clear opinion that is critical of UK Govt. military policy; such a communication, when published, being detrimental to Army discipline and morale.

Reported by: Lieutenant Colonel I.S. Moncrieff on 7th July 2013

You have been awarded an administrative sanction of:
A formal warning as to your future conduct

Name of Deciding Officer: Major P.B. Mayer

2. The reasons for the award are:
Behaviour that does not comply with the standards of conduct required of Service personnel
3. This sanction to be effective from **13th July 2013**
4. This sanction will be recorded as a Regimental Entry and details will be visible on your CR book for 3 years.

Signed for: (Comd) Colonel W.A.H Jones, MC

"I thought I'd asked you to put that bloody letter away,

Sands. What's the matter with you? Are you deaf or something? And don't blame anyone else. You brought this on yourself."

The subject of the letter stared at the contents before folding it with an air of resigned resentment and sliding it into an inside pocket.

"Concentrate on the job in hand, will you, Sands? Where's the bloody pick-up point? Come on, you're supposed to be the navigator."

The Lynx helicopter turned high over the Galloway Hills and made a second sweep along the eastern shore of Loch Macaterick. The wild beauty of this remote part of south west Scotland had come as something of a surprise to the two young pilots, both of whom were viewing it for the first time from the air. The hills were studded with spectacular lochs and boulder-strewn ridges, whose names, The Awful Hand, The Dungeon Hills and The Rig of the Jarkness, added a melancholic touch to the spectacular, if inhospitable, scene unfolding below them.

Despite the surprising warmth of the autumn sunshine, the atmosphere in the cockpit was decidedly chilly.

"Enlighten me on something else, Sands, if it's not asking too much of you. And I'm not talking about your bloody letter now. But by what right do you consider you're entitled to inflict unsolicited political opinions on fellow officers?"

"By what right? How about freedom of speech?"

"Stop taking the sodding mickey, Lieutenant, you know what I mean. You're not on some university soap-box now. I mean, last night in the officers' mess, what the hell was that all about?"

"There you go, that would be an example of freedom of speech. Trust me, it's an interesting concept. You should try reading about it sometime."

"Ok, here we bloody well go again. That's just what I'm talking about. Don't be so damned insolent, Sands; you know exactly what I mean. There're plenty of brave men in your own regiment who died fighting to protect your precious right to freedom of speech. How about showing a bit or respect for their sacrifice, if nothing else?"

"What, by shutting up, you mean? Rather undermines the strength of your argument, wouldn't you say?"

"No, I bloody wouldn't. And in case you're the slightest bit interested, do you recall what the Colonel called your pathetic little outburst last night?

Sands laughed. "Are you really serious? Last night?"

"That's what I'm talking about."

"You're talking about the old man and his drunken claptrap? Who could possibly forget? But I'm sure you're going to remind me anyway."

"*Reprehensibly discourteous* were his exact words."

Birch enunciated each syllable with relish. "I'd suggest you reflect on that the next time you want to dispense an unwanted view."

"A generous piece of advice," Sands riposted. "However, it hasn't altogether escaped my attention that, in your estimation, being drunk and offensive doesn't disqualify the Colonel from expressing *his* opinion."

"That's a completely different matter, as you damn well know. Being drunk in the officers' mess isn't a crime - far from it - but talking politics is. Or, at least, it bloody well should be. You were discourteous, plain and simple. And he wasn't the only one who'd formed that opinion. Trust me, you got off lightly. He was being generous; just try asking the others what they thought of your post-dinner performance. Utterly contemptible: that's what your behaviour has become."

"Look, sir, I was just pointing out one blindingly-obvious fact. For the past ten years the British army has been championing free speech and democracy in every far-flung location across the globe, but with one notable and singular exception: its own regimental officers' messes."

"Yes, yes, Sands, I know what you said. I was there. Dear God, do I need to keep reminding you? You don't have to repeat it *ad nauseam*. But what the hell kind of response did you expect? And whose side are you on, anyway? You can't be an officer in the Army Air Corps and a barrack-room lawyer.

It's one or the other, Sands, one or the other."

He paused, waiting for a response from his young co-pilot, but none was forthcoming. Was that a flicker of amusement he detected crossing Sands' features? This level of animosity between a pilot and his navigator was most untypical. It was neither tolerable nor healthy. Normally, both officers would be on first name terms, exchanging inconsequential familiarities, not bickering and hurling barbs at each other.

Enraged, Birch ploughed back into the attack for one final assault. "Damn it, Sands, you're not cut out for the discipline and personal sacrifice of regimental life." But as soon as he'd finished speaking, the senior pilot felt belittled by the absurd pomposity of his remark.

His junior colleague sat in silence beside him, smiling inwardly while scouring the landscape below for signs of life.

Sands' quick mouth and sharp mind had long-since marked the young pilot out as a potential threat to a number of the regiment's less adroit and resourceful officers. This intellectual spark and outspokenness were not always welcomed in the officer's mess, where Sands' more provocative contributions evoked a guarded, weary response from those in authority.

"Come on, come on, where are you?" Birch mumbled. Sands had really succeeded in getting under his skin this time. "Three hundred square miles of sodding wilderness, and nine brainless soldiers."

"Down there," pointed Sands, "north east point of the loch."

The helicopter banked to the right, descended swiftly and landed on an open stretch of land near the loch. Two minutes later the pilot and co-pilot were introducing themselves to their new passengers. One of them, a burly NCO, had stepped forward with a wave and a broad smile.

"Afternoon, Sergeant, I'm Captain Birch and that officer over there is my co-pilot, Lieutenant Sands." He gestured over his shoulder at his colleague who was busy opening the helicopter's entrance hatch.

The dismissive manner of Birch's introduction spoke volumes about his character. In Sands' estimation, the pilot's leadership style was defined by the paucity of his man-management skills and by the calculating and ruthless pursuit of his own interests. The open contempt that he displayed towards his subordinates, especially Lieutenant Sands, appeared to be in precise inverse proportion to the exaggerated esteem in which he held himself and all those who were in positions of authority over him.

"Afternoon, sir, I'm Sergeant Rattigan," the other man yelled back in response. "Are we pleased to see you two? After two weeks in the outback, we could all do with a right hot shower and some decent grub."

"What have you been up to, Sergeant, substituting a Scottish bog for Afghanistan?"

Over the years, Birch's mode of address had begun to resemble a partitioned zone in which two combatants, in the form of condescension and contempt, were fighting for supremacy in an endless war of attrition.

"Yes, sir, a two week survival, evasion, resistance and extraction exercise."

"Well it looks like we're your extraction, Sergeant, so let's get cracking. Lieutenant Sands will take you through the pre-flight briefing."

Sands coughed deeply and began her drill. The men were anxious to get on board and paid scant attention to her.

"Okay, were going to be flying over the sea for a short period so you'll all have to don an aviation flight jacket and immersion suit. In the unlikely event that we have to ditch at sea, the emergency flotation equipment will automatically inflate. There's a single action door release on both escape hatches for the rear cabin. The soldier sitting next to it will be required to operate it in the event of an emergency and if instructed by me. Oh, and it's going to be a full flight so you'll all have to budge up. Is everything clear? Then let's get cracking before the mist starts rolling in."

This no-nonsense address was typical of Lieutenant Sands. She was one of a very small number of female pilots in the British Army and had had some high-profile difficulties adjusting to the pervading masculine ethos of the Army Air Corps. One thing she had made clear, though, was that she had no interest in training as an Apache attack helicopter pilot. Her passion lay with flying Lynx helicopters, airlifting troops and supplies and evacuating casualties from combat locations. Compared with some of the recent missions she'd flown in Afghanistan, this flight promised to be a routine affair, a perception that was shared among the passengers as the helicopter took off in the dusk.

But within minutes, as they headed out over the water, events conspired to offer up a very different outcome.

There was a strange unfathomable atmosphere lurking ahead of them and it didn't take long to stimulate the antennae of the two pilots. The further they headed out over the Solway, the more they all began to sense it. Even those men seated furthest from the cockpit windows started to peer forward.

Contrary to forecasts the weather was starting to close in. A vague green glow appeared to infuse the air around them. It shimmered with a liquid effervescence.

"That's bloody strange, Sands. What the hell's that? Ever seen anything like that before?"

"Aurora Borealis? But not at this latitude, and not at this time of year. I think we need to head round it."

"I'm not so sure. There're no warnings of unusual weather phenomena, are there?"

Suddenly and without warning the aircraft found itself enveloped in a dark, impenetrable cloud. "Where the hell's this come from?" yelled Birch.

Sands' instincts kicked in. "I don't like it, Sir. We need to divert course now. We've got to get out of this."

"What's going on, sir?" yelled Sergeant Rattigan.

"Tell your men to keep their heads down, Sergeant. Hang on, all of you."

Birch's warning was met by a shattering change in cabin pressure. The pilot and his navigator screamed in agony as they fought to retain consciousness and their control over the

Lynx. Their disorientation was compounded by an intolerable ear-splitting sound. It was this high-pitched mechanical scream, more than anything else, that tested the mettle and nerve of every soldier in the platoon. The passengers were pinned terrified to their seats by their safety harnesses, but still the men's limbs whiplashed around the cabin.

The sky outside had become impenetrable and the warning devices continued to scream within the cockpit. Everything appeared lost.

But just as suddenly, the atmosphere on board became still and quiet. A strange, awful calmness prevailed. The Lynx was going down. It was obvious to everyone on board. For a moment the crew seemed to be regaining control of the helicopter. But it was to no avail.

Down went the aircraft and all the soldiers in it, down into the sea. It was all over in seconds.

The only thing that could be said with any certainty was that it was a controlled, expert ditching. Thanks to Sands, the evacuation of the aircraft was conducted without loss of life or serious injury and the two life rafts were deployed in accordance with safety guidelines. Ten men and one woman escaped into the rolling fog that was sweeping over the Solway Firth that evening. The evacuation was completed only seconds before the Lynx turned turtle, sank in deep water and started to rust with every foot that it descended.

As the soldiers catapulted panic-stricken out of their doomed aircraft and into the two inflatable dinghies, they toppled into a bewildering new world of fear and uncertainty.

While they fought for control of their senses, the fog hemmed them in on all sides. The life rafts drifted away from the great shifting hulk of the Lynx. An explosion of smoke and glowing light, followed by a final terrifying death rattle, confirmed that the aircraft had sunk. Disorientated, shocked and fearful, the soldiers had lost all sense of direction. They were disabled by a sense of foreboding and uncertainty.

As the two life rafts started to drift apart, Captain Birch shouted into the void. "Sergeant, can you hear me? We've lost sight of you in the fog. Are you all okay?"

A distant voice responded from the second life raft. "Yes, sir, we're drifting into shore with the tide. Everyone in Charlie fireteam is safe and accounted for. That's five, including me."

"Same here," replied Birch. "Six accounted for and no injuries: four of your men, plus Lieutenant Sands and me. Keep your emergency locator transmitter activated."

"Yes, sir, we're drifting quite fast now." His voice was becoming less audible, even as he spoke.

"Okay, Sergeant. When you get to shore keep your group together till the fog lifts and wait to be picked up. Good luck."

The sergeant didn't reply. He was already out of earshot. And within hours, like the rest of his hardened little section, he would be confronting a series of events that would leave him questioning his sanity.

Birch, meantime, leaned back against the comfort of the life raft and tried to take stock of the situation.

He was in a state of shock, like the rest of his small crew, but he'd been trained to take control and make decisions under demanding circumstances. Despite that, he couldn't stop shaking. His mind started to cloud over; fleeting images of a looming board of enquiry, of an impending Court Martial overwhelmed him.

"Ok, when we get ashore we stick together," Sands said. "We're not certain where we are, so it's best if we let the rescue services find us. As long as we stay with the life raft we'll all be picked up safely. Isn't that right, sir?"

Birch still seemed preoccupied and failed to respond.

"But what happened out there, ma'am?" asked a nameless soldier. "How did we all survive? Did you see the speed at which that thing went down?"

"Yes, Corporal, I saw it. We just suddenly lost all power."

Captain Birch was jolted back to life. "There was no warning, Sands, you were right next to me."

"I know, sir, there was nothing we could do. It was a miracle you got us down. Are your men all alright, Corporal?"

The three privates nodded; all were young men, all shaken

and all psychologically drained. Despite their toughness and durability, open water was not an environment in which they were best equipped to function. Sands noted that the only noise to be heard was the collective chattering of her companions' teeth. The fog had succeeded in dampening every other sound.

As the life raft drifted on through the darkness, Captain Birch sat disconsolate and silent; his sole concern now was for the damage that the crash might do to his future career. His preoccupations were misplaced but he wasn't to know that. In subsequent days he would have to confront an unimaginable reality; that the wreck of his Lynx would never be found, that neither his own fate, nor that of his ten companions, would ever be accounted for, and that no one would ever be held responsible for the events that befell them on that fateful evening.

It was high tide, and half an hour later the gentle swell jettisoned them through the breakers on to an invisible muddy beach. The blanket of fog dulled their senses; their disorientation was complete. "Anyone see a light anywhere?" "Rattigan, have you come ashore yet?" "Hello, there, where are you?" A collective of anxious voices propelled unanswered messages into the opaque mass of damp cloud through which they had plunged and become enmeshed.

"Damn, no signal. Anyone else got a phone? Corporal, do the others have the radio?"

"Bottom of the sea, sir."

"Brilliant. Don't suppose any of you've got a phone?"

"Not permitted, sir. Not on survival training. Haven't we got a flare gun, sir?"

Sands leapt back into the beached life raft, tore open the marine survival kit and pulled out a plastic flare pistol and some cartridges.

"Go on then, Sands, give it your best shot. At least the other group should see it."

The brilliant orange trail arced up into the sky and burst into a distant, warm glow, barely visible to the naked eye.

"Right, the fog's too thick to go blundering off along the shore looking for the others," said Birch. "We'll improvise a shelter here and once the cloud lifts we'll start looking for help. We'll take it in turns to listen out for search parties and keep an eye out for a break in the fog. Corporal, get two of the men to act as look-out and relieve them in an hour. Lieutenant Sands and I will take the third watch. Now let's get a fire made."

Corporal Crawley pointed at two of his men, jerking his head to one side as he did so to indicate the direction in which he wanted them to go.

"And don't go wandering off."

He understood his men well and they had an easy rapport. As a fireteam they functioned with great cohesion and his authority went unquestioned. He felt a greater bond with them than he had ever experienced with any other group at any point in his life. And for what was left of the rest of his life he was to be tormented by his decision not to take the first watch himself that night.

THREE

Robert Jamieson is a well-respected figure. Born and educated in Edinburgh, he trained as a lawyer in London and practiced as a solicitor for twenty years before assuming his current role as coroner. Over the years, his subordinates have learned, at not inconsiderable cost to themselves, that his natural diffidence masks a keen intelligence and a sharp tongue. Despite his tendency to indulge his staff, they're not likely to misinterpret his over-solicitous manner as a sign of weakness or lack of resolve. But today his open features carry a worried countenance. He is attempting to contact Sterland Morris by telephone, a task that has proved exasperating over the preceding two days. The two men share a similar age, but in every other detail are separated in outlook, manner and appearance by a gulf so wide that it would take an unimaginable series of events for them to forge a friendship.

The phone is answered, sending the coroner into an accelerated spin. "Hello, Dr Morris, it's Jamieson here, in Carlisle. I'm sorry to disturb you, but I've been mulling over some of the things you raised with me in our recent phone conversation. If you have a moment, I wonder if you'd mind filling in a bit of background detail that might explain the anomalies we appear to be facing."

"By all means, go ahead. What can I help you with?"

"Well, first of all, what about the location of the find?" asks Jamieson, as he checks off the first of a series of questions on the notepad in front of him. "What was the significance of Burgh by Sands to the Romans? I'm curious as to whether the hoard's location has any relevance to the nature of the find. "

"Possibly. The site itself was originally near a fort on Hadrian's Wall; Aballava, to give it its Roman name. It was of no great importance beyond the fact that it guarded two fords across the Solway Firth. According to a Roman chronicler, Ptolemy, these were often used by raiding parties from the barbarian northern tribes, the Novantae, specifically, but also the Selgovae."

"But the hoard, itself; you say it contained substantial amounts of valuable coinage? Would this scale of find be consistent with what we know about the Roman settlement there?" Jamieson's pen moves down the list, and is left poised over the next question on his notepad.

"Well, Aballava would have been garrison to between five and eight hundred auxiliaries; not legionaries, you understand, but professional soldiers, none the less, and none of them Roman citizens. They'd have been raised from distant parts of the Empire and, according to the *Notitia Dignitatum*, by the middle of the third century Aballava would have been home to a division of Moors recruited in North Africa. It's fair to say there would have been a lot of local trade and a lot of coinage in circulation. There would certainly have been a small township outside the walls of the fort and a lot of trade and commerce entered into along the length of the wall itself."

"But what I'm interested in is the wealth associated with the individual who buried this hoard. Is it possible that it could've been the property of a common soldier from the period?"

"Almost certainly not. We know that the average annual salary of an auxiliary was roughly 25 gold aurei. The hoard contained well over 1000 aurei, along with a number of valuable artefacts. The basic maths wouldn't add up to support such a proposition. You have to remember that despite the fact that an auxiliary signed up for twenty five years his combined income for that entire period would still have fallen well short of the sum buried. No, this is much more likely to have been the property of an extremely wealthy Roman citizen or senior administrator."

"But I don't understand why anyone would bury such a fortune and then not return to reclaim it. Had Roman military and social structures fallen into complete disarray? Had security collapsed along the borders of the empire?"

"Not just along the borders," Morris replies. He's aware that he's well into his stride by now. "The Empire was in total crisis by the middle of the third century. The Emperor Valerian, whose reign would have coincided with the burial of this hoard, had been taken prisoner by the King of Persia who used him as a footstool before flaying him alive, stuffing his skin with straw and then preserving him for a number of years as a trophy in the main temple. Such events hardly support the popular notion of unbridled Roman military hegemony."

"Indeed not. Is it likely, then, that whoever buried the hoard did so during a period of military incursions over Hadrian's Wall, acting as a response to an imminent perceived threat?"

"No, strangely enough, that doesn't seem likely. Despite the crisis in the Empire generally, this was an extended period of relative peace along the wall. Don't forget that the average Roman soldier was pretty brutal, ruthless and lawless. In northern Britain the Romans had as good as cowed the local tribes into a resigned submission by the end of the previous century. Are you familiar with the famous quotation, "To ravage, to slaughter, to usurp under false titles, they call empire; and where they make a desert, they call it peace."? Do you know where it comes from?"

"It sounds familiar, certainly. If I had to hazard a guess, I'd plump for the Napoleonic era, or for some great hero of national liberation - Gandhi, perhaps, or Ho Chi Minh. It has a contemporary resonance."

"Actually, you could hardly be more wrong. According to Tacitus, it's the words of Calgacus, the Pictish leader, before he went into battle against the Romans in central Scotland in AD 83. It took a Roman historian to tell it the way it was."

"Good God, it does sum up the current situation in Iraq, though, doesn't it? Do you sometimes think that mankind hasn't learned an awful lot over the last two thousand years?"

There's silence on the other end of the line, giving Jamieson ample opportunity to ponder on his remark. It is most unlike him to talk so unguardedly. He's prided himself throughout his career on his diplomacy, tact and prudence. He's a pragmatist. He's never been aware that he harbours political convictions, and certainly none that he'd be prepared to express to a stranger over a telephone line.

"Funnily enough, the thought has crossed my mind on occasion. Now I must get back to work if there's nothing more I can help you with."

"No, no, that's fine," says Jamieson, nonplussed, and reprimanding himself under his breath. "You've been very helpful, Dr Morris. Thanks very much."

Morris returns the handset to its cradle, chuckling to himself. He does tend to have an effect on people.

FOUR

The fog engulfed Birch and Sands in a timeless world of fear and silence. They stared sightlessly into the night's sky, their attention focused on any sound cue that might indicate rescue was at hand.

The odd word of conversation reached them from further up the beach where the two privates kept watch. But otherwise there was no sight or sound of any human activity. The corporal dozed in the warm glow of the fire. Birch stared at him, envious of his relaxed demeanour. How could someone snooze at a time like this when the whole world was searching for them, not knowing whether they were dead or alive?

Birch leapt to his feet, and kicked the corporal's boots. "Come on, Crawley, snap to it. I'm going to wander up the beach for a bit to see if I can see any life. Keep the fire burning strongly so I can see you. And, Sands, time to set off another flare, I think." He turned and walked up the beach. Within ten metres his outline had been swallowed by the fog.

Sands reloaded the flare pistol and dispatched another orange fireball high over the Solway Firth, its glow adding an artist's finishing touch to an already ghostly scene.

The sound of human voices came cascading down over the beach. Then other sounds; was that a horse? Where were the noises coming from? The corporal and private leapt to their feet, shouting as they did so.

"Stog, Thommo, what's going on? We're over here!"

"Look over there, it's a man on horseback! I'm sure it is."

Something wasn't right. Voices were raised, but not in welcome; instead the tone that carried its way to the fireside in the fog was one of anger, fear and aggression. It was clear that

Stogdon and Thompson were in trouble, but where were they?

"There he is! There's Thommo!"

A figure plunged at them in slow motion through the fog, Christ-like, arms outstretched, mouth agape, beseeching them to come to him. Behind him towered a huge devilish shape, helmeted, shining, malicious and vengeful. He sat astride a huge horse that ploughed its way through the sand, the sound of its hoofs muffled and yet unmistakable.

"Thompson, over here!" they shouted in desperate unison. They reached out as they advanced towards him. But he didn't seem to be moving forward any more; he was upright but frozen still as the horseman bore down on him from behind. He appeared to be overcome by an immense weight that prevented any forward momentum and he began to sway. The object that obstructed his flight was protruding though a blood soaked wound in his chest. His body had been pierced through its core by a metal javelin thrown with huge force from behind him.

The corporal and private leapt forward to catch Thompson's body as it toppled and both fell backwards as the horsemen reared past in a frantic gallop, the light of the fire reflecting madly off his metallic body. Birch leapt out of the fog and attempted to seize the reins but he was slammed to the ground by a flailing hoof. The horseman circled the fallen officer with his new javelin poised to strike, while the corporal and private tried in vain to reach him.

The horse was distracted by the two soldiers, making it difficult for the rider to steady his aim, and as Birch regained full consciousness he was accorded the curious privilege of staring into the face of death. He rolled on the sand to avoid the lunges of the javelin but the more he struggled the more he felt pinned by the inevitability of the outcome. With a final tug of the reins the rider positioned himself at arms length from the stricken officer and raised his javelin to its full height above his head. Birch saw the flash of the javelin's point as it reflected the fire's flame and at that moment he closed his eyes to avoid witnessing his own execution.

What Birch missed, however, was the blinding explosion which engulfed the rider above him and erupted into an inferno of flame and smoke, his cape and leggings combusting, his hair and plume alight. The sparks cascaded down on to Birch and the two soldiers nearby. The horse wheeled around in hysteria, the rider screaming in shock and pain. The animal plunged headlong back into the fog carrying off the grotesque human torch as it went, smoke and the smell of burning flesh trailing in its wake.

Sands ran up to Birch, the discharged flare pistol still smoking in her hand. She helped pull him to his feet. In the distance they could detect the shape of the burning rider as he was carried off, anchored in place by his stirrups and serenaded to his final resting place by the shrieks of his demented stallion.

They looked around; Thompson was clearly dead. The corporal collapsed to his knees next to him, sobbing aloud.

The others stood dumbly for a moment looking at him in complete shock. Finally the private urged him to his feet. "Come on, Corp, we've got to find Stogdon."

"Hang on," cautioned Birch, "we need to arm ourselves. Sands, grab the paddle. Have you men got survival knives on you? Ok, spread out then and let's comb this beach. Stogdon, can you hear us? Where are you?"

They stumbled along in a line, Birch with his small flashlight, all in varying degrees of shock, with the corporal worst affected. Within a minute they were out of sight of the fire and hemmed in by the dark.

Now they were fearful for their own lives again. Who the hell was out there? And why had they been attacked?

When they stumbled upon Stogdon he was in a wild and disoriented state, shocked and bleeding from a head wound. From what little he was able to tell them, he had been hiding in the dunes while they'd been searching for him. He'd been attacked without warning. He had been able to fight off his assailants but only by stabbing one of them with his survival knife. He wasn't sure if he'd killed him.

29

Sands and the corporal volunteered to do a further quick sweep of the beach to see if they could find any evidence of a body. Birch and the corporal helped Stogdon to his feet and began supporting him back to the warmth and light of the fire, which was just visible in the distance. Birch marked the soldier down as the worst kind of insensate brute, remarkable only for his primordial strength and his refusal to submit. Shortly afterwards they were joined by the two others who had returned from their search mission with unwelcome news.

"I'm afraid he's dead; stabbed through the neck. You must've put up one hell of a fight, Stogdon," said Sands.

"They came at us out of the fog. Swords, armour, spears. It was all in self-defence. Look what they done to Thommo, the bastards. They had a horse, they was proper fiends - evil."

"They were real enough, though, and the one you killed was wearing this hooded cape. Here, wrap this around you and try to keep warm," said Sands, throwing it into his lap. "Corporal, you'll find proper bandages in the life raft survival kit. We've got to try and staunch that bleeding."

Sands pulled Birch to one side. "Sir, we've got to get off this beach. It's not safe to remain here."

Birch bridled at this intervention from a subordinate officer. "Lieutenant, it won't have escaped your notice that this is a murder scene. We can't just up sticks and leave the bodies to the elements."

"Sir, your first duty is to the continued safety of your surviving men. We must get them to a place where they can at least defend themselves from further attacks. Let's get them inland where we can at least survey the scene from a safe distance. Whoever perpetrated this is heavily armed. And judging by the amount of footprints around the body there was a number more involved who we haven't seen yet. They know where we are, they can see our fire, and they probably know that we've killed one, if not two of them, already. We've got to disperse till dawn and wait safely till a search party can find us. And Thompson's body is above the high-water mark. It can't be washed away."

Birch spat on the sand and cleared his throat. "Ok, you three, we're going to move off the beach for the night. Grab any supplies that we can use, take whatever we can find in the marine survival kit and let's get going. We're going to have to leave Thompson's body here till the morning when the emergency services will have to deal with it. Ok, Stogdon, think you can cope? Then follow me."

The group set off inland, torch light extinguished. They navigated a way through the sand dunes at the top of the beach and found themselves in a more sheltered area of rough pasture land. After a few minutes they encountered a turfed dyke that they followed inland for several hundred meters, the ground rising as they marched. At the point at which the dyke turned to the right, Birch ordered the group to set up camp in a leeward position that afforded them protection from the wind.

They all knew that they would be unable to sleep. Although tired, cold and hungry, and having shared out what was left of their personal rations, they agreed to keep each other awake through the long dark hours that lay ahead. Once Stogdon's wounds had been cleaned and stitched up, the soldiers needed to talk, to explore and expiate their perceived culpability. This was not going to be a night that they could doze through; the horrific events of the day would see to that.

And much as they mourned the tragic loss of Thompson and shuddered at the horror of the conflict of the beach, there were other thoughts gnawing away at them. What had caused the Lynx to crash without warning and how had they all survived the ditching at sea? They knew that something very strange was happening to them that none of them could explain, let alone control. But uppermost in their minds was a commonly shared anxiety for the safety and well-being of their comrades in the other life raft. They hoped to God the other soldiers were alright, but somehow they all doubted that they were.

FIVE

First light saw the five soldiers spread-eagled face down into the green landscape. Seconds before, peering through a gap in the fog, they'd caught a sudden glimpse of a strange scene unfolding on the beach below them. What they'd witnessed had been sufficient to provoke them into a spontaneous and undignified dive for cover.

"That's no search party. Them bastards are back."

"Keep down, everyone. Sands, pass me my field glasses." Birch crawled forward and peered over the top of the dyke.

"Jesus, there's at least twenty of them; six on horseback. What the hell's going on? They've got Thompson's body; they're loading it on to a horse. Damn, the fog's swept in again. What are they wearing?"

"They're dressed like Romans, sir."

"What? Sod off, Sands. Don't be absurd."

"They're the same people that attacked us last night, sir. Their clothes and their weaponry; it all fits."

"What fits? Nothing fits. Romans - don't make me laugh. They're just as likely to be some modern satanic cult, or aliens, maybe. Had you considered that they might be aliens, Sands?"

Stogdon suddenly spoke up. "They were speaking proper weird when they attacked Thompson and me. They sounded right off their heads."

Corporal Crawley glanced at Stogdon with concern. "I agree with Lieutenant Sands, sir. You didn't see that body on the beach close up. It looked like a Roman soldier to me."

"What, and you're an expert are you, Corporal?"

"No, sir, but the Lieutenant found something on the body."

"Oh, I see, holding out on us were you, Sands? And what have you got to show us?"

Sands dug into her flight suit trouser pocket and pulled out a circular object with a handle made of a dull dark metal. The bottom half of the object, which was four to five inches in diameter, was wrapped in a fine leather cloth. The men stared in fascination as Sands gently began to unwrap the object.

"He was wearing it above his wrist."

She turned the object up upside down, revealing it to be entirely cast as one piece of metal. And as she did so, out of it fell a number of small brown and silver coins.

"It's a bronze arm purse. And these are Roman coins that were the property of that dead soldier."

Corporal Crawley whistled in amazement. "I told you we found something."

"So, Lieutenant, what is it that makes you such an authority?" Birch asked.

"Just the evidence of my own eyes, sir - that and the fact that I studied Classics and Ancient History at Cambridge."

The two privates exchanged a knowing glance, each enjoying this brazen piece of one-upmanship. No matter what miserable circumstances they found themselves in, these men were always capable of extracting some pleasure from seeing the authority of a pompous officer deflated by a subordinate.

Sands now had the wind in her sails. She was not going to waste this opportunity to display her knowledge, and it was clear the men were transfixed by what she had to say. "This silver coin is a *denarius*, roughly equivalent to a day's pay to our dead friend out there. Probably had the same worth as today's ten or twenty pound note. The bronze coin is a *sestertius*, roughly equivalent to the present two pound coin; there were four of these to the *denarius*. The smallest denomination I recognise is this one, a copper coin called an *as*, and worth about fifty pence or so. The rest I don't know but they will probably be equivalent to pennies by today's standards."

"So what're you saying, Lieutenant; that we've stumbled upon some rogue Roman Empire re-enactment society with a taste for murder and dressing up? Grow up, Sands, for God's sake."

"No, sir, I'm not saying that."

Sands choose her words with care. "What I am saying is that

the helicopter crash may have somehow thrown us off-kilter. We've become disconnected from our own time zone."

"You what?" gasped Birch.

"Hang on, man, now you're really fucking with my head", said Stogdon. "I can't be dealing with this no more."

"Get a grip, Sands," warned Birch, "you're putting the bloody wind up everyone. We've got enough to worry about without you spouting fantasyland bullshit. Start acting like an officer, for Christ's sake."

Silence ensued for a few moments as Sands held her tongue. Suddenly Stogdon and Crawley jerked upright, pointing inland as the sun fought to illuminate the landscape.

"Look, sir, the fog's starting to lift."

"Thank God for that. Now we've got a chance of being rescued from this nightmare."

As the mist drew back and the sun broke through, a brilliant surge of radiance was released that lit up the landscape in a way that none of the watchers had ever experienced before. The vision that was revealed was one that left them speechless and overwhelmed. The mist rolled back like a series of great curtains being drawn apart to reveal an ever-increasing series of wonderful backdrops. They sat, an awe-inspired audience witnessing the birth of a truly unforgettable event.

The first scene to be revealed was the lush, rolling landscape free of fences, hedgerows and the imprint of any organised agricultural activity. Then came the swift realisation that the conventional built environment and all its ephemera had been expunged; no brick, no concrete, no asphalt, no metal, no glass. That meant there was no sign of villages, of roads, of cars, of pylons, of windows. Finally, as the full glory of the scene was revealed, a new wonder was presented to their astonished eyes. Here, at last, was the mark of man! Mankind did exist in this virgin landscape. There, in the distance was a vast, continuous, magnificent turf and stone wall standing fifteen feet high and stretching westward down to the sea and as far as the eye could see in the other direction.

Dumbfounded, this small group of twenty-first century

soldiers fought to absorb the evidence of their own eyes.

Where was this place?

"What the bloody hell is going on?" whispered Crawley, astounded by the magnificence of the sight that faced them. "Anyone know where we are?"

All were too stunned to respond. The small group stood speechless, unable to react. Slowly, however, an inevitable explanation began to dawn on them. In silence they contemplated the same possibility. Maybe Sands was right, after all. Even she found it hard to believe the evidence of her eyes. The proof was laid out before them, but it still defied logical confirmation.

Sands groaned.

The others turned to look at her in a state of wonderment. Now they could see and understand everything that had formerly been obscured and confused. There, look, there! There was Hadrian's Wall, with a small fort built into the wall every mile or so, and between them a couple of evenly spaced turrets about a third of a mile apart. Early morning smoke was rising from each of the fortlets and turrets as men went about preparing their breakfasts and heating water for their ablutions. They were doing just what we do. And over there, to the right, was a small column of men walking along the wall. They must be changing guard.

They all started to talk and point at once.

"I'm seeing it, but I don't believe it," someone said.

"What the hell is happening to us?" added a second.

"This cannot be happening," muttered a third.

"What's going on, ma'am? This ain't no sodding joke. Someone tell me I'm dreaming."

"I hate to tell you, but you're not dreaming, Private."

Sands bent down and wiped the dirt from her knees. "Welcome to Roman Britain."

Stogdon leapt to his feet, agitated and gesticulating. "You know what, yeah, you're doing my bloody head in. Ever since you picked us up yesterday everything's been fucked up. What are you up to? What's your game? What the fuck's going on?"

"Calm down, Stogdon. I'm as confused as you. We all are."

"Well, she don't seem confused. She's been one step ahead of us all along. How does she explain that?"

Birch leant forward into Stogdon's face. "Shut up, Stogdon, you're not helping matters. We've got to keep our heads."

Stogdon mimicked Birch. "Ooh, we've got to keep our heads, have we? What bloody good is that going to do us? As far as I'm concerned you got us into this fuck-up, and you're sod-all use to us without your helicopter."

"Watch your mouth, Stogdon. You may have had a crack on the head, but I'm still in command of this group." As soon as he spoke, Birch realised how hollow his assertion sounded.

"Well, what's the plan, then, big man?"

Sands stood between them and pushed them apart. "That'll do, there's absolutely nothing to be gained by falling out with one another." She half-turned away from the officer. "Now you three know how to survive behind enemy lines, right? Isn't that what you've been training for? Well, here's the ultimate test. You're the experts in this situation, we're not. If we're going to survive we're going to have to pool all our knowledge and resources. Agreed?"

They all nodded, grateful for her calm leadership.

"Ok, now, Corporal, what's the first thing we should do?"

"A quick recce to identify the best source of shelter, warmth, water and food, ma'am."

"Right let's make that our priority."

"Do we need to make a signal to attract help, ma'am?"

"I don't think I really need to answer that, Corporal, do I? No one is going to be riding to our rescue."

"No, ma'am," Crawley confirmed. "Captain Birch, pass me the field glasses, please."

Birch, fuming, bridled at the request. However, any thoughts of attempting to re-assert his authority dissipated when he caught the steely glint in the corporal's eyes.

"This is insane, right fucking insane," Stogdon mumbled to himself, as his corporal took the glasses.

Crawley lay down on top of the grassy dyke. As he surveyed

the surrounding country he began a running commentary.

"Ok, let's see – well, they've cleared the beach completely. Both bodies have been removed and the life raft's disappeared. There's a number of stone-built look-out posts positioned along the coast; we must've landed slap-bang between 'em but the fog would have hidden us from view. They must've been alerted by our flares, though. The wall's continuous; it looks like the only way to traverse it is by going round it over the mud flats at low tide or by going over it."

"What about the milecastles?" enquired Sands. "They've got gates on their south walls; maybe they've got corresponding gates on the north wall to allow access?"

"Yeah, but I don't see us being welcome callers. We've already killed two Roman soldiers." He trained his field glasses to his right hand side. "However if you look over there a couple of miles you'll see what looks like a much bigger fort with a fair amount of life around it. That might be worth having a closer squint at."

The soldiers peered into the bright sun in the direction that Crawley indicated. The walls of the fort were visible, although masked by the smoke that rose from the informal settlements peppering the southbound approach road.

"I reckon we could make our way over there without being seen. There's also a wood several miles to the rear which should provide us with shelter and a source of fuel. Sir, I suggest we leave the others here to forage for food and improvise a camp. You and I could reconnoitre further east to do a bit of intelligence gathering and look for possible ways to traverse the wall. It may be safest for us to get out of occupied territory as soon as possible. And that's going to mean heading north."

"And who do you thinks is occupying the territory on the other side of the wall, Corporal?"

"Not the bloody Romans, sir, that's for sure."

Sands stirred. "I know, Corporal, but we're going to have much greater opportunity to forage on this side of the wall. We should weigh up our options carefully before we head off anywhere. The Romans at least represent civilisation in this part of the world."

"Look, ma'am, whichever way you look at it, we're stuck behind enemy lines. We have to evade capture and extract ourselves to a neutral location. Them guys are the occupying power and they don't like us a whole bunch. Ask Thompson."

"I can't believe this is happening," interjected Stogdon, who was growing increasingly agitated. "Thommo can't be dead. I must be proper tripping."

Birch, ignoring Stogdon's appeal, glanced at Sands and Crawley. He raised his hands in front of his chest to call for silence. "Ok, here's what we'll do, right? We'll investigate the wall like Corporal Crawley suggested, gather some intelligence and make a decision in a few hours as to our plan of action. Sands, you stay put with the two privates, forage for food as best you can and try and improvise an overnight camp in the wood down there. In the meantime Crawley and I will follow the wall further east for several miles so we know what we're facing. We'll meet you back at the wood by mid afternoon. I'll blow my whistle once to let you know we've arrived. Ok, Corporal, are you ready?"

As Crawley got to his feet he focused his gaze on the two privates. "Make sure you set some snares, lads. We'll be back soon and we're all going to need some protein tonight."

Birch and Crawley set off, heads down and stooping low, hugging the natural contours of the landscape as they went. With Crawley taking the lead, they made impressive progress, skirting around the perimeter of the nearby fort and across the road, their presence invisible to the watchtowers that were dotted along the wall, a mile or so to their north.

"He's good your corporal, isn't he?" said Sands.

"He's the best there is, ma'am."

"And what about you guys? Are you the best there are, too? Because if you're not, then we're well and truly screwed, you know that, don't you?"

"Yes, ma'am, but this ain't exactly what we signed up for."

"I know, but it can't be any worse that Afghanistan, right?"

"Too bloody right, ma'am, but at least we could call in some back-up when the going got tough."

"Ok, we're agreed, then. It's all down to us now, right?"

The two privates nodded.

"So let's have a closer look at what we're going to have to deal with. Can you get me to within a safe viewing distance of that fort over there, without us giving our presence away?"

"It's what we was trained to do, ma'm. That and kill Romans."

Sands noted that Stogdon was showing signs of getting his act together.

"But admit it, you're both dying to have a closer look at them, aren't you?"

The privates shot her a wary glance. One thing they didn't care for was enthusiastic amateurs. They had a nasty habit of getting you killed.

"This ain't no training exercise," warned Stogdon. "We ain't got no clue what we're up against here. Just keep your head down and do exactly what we say."

"That's the spirit, Stog," she thought. "And try not to think too much - it's clearly not going to do you any favours."

SIX

After twenty minutes spent scrambling and crawling over the rolling landscape, the two privates delivered Sands to a viewpoint from which they were well hidden but had a clear, uninterrupted view of the fort and settlement below them. Now that the fog had lifted, the scene was illuminated in the early morning sunlight.

A well-made military road ran down the slope to their right and proceeded through a ramshackle settlement of maybe fifty buildings of varying size that hugged the southernmost entrance to the fort. It was clear that this little township was populated by civilians, probably traders, blacksmiths, tavern keepers and the like, and existed to benefit from its proximity to the military garrison. The stone fort was of an imposing size, oblong in shape, the outer walls stretching for one hundred and twenty to one hundred and fifty yards on each side, with a monumental gatehouse in the middle of the southern perimeter, and a series of turrets adorning it every thirty to forty yards. Beyond the fort, the mud flats of the Solway Firth lay a couple of miles to the north.

The three soldiers drank in every detail of the scene that sat before them. Their professional caution was undermined by the astonishing sights that they were desperate to relay to each other through a series of nudges, whispers and involuntary exclamations and expletives. The dreamlike brilliance of the tableau affected each soldier in a similar manner, a nervous existential angst mixing with a fascinated appreciation of the privilege afforded them as visitors from an alien timeframe. Despair and desire vied for possession of their souls.

Sands fell back on literary cliché to articulate her jumbled emotions. "An English writer once described the past as a foreign country. If so, I'm a wide-eyed tourist who's had her passport, credit card and map jacked."

"If you're a tourist, ma'am, you're right bloody lucky," said one of the privates.

"Check that, mate," nodded the other. "I'm more like an illegal immigrant cuffed to a police van with a bleeding great boot on my neck. I've been in some proper hairy fire-fights, but I wouldn't rate my chances of getting out of this one in one piece."

"What I can't get my head around is this," replied his pal. "As a soldier, when your number's up, your number's up. Ain't that how we face the shit that gets thrown at us?"

"I hear what you're saying, bro'. When you've had it, you've had it."

"But now I've discovered my number's not up at all. My number's so far bloody down that it's disappeared from view. I must be immortal."

"Thompson's number was up, though. I just think we're going to get the chance to die lots of times."

"That's true, the poor bastard! And he didn't even know what hit him."

"This is all so screwed," confirmed Stogdon.

Sands broke the reverie. "Come on, lads, keep your chins up. We've still got a job to do. Let's get back to the wood and start building a camp for tonight."

Stogdon motioned them to get their heads down, pointing to movement around the fort. "Hang on, ma'am, there's some action around the gatehouse; looks like a patrol is making its way out. Tell you what, let's move further back so that we can't be seen from the road."

They crawled back from where they'd come. A couple of hundred yards of undulating ground now separated them from the roadside. The fort was out of clear line of sight but they could observe the approaching Roman patrol at close quarters without being seen themselves. While the sound of marching feet sounded familiar, the voices that reached them on the prevailing wind were unintelligible to the two privates.

"Latin," whispered Sands.

As the troops moved past them down the road, the three soldiers stole quick glances at their retreating shapes, their astonishment growing as an unmistakable realisation dawned on them.

"Bloody hell, Ojo, some's as black as you are!"

"Some of them are blacker than me, mate. Look at them two in the rear rank."

Private Ojokwu had scarcely spoken a word since the helicopter had crashed, but all that was about to change. "They gotta be Africans. What you think, Stog?"

"Well, they ain't bloody English, that's for sure."

"Ojokwu is right, Stogdon. They're Africans, Moors probably, from North Africa. You know, Morocco, Algeria."

"Give over, them geezers is supposed to be Romans, man. Romans ain't black."

"You can see it with your own eyes, Stogdon," whispered Sands. Her cheek was pressed against the damp grass, her face inches from his. "You may not like it, but there were black Africans living and working in Britain hundreds of years before the English turned up."

"Sod off, ma'am, with respect. The English have always been here. That's why it's called England, see? It's dead simple."

"So, you're a good Anglo-Saxon, are you?"

"Yeah, pure-bred English, one hundred percent guaranteed, stamped through like Blackpool rock."

"Well, in that case, don't bank on meeting your ancestors." She paused to give her next words maximum effect. "The Angles and the Saxons ain't turning up here for centuries."

"You what?" he gasped in disbelief, the twinkle suddenly gone from his eye. "You tripping?"

"Your clan's stuck in Denmark. They'll have to wait for the Romans to sod off out of Britain. Face facts, Private, the Stogdons are gonna be at the end of a very long queue if they plan on immigrating."

Ojokwu snorted. "You heard her, Stog. Go on, piss off back to your own country. We shoulda just kicked your lot out -

kept Britain black."

Stogdon lifted his face up off the grass and shot his companion a disbelieving glance. "I swear this is proper screwed, man. Bare fucked up."

"Yeah, so you keep saying. Get with the programme, Stog. We're all immigrants now."

Sands smiled to herself. "Keep it down. These guys are out looking for us. If we get caught, they won't be extraditing us."

"I reckon them's the geezers what attacked us."

"I'll tell you what, they'll certainly be up for a spot of retaliation. What are they up to?"

The trio kept the Roman patrol under close observation as it fanned out across the countryside north of the wooded area. They watched as they encircled the wood and then flushed their way through it. The patrol appeared more interested in the wild pigs they drove out of one edge than any possible human hiding places within it. After an hour, the Roman soldiers returned to the fort carrying a large boar suspended from a tree branch.

"Ok, ma'am, it's safe now to start setting up camp for tonight," confirmed Ojokwu. "They won't be back for a while. And we've got to get some food to eat. The wood will be the best source of forage around here."

Within half an hour the two privates had taken command of the situation; Stogdon volunteered to set snares and to begin building a camp while Ojokwu took Sands off with him to forage through the trees for wild vegetables, fruit and fungi.

"Take your cap off, ma'am, we going to need it to carry what we find."

Sands obeyed Ojokwu without question. She already recognised that these two soldiers possessed practical soldiering qualities that surpassed her own. She would have her uses, of course, but for now this pair was out of her league when it came to surviving behind enemy lines. Her time would come. She was confident enough in her own abilities to know that she would play a crucial role in tackling whatever events lay before them in the long term. Birch, however, would pose a problem; she knew that she would have to battle to wrest authority from him.

As they foraged for vegetables and fruit, Ojokwu worked with expertise. With each species of plant they encountered, he explained its suitability as a food source. On the edge of the wood Ojokwu located ground elder and sorrel as well as stinging nettles and chickweed - good to add to salads, he explained - and wild rosemary.

Sands discovered a blackberry bush that yielded a good supply of ripe fruit. But her curiosity was most engaged by the wide range of wild fungi that Ojokwu brought to her attention. Within a short period of time he had identified a cornucopia of grotesque looking and unlikely-sounding edible mushrooms and fungi; as well as the more common horse mushroom and chanterelles they were soon collecting considerable numbers of shaggy ink cap, giant puffball and jew's ear mushrooms.

The act of harvesting wild plants gave the two of them a welcome focus away from the mental turmoil that had been consuming them. They communicated together with gentleness and whispers, as if under a spell. At one point Sands found some mushrooms under a large oak tree and revealed her find to Ojokwu with satisfaction.

"No, not them!" he warned. "Never touch them ones. Have a good look so you can avoid them. No, I'm proper serious, that's the death cap mushroom. See the olive brown colour of the cap and the white gills underneath? See how they're not directly attached to the stem? Half a mushroom can do you in. They can be dead ringers for field mushrooms, you get me?"

"I get you. Is the effect instantaneous?"

"No, it takes twenty-four hours to kick in - breathing problems, vomiting, dehydration - but there's no known cure, so by then you're proper hosed. You're dead within six days. Massive organ failure; it destroys the liver and kidneys. Here, smell the flesh of the mushroom. What's it remind you of?"

Sands leaned forward with care and sniffed the portion that Ojokwu proffered her on the tip of his knife.

"It smells kind of perfumed, not pleasant, though. It's like a smell of rotting roses or something."

"Yeah, for real. Don't forget if you plan on eating fungi."

"Thanks, Ojo, I'll remember. D'you know the Latin name?"

"*Amanita phalloides*. Is that the same thing?"

"Yeah, Latin's the language of scientific classification."

"Is that why you can speak it, then?"

Sands laughed. "No, I was interested in Roman history."

"Don't mean to be rude, like, but wasn't that a bare stuck-up thing for a kid to be into?"

"Yeah, I guess, but when I was a teenager I was brought up by an uncle who worked at the British Museum. He's a curator of Roman art and archaeology. Poor sod, he must be wondering what the hell's happened to me."

"You think that we've just stopped existing back there, in the twenty first century?"

"Who knows, maybe this is just a bad dream."

"Well, if it is, I swear I'm proper dreaming it, too."

"Maybe it's a collective nightmare then, and we'll all end up safely back in our beds tomorrow morning."

"I don't think so, ma'am, this all feels far too real to me, you know what I'm saying?"

"Yeah, but call me Kal, Ojo, that's my name. I was never one for pulling rank."

"Ok, Kal, but don't call me Ojo. My real name's Titus."

Sands burst out laughing. "Hey, Titus, you're going to be right at home here! That's a noble Roman name."

"You think?" Ojokwu smiled at her. "I can proper tell Cambridge weren't wasted on you, ma'am."

"Watch it, Titus. The name's Kal. Have you got that yet, my Roman friend?"

"Yeah, man, but no way I'm Roman. I'm thinking you should just stick with calling me Ojo after all."

They chuckled, appreciating the warmth of their exchange. It represented a brief distraction from the extreme challenges that lay ahead of them in this alien, disconnected time zone.

SEVEN

"Hello, Mr Jamieson, it's Sterland Morris here. I'm sorry to disturb you. Do you have a couple of minutes to talk?"

"Certainly, Dr Morris. What can I help you with?"

"It's a personal matter, I'm afraid. It's concerning the army helicopter that's been lost over the Solway."

"Oh, Lord, you mean the one that went down last night? What a nightmare; it's been complete mayhem up here, as you may well imagine. The press, emergency services, army, navy, M.O.D - even Number 10's contacted the Chief Constable."

"Yes, I can imagine. But, the thing is," and here Morris pauses for a second to compose himself, before continuing, "I have a more personal interest in the fate of the crew. My niece, you see, was one of the pilots."

Jamieson is pole-axed. "Oh, good heavens, I'm most terribly sorry, Dr Morris; I had no idea."

"It's okay. There's no earthly reason why you should have," replies Morris, touched by his colleague's concern.

"You must be beside yourself with worry. Is there anything I can do to help?"

"Well, to be frank, you're the only person I know up there, the only one who's actually on the spot."

"Of course, I quite understand. What can I do to help?" Please ask me anything. I'd be only too happy to assist in any small way I can."

The tone of genuine disquiet in Jamieson's voice has struck a chord with Morris. He begins to open up. "You see the thing is, I raised her as my daughter after my sister and her husband died when Kal was only fourteen. We are very close – and I just can't stand this lack of news, not knowing one way or the other."

"Yes, it must be appalling for you."

"I just can't understand why there's still a complete embargo on news, for family as well as for the media. What the hell is going on up there? Have you any idea what they've found yet? It's getting on for twenty-four hours since the helicopter was reported missing, for God's sake!"

"All I can tell you is the official line, really, which is that there's still no confirmation as to the fate of the crew. What we know is that they lost contact with the helicopter in thick fog at about five-thirty yesterday afternoon somewhere over the Solway Firth. The expectation is that they must have ditched at sea. The water's been crawling with craft and divers all day but there's been no sign of chopper or crew. The search is ongoing but is likely to be called off for the night. As you know, there's still been no official statement. I've tried talking to some of the officers at the Police Station here in Carlisle – they've been down there all day keeping the crowds away – but they're as much in the dark as the rest of us."

"And have they really found nothing all day?"

"Well, nothing of any relevance, anyway. They've been identifying and hauling up large chunks of heavily corroded metal from the sea floor but that's only going to be of interest to the marine archaeologists. Nothing at all, I'm afraid, not even a life-jacket. I'm sorry to be so negative but it obviously looks very bad."

"Yes, I know, Mr Jamieson…"

"Robert, please."

"Yes, I know, Robert…but I just can't believe it till I hear it. I feel completely useless sitting down here. I'm going to fly up there tomorrow morning and see if there's anything I can do to help. I'd just rather be on the spot for when there is news."

"Of course. Well, look, you must come and stay with us while you're here. You'd be very welcome. I'll tell my wife to expect you. When might you be up?"

"There's a flight from Stansted gets me into Newcastle at five past eight tomorrow morning. I've rented a car – how long to drive over to Carlisle, d'you reckon?"

"It's about fifty miles; shouldn't take you much more than

an hour. Do you want to come straight to my office?"

"That's very kind of you. I do appreciate your offer of accommodation. I'll see you at about half past nine tomorrow morning. Oh, and one more thing; you don't happen to know where they're storing all that old corroded metal they've dredged up, do you?"

EIGHT

While his two comrades had been foraging for food, Stogdon had made good progress on setting up camp. He'd erected a lean-to shelter by stretching the Roman hooded cape between two lengths of twine tied at waist height to a pair of pine trees spaced about three meters apart. The cloth was anchored to the ground with stones laid along one edge with extra support provided by a central line attached to an overhanging branch. Isolation from the ground was provided by a generous bed of pine needles. A quick glance revealed that the beauty of this shelter lay in the speed with which it could be dismantled, leaving no sign of its existence to attract Roman patrols or inquisitive locals.

"This'll do us for the night," said Stogdon.

Sands eyed the structure with suspicion. "Can we get all five of us under that?"

"Not with any comfort but one of us will always be on watch anyway. When we've decided on our longer term plans we can build a more stable structure."

"If we live long enough, you might get a chance to experience his debris hut shelter," said Ojokwu. "It's a marvel of ancient engineering. Ain't that right, Stog?"

Stogdon ignored him. "That Roman garment's right well made, you know – waterproof, too."

Sands ran her fingers down the hem. "It's a *Birrus Britannicus*, a high-end British export. The rich and powerful will be wearing these in Rome. It's a glorified hoody, really, but warm and waterproof. We need to try and get hold of a few more of them to make ourselves less conspicuous. This one is top quality, though. Whoever owned it must have been a man of influence or wealth, probably an officer."

"There'll be a good price on your head, then, Stog. Nice one!"

"Sod him, you saw what they done to Thommo. I just hope them other two's okay."

A short, sharp whistle made them start.

"That'll be them!"

Ojokwu returned their signal and within a minute Birch and Crawley staggered into the camp. After a short reunion, Ojokwu and Stogdon turned their attention to feeding the group. None of them had had much, if anything, to eat all day and they all felt weak and dispirited. Towards the end of the day Stogdon had snared a brown hare which was now roasting on a spit over the open fire. It was soon accompanied by an array of baked frogs and fungi and assorted wild plant leaves.

As they sat around the fire exchanging news, Birch gave a brief report on their reconnaissance mission. "We followed a trail running east two miles south of the wall; far enough away for us to be pretty inconspicuous, at least. We ran across a few locals who didn't seem too surprised to see us, but gave us a wide berth. We had to hide at one point from a Roman patrol that seemed to be more interested in stealing chicken eggs than soldiering. Worth noting that there definitely are farms out there if we run out of food. Anyway, we pushed on for about five or six miles checking the wall for any weak points as we went. Finally we hit a decent-sized village and, just north of it, a huge fort, twice the size of the one near here, and we were able to have a damn good look at it. We watched troops coming and going for a good hour and there are two pieces of bad news to report, I'm afraid."

At this point Birch paused and exchanged a glance with Crawley; they were both very subdued. "The first piece of bad news is that they have cavalry, lots of cavalry. Within five miles of here the Romans have got in the region of one thousand mounted troops."

"Jesus Christ, this is just supposed to be a god-forsaken outpost on the edge of empire," muttered Ojokwu.

"Well they've got overwhelming force of arms, outpost or not. For the first time it made me realise the scale of what we're dealing with here. They can get huge numbers of troops in and out of that fort, both north and south of the wall, in a matter of minutes."

"And what's the second piece of bad news?" asked Sands.

Birch and Crawley once more exchanged a glance; and this time, Crawley spoke.

"It's about Private Thompson." Everyone stopped breathing at the mention of his name. "Thommo…John Thompson… He…" Crawley gulped for air, unable to continue momentarily.

"What about him, Corp? What about Thommo?"

Crawley's face distorted as he concentrated on picking his words. "Private Thompson's body," he began, before pausing in clear distress.

"What, Corp, what about it?"

"…was on display."

Ojokwu and Stogdon jumped to their feet in agitation and started to walk around the clearing. Sands sat on the ground shaking her head. The corporal had tears in his eyes as he spoke.

"I didn't realise it was him to begin with. They'd hung him from a pole on the outskirts of the village outside the fort. His body had been badly mutilated - and they'd performed every humiliation on him you could imagine."

Birch nodded. "It was Thompson, alright. They'd topped him off with his regimental cap as a final insult."

"So much for fucking Roman civilisation!" spat Stogdon.

Sands rubbed her head with weary resignation. "This is what we're up against from now on. What Thompson got is nothing compared with what lies in store for the rest of us if they manage to capture us alive. He, at least, had the satisfaction of being dead before he was mutilated."

"You're a cheery sod, aren't you, Sands?" Birch countered.

"Just telling it the way it is – or was. There was nothing benign about Roman rule. They were happy to use death as a method of terrorising native populations. Violence and oppression were the currencies they dealt in. So if you really want to know what the Roman's ever did for us – try a public crucifixion for starters."

"And we always thought that the Romans were the good guys – keeping the barbarians from the gates."

"Well, they were if you lived in Rome – but not if you were a down-trodden Briton. This is an occupied country and the people manning the frontier are mercenaries brought in from all over the Roman Empire to subjugate the native population. The guys we've been fighting aren't even Roman citizens yet – but they will be after they've served in the army for twenty-five years. That's the ultimate aim of all these guys: citizenship and the gift of a plot of land. They get a better deal out of the Romans than we've been giving the Gurkhas when they join our armed forces."

"We're grateful for the history lesson, Lieutenant." Birch's sarcasm created an uneasy, momentary silence. "But, it doesn't help us decide what our next move should be. I'd like to discuss what we are going to do and what our strategy is going to be? Do we stay where we are, south of the wall where there will be at least some form of law and order, or do we cross the wall and head north into the unknown? Do we risk giving ourselves up to the Romans or remain outlaws trying to survive off the land?"

"That's a bloody stupid question, sir", interjected Stogdon.

"I've warned you, Private, watch your mouth. I'm still your superior officer."

"Superior? You ain't got a bloody clue, have you?"

"Come on, Stog, we're all in this together, remember?" Crawley cautioned.

Birch chose to meet the challenge head on. "Go on, then, Stogdon, if you're such an expert then please enlighten us." Despite his bravado it was clear that Birch's authority was on its last legs.

"Ok, sir, here's how I see things. Over the past twenty-four hours your one contribution to this group has been to crash the helicopter that landed us up in this shit in the first place. Since then, you ain't made one leadership decision off your own bat. If it wasn't for the four of us you'd be still sitting on that bloody beach riddled with Roman spear holes. Who's been making all the decisions? She bloody has and he bloody has," he said pointing at Sands and Crawley. "You're completely out of your depth and you're a danger to any poor fucker that has the bad luck to be under your command. And you know something else? I really don't give a bloody toss whether we go north or south; it's unimportant to me. And do you know why? Because there's only one thing I'm worried about and that's what's happened to the Sarge and Charlie fireteam. You know what, yeah? To hell with whether we're alright; I want to know that they're alright. And if they're not, I want us to do something about it. Is that clear enough for you, sir?"

"Perfectly - you've just talked yourself into a charge of insubordination. Corporal, make a note of that."

Corporal Crawley shifted in his seat. "That ain't going to help matters, sir. I know Stogdon could have been more respectful in how he expressed himself. But in this case I happen to agree with everything he says, even though I'd have said it more diplomatic like."

"I see, and what about you, Ojokwu? Are you part of this mutiny, too?"

"If you want to put it in them terms, yeah. But remember, sir, them's your words, not mine. I just happen to agree you ain't the right person to lead the group in this situation."

"All sticking together, eh? Ok, Lieutenant Sands, it looks like you and I are in a minority of two in this matter. You men have no authority to overthrow your officers in this way."

"We're not challenging her authority, just yours," corrected Ojokwu.

"That's ridiculous! Lieutenant Sands will do what she's told and will back the authority of her fellow officer."

"No, I won't, Sir."

"You what, Lieutenant? Pull yourself together, woman, and do what you're told. I'm giving you a direct order."

Sands met his startled gaze head on. Her voice was calm and measured as she responded to her superior officer. "Captain

Birch, if we are going to have a chance of meeting up with the other group then you're going to have to relinquish your command."

Birch started and shook his head in astonishment.

"Lieutenant, for God's sake, this is mutiny. Think about what you're doing. I hold a Queen's commission. Who the hell is going to take command – Private Stogdon, perhaps?"

"Perhaps he could. He's certainly opinionated, and he's clearly decisive. But under the circumstances, I think I'd be the best choice."

"You?" replied Birch, dumbfounded. "For Christ's sake, Sands, this isn't a game. Have you taken leave of your senses? What makes you think you're so uniquely qualified to take command?"

"Firstly, I'm the only one here who speaks the language of the local population. Correct me if I'm wrong anyone?"

"Don't be so bloody ridiculous," countered Birch.

Crawley spoke up. "Not me, ma'am, I can't even say grace in Latin."

Sands appreciated his implicit support. "No big loss, Corporal. Christianity hasn't penetrated here anyway."

Birch attempted to reassert control. "This is no time for your clever quips, Sands. This is deadly serious. Think of what you're doing, for Christ's sake."

"Secondly," she continued, "I have a unique knowledge of the history, culture and *mores* of the people we are going to be dealing with."

"What's *mores*, Lieutenant?" asked Ojokwu.

"Never mind that, Private," Birch attempted to interrupt.

"Roman customs and values," she responded, cutting across her superior officer. "It gives me an insight into their behaviour and beliefs. If we're going to be able to take them on, then we have to be able to understand what motivates their actions."

"Hearts and minds, yeah?" deduced Ojokwu. "Is that what you're on about? Understanding the enemy's psychology?"

"Exactly. You may not know it yet, but I'm the best

intelligence officer you could find under these circumstances."

"I think I'm beginning to get the picture, ma'am," said Corporal Crawley. "And I like what I see."

Ojokwu spoke up next. "Ok, Lieutenant, you've convinced me. I'm prepared to serve under your command."

"Oh, for God's sake, this is absurd. Think about what you're doing," muttered Birch in desperation.

All eyes now turned to Stogdon who had been prowling around the fire as Sands spoke. "You know what, ma'am, you've talked yourself up well; but let's hope that's not all you can do. You've got my support for as long as you don't screw up like big-time Charlie over there."

"You'll regret that decision, Stogdon," Birch warned. "I know what she's like, you don't. You don't know what you're letting yourself in for. None of you do."

"Well, in that case I will take command," she confirmed. "And I'm going to issue my first two orders. Number one, we're on first-name terms from now on. My name's Kal, so please drop the ma'am stuff. Number two, you, Stogdon, what's your first name?"

"Just call me Stog."

"Ok, Stog, you are going to have to drop the attitude from now on. You speak to all of us now with respect, including Captain Birch."

"Anything you say, Kal."

"I mean it, Stog. Only one thing counts from now on and that's finding the other group. If you don't work with all of us collaboratively then you will sabotage our efforts."

"Ok, I'm proper cool with that; you can count on me from now on." Stogdon then nodded towards Birch. "But you may need to smooth his fucking feathers down a bit."

Birch bridled at the taunt. "I'm not accepting what's happened, Sands, and you can forget the chummy first-names, I'm not having that either. The name's Birch. As far as I'm concerned this is mutiny and betrayal and I won't forget it. But it seems that I've no option but to work with the team for the sake of all our lives."

"Ok, Birch, fair enough. That's all we can ask from any of us."

"Good." said Crawley, "My name's Mal, but I answer just as well to Crawley. Now what's the plan for tomorrow?"

"Here's what I've been thinking," replied Sands. "It strikes me that there are two things that we really have to do if we want to track down the other guys. The first is for some of us to return to the last place we saw them and see if we can follow the coast along in the chance of picking up any sign of where they came ashore. Mal, I thought you could take Stog and Ojo with you."

"Yeah, that's fine. If we have a chance we could scavenge for shellfish and maybe run out a line or two. We have some fish hooks."

"Now you'll have to be very careful of Roman patrols because the wall seems to come right down to the sea. The other thing I'd like to know is whether those fords across the mud are really passable at low tide. You never know, but we might be forced to escape north via the mud flats at some point. The more information you can provide us with, the better. Can I leave you to arrange the details?"

"Yep, no problem, and you want us to take Birch with us?"

"No, I have plans for me and Birch. He's going to cover me when I make a visit to the village outside the fort tomorrow."

"You what, are you mad?" exclaimed Birch. "You don't have to prove anything to me. If you get caught then we've as good as had it."

"Don't worry, this isn't all about you, Birch. I've thought it through. I'll wear the cape to cover myself so I don't stand out. I can nose around a bit and use my knowledge of Latin to pick up some local intelligence. If the worst comes to the worst, it'll simply turn into a shopping expedition. I've got a bit of money from that dead Roman's purse."

"What do you want me to do?" asked Birch. "I don't think I could carry off a convincing conversation if approached."

"Your job will be to hide out of sight and watch everything that happens through the field glasses. If anything happens to me then you've got to let the others know. But I don't want you stumbling down by yourself in your army fatigues to try and help me out. That way you simply get us both killed. Is that clear?"

"If you say so; but you're still taking a ridiculous risk."

"It's called decisive leadership – leading from the front. It's what I get paid for."

"Can't argue with that," said Ojokwu. "But how're you going to avoid getting nabbed tomorrow? You can't just walk in looking like that."

"I'll strip off all my outer clothes and just wear the *birrus* fastened together with a clasp; maybe my regimental badge or belt buckle would do the trick."

"Ok, but you've got to lose any other form of identification, jewellery etcetera, and what about your footwear?"

"I thought barefoot, or maybe socks?"

"No, I think Stog, here, could improvise something more convincing-looking, and comfortable, than bare feet. What d'you say, Stog?

"No problem," said Stogdon, "give us your inner soles and boot laces and I'll knock together a shit-hot pair of sandals."

"Thanks, Stog, size six, preferably. Must look presentable, don't want to let the British Army down."

Stogdon sucked his teeth. "Bloody women, but seeing as how it's you, ma'am, I'll do the best I can."

"Great, I'll pick them on my way in to town, then."

"Have you two quite finished your pathetic little joke?" interrupted Birch. "It's all very well having a laugh about it but she'll be taking her life in her hands in that village tomorrow.

"Lighten up, Birch, by the time we've finished with her, she could pass as an extra in 'Spartacus'," said Stogdon.

"I just think you won't be able to pass yourself off without attracting attention."

"I've thought about what I want to say," said Sands. "I feel properly prepared. If the worst comes to the worst, I've got hundreds of classical quotes to fall back on."

The rest stared at her.

"That was a joke, guys. At least we've got to try something."

"Exactly how good is your Latin, Sands?" asked Birch.

"It's got to be more fluent than most of the local population. It's a calculated gamble. But I promise I won't be taking any unnecessary risks."

NINE

That night the group took it in turns to sleep under the improvised shelter. They kept each other company in pairs by maintaining guard and feeding the campfire with fresh wood to help keep the worst of the night's chill at bay. There was one light shower but otherwise calmness prevailed; fear had been replaced by a clear sense of duty and obligation. Tomorrow they were going to set out to locate the other members of their platoon.

At about two in the morning, Sands found herself sharing guard duties with Crawley. They were both grateful for the chance to talk and to measure the weight of their uncertainties.

"Look, Mal. It's clear to me that you're going to have to lead these soldiers when it comes to operational matters. Stogdon and Ojokwu trust you implicitly and Birch will respect your experience as a combatant, which is something I'm clearly not. Are you going to be okay with that? Because I'm going to have to rely on you a lot from now on."

The corporal smiled at Sands. "I gotta hand it to you, Kal, you proper know how to handle people. You've got Stog and Ojokwu on board already. And you can rely on me all you like. Tell me what role you'd like me to play and I'll be right happy to do it. You've dealt with this whole situation with much more command than anyone else."

"I think it probably seems less alien to me, this whole nightmare situation. I feel like I'm in a dream but in a way that I'm controlling, if that makes any sense?"

"No, not really," he replied. "I just feel like I'm in a nightmare, full stop. The worst thing is losing Thompson. When I wake up tomorrow that's what I hope I've imagined. If only he was still with us I wouldn't give a shit about the

Romans. I can't get my head around that side of things anyway. But I'll never be able to forget the sight of his body hung up on a pole like that; that's what's keeping me awake."

"Yeah, I know. But if you don't sleep then who's going to keep these other guys safe tomorrow, hey? We've got a duty of care now to all members of Her Majesty's armed forces currently serving in the Roman Empire. And by my reckoning that makes a grand total of ten people, including you and me, and five of those are currently unaccounted for, presumed missing in action. But we're going to find them, I promise you that. You, me, Birch, Stogdon and Ojokwu are going to track them down, you got that?"

"Yeah, thanks Kal, I got it."

The following morning everyone woke early. Nothing could disguise the fact that they'd had a lousy night's sleep. The weather was dull but fine. Ojokwu had collected a fresh crop of field mushrooms that had sprung up overnight in the adjoining rough meadow and had baked them for breakfast in the dying embers of the camp fire. Afterwards, the camp was cleared, leaving precious little evidence that they'd ever spent the night there.

The relative security that they'd all felt the night before, encased as they were under the blanket of a primordial sky, had now dissipated and been replaced by a dry-throated uneasiness. There were no quips or barbs being thrown around this morning; all was quiet and personal exchanges were perfunctory and distracted.

Finally, Sands pulled the group together. She drew a map in the soil with a stick.

"Ok, this is what we know so far of the immediate vicinity. The wall starts over by the sea at a location which we know as Bowness on Solway. It was somewhere immediately south of here that we came ashore. It seems perfectly likely that the other team came ashore north of this fort. If we move east along the wall we come to two smaller forts located a mile or two apart. The third of these forts is the unnamed one that is immediately north of us and which I plan to visit this morning. We can't get to the shoreline to the north without crossing the wall, so you three are going to have to head back due west for about four miles to hit the sea. Somewhere, I'm sure, there are some ancient fords across the mudflats of the Solway Firth. Your job is to recce the coast at low tide and to find those causeways – we may need to use them to escape north at some point. Take the field glasses with you and try to survey the area as accurately as you can, bearing in mind that we may need to cross under cover of darkness."

"The other important information that Birch and Crawley brought back yesterday was that there are two forts five miles east of here, one of which is a sizeable civilian settlement about two miles south of the wall itself. It's likely to be the town that we now know as Carlisle."

"Do us a favour," scoffed Stogdon, "I knew that Carlisle was the town that time forgot, but that's plain taking the piss."

Sands ignored the interjection and ploughed ahead. "The Roman name of the large cavalry fort on the wall itself completely escapes me. I know it, but my mind's a blank. The anglicised name is Stanwix, so we'll refer to it as that for the time being. Anyone else have anything else to add?"

"I know that there'll be rich pickings along the shoreline, especially at low tide," volunteered Crawley.

"Yeah, mussels, cockles, oysters and razorfish should be easy to collect," added Ojokwu.

"And the Solway Firth fishermen have always been famous for the way they net salmon," said Birch. "I remember them working along the tidal flats when I was a teenager."

"The sea's going to be our best and most reliable source of protein," concluded Crawley, and the others nodded agreement.

"I accept that, but if we are forced to move inland to evade capture then we have to have a staple that we can carry with us," argued Sands.

"Like what?" queried Ojokwu.

"Like grain," replied Sands. "That way, we don't have to forage everywhere and we can make our own porridge and bread as we march. Bread is the staple of the Roman army's diet. Each soldier will consume a third of a ton a year."

"Well, I guess that solves our roughage problem, then," conjectured Stogdon.

The others laughed, Birch the loudest. He clapped his hands together with delight. "So wheat it is, then. I hope you've got your shopping trolley, Sands, because you're going to need it."

"Hey, Birch, you're coming with me, remember? I shop, you carry."

"I'll carry, but I'm not going down into that shit-hole."

Crawley turned to his two privates. "Ok, lads, now let's start getting ready, we've got a long day ahead of us. And you, Kal - let's get you dressed."

"Hang on. I know you mean well, but I've been getting myself dressed for years now."

Crawley reddened. "Sorry, I didn't mean nothing by it."

There was a momentary, awkward silence before Sands terminated the conversation. "Ok, let's push on, then," she said, ensuring that she had the last word.

TEN

Birch accompanied Sands as far as the Roman road that led to the *vicus* and on to the fort behind it. He kept Sands preoccupied by pestering her for Roman vocabulary and common phrases; it was clear he'd soon have to communicate for himself.

Sands felt calm. She'd already determined that Thompson wasn't the only one of their number who'd died. She'd already visualised the tragic reports on the television, the shocking on-the-spot breaking-news items, the distraught family members, the appalled colleagues and the panicked senior brass. And she'd thought most of all about her Uncle Sterland, about what a terrible blow it would be to him to lose his adoptive daughter, about how he must be suffering. It helped her to visualise these events taking place two thousand years hence, and it helped her feel less fearful in her present incarnation, if that, indeed, was what it was. But exactly what was it that she was experiencing? Was it re-birth, perhaps, or a pre-birth, even, or just possibly a pre-incarnation? Whatever the name for it, she was aware of one thing more than anything else. She felt hugely powerful and self-actualised, felt a sense of herself as a truly autonomous, unshackled person, a feeling that she'd experienced once before, under tragic circumstances, when her parents had been killed and she'd found herself alone and adrift in the world.

While Birch continued to pester her for fresh Latin vocabulary, her mind was absorbed elsewhere. A quotation was rolling around her brain – an existentialist maxim, perhaps, from Camus, maybe, or Sartre? Yes, it was Jean-Paul Sartre, the one about personal responsibility and freedom. What was it again? Something about man being condemned to be free; because once thrown into the world, he is responsible for everything he does. Now she had a real understanding of what it meant to be thrown into the world. The world into which we are hurled is not normally peopled with vicious Romans, she thought, but it is a far more fearful place for all that. We spend our entire lives under a dark shadow of fear, of not doing the right thing, of failing to live up to expectations, of letting people down, of living, of not living, of dying, particularly of dying. But Sands was aware that she was already dead and yet she felt free. How could that be?

As they approached the road, Birch brought her out of her reverie. "Ok, you're on your own now; I'll wait for you here. Remember, we don't take any unnecessary risks." He adjusted her cape and re-fastened the military badge that held the garment together across her chest. He looked at her and tried to imagine her as an ancient Briton. Her appearance seemed plausible enough; muddy feet, roughly made sandals, dirty face, damp-looking *birrus*, and, judging by the enthusiasm with which she clasped together the edges of her cape, no undergarments to speak of. "Well," he pronounced "you've got a fighting chance of pulling it off."

She nodded, turned and started to walk the remaining mile into the village. The closer she got to her destination, the more she felt past and present coalescing into a uniform time register, until, at last, all she had left to focus on was the unpredictability of the future and the mysteries it held in store, like a series of locked promises.

Sands started to feel unbalanced, her senses immersed in the hyper-realistic quality of the village scene she now proceeded to enter. She became overwhelmed by a sensation of intensely saturated colours and over-sharpened detail, almost as if she was progressing through the pre-determined stages of a computer-generated video game, or viewing everything through the distortion of a massive prism. It felt alien and yet reassuringly mundane.

She floated through the outskirts of the village without attracting any attention and, although the whole experience had a trance-like quality to it, she was still able to pay detailed attention to the events going on around her. She counted each building, noted each doorway, chimney, window, courtyard and shop. She took stock of every item on sale, every service on offer and every trade being practiced.

The *vicus* sprawled in an untidy manner over at least five acres, an area approximately the same size as the fort itself. She counted twenty-eight different businesses and service providers. There were traders, merchants and small-scale peddlers selling trinkets and bric-a-brac, and the more predictable range of basic service providers such as weavers, cobblers, blacksmiths and metal goods repairers; all the services, in short, that any military garrison would need to sustain itself in comfort and convenience. Closest to the entrance of the fort, Sands came across the inevitable entertainment quarter, containing a tavern, a couple of gambling houses and a large building that seemed to serve as both a brothel and a laundry, among other things.

The commercial structures were constructed with timber frames and the walls made of traditional wattle and daub, a method by which woven sticks and branches were fixed between the frames and then overlaid with a mixture of earth, clay and straw. One or two of the grander buildings contained upper storeys and most enjoyed open frontages onto the street from where business was transacted. Yards, storage spaces and workshops appeared to lie behind the front of the buildings with living accommodation presumably right at the rear. Some of the more outlying buildings had the appearance of small-holdings with extensive market gardens attached and finally there was a small scattering of rudely-built domestic buildings of poor-quality construction.

As she finished her circuit of the *vicus*, Sands found herself to the east of the fort and less than one hundred metres from Hadrian's Wall itself. Her attention was drawn to an imposing stone building, raised higher than the others around it, which seemed to consist of half a dozen rooms. It lay just below the wall, a decent stone's throw from the fort's east gate and was connected to it by a paved path which supported a constant traffic of auxiliaries strolling backwards and forwards along it. Judging by the relaxed demeanour and wet hair of those returning from the building, and the steam that was escaping from the vents and clay pipes around its base, Sands surmised that this must be the military bathhouse. She made a careful note of the size of the guard detail outside the bathhouse and the procedure that was followed to effect entry. Sands was struck by the poor discipline of the troops manning the fort's east gate; they were a bored detail, waving men through without care or proper scrutiny.

After a few minutes she returned south via the outer circuit road. This hugged the edge of the small township and gave on to rough-looking, enclosed pasture that supported the garrison's small dairy herd. By now she had done a complete tour of the *vicus*. She'd concentrated on the strategic layout and plan of the buildings as she had progressed on her tour, but it was only now that she realised that she had failed to pay any meaningful attention to the local inhabitants. As she returned to the now familiar main street, she noticed that individual traders and pedestrians were starting to acknowledge her openly. A pair of North African auxiliaries walked past on the other side of the street, showing a fine contempt and disregard for the local inhabitants that they encountered en route. An idle curse here, and a half-hearted shove there, spoke volumes for the power that these soldiers were able to wield on the street without any fear of recrimination or retaliation. The native population was certainly cowed by the military presence, despite deriving a healthy living from trading in such close proximity to it. Sands hurried past with her gaze averted, and with unsettling memories of Kandahar, Basra and Baghdad jostling her conscience. Suddenly she found herself outside the shop frontage of a merchant who sold a range of grain and fresh vegetables, as well as hardware and cloth goods.

The trader greeted her, and Sands responded in strict, formal Latin as if reciting from a secondary school primer. He examined her with curiosity, and enquired what she would like to buy. He went through the foodstuffs on display, pointing to, and naming, every item as he went, sensing, somehow, that he was dealing with someone for whom this was an exceptional and demanding activity, and one which required huge powers of concentration. She heard all about the wheat, barley, oats, spelt and rye on sale and the lentils and chickpeas and the wide range of imported spices available too. Her personal preference, intensified by a deep hunger, tended towards the spectacular non-uniform cabbages, broad beans, carrots, radishes and garlic on display.

Sands struck up a rapport with her fellow-countryman. After a few minutes of bargaining over prices, the process of Roman shopping seemed very familiar to her. She bartered with enthusiasm and was puzzled by her decision to reject the man's lentils on the grounds that they were over-priced. "Compared with what?" she mused to herself.

Finally, and with rare satisfaction, Sands brought the transactions to an end. She'd bought five kilos of wheat and paid a supplement to have the grain threshed. In addition, she purchased a frying pan and a camp-kettle and some salt for seasoning and preserving meat. The merchant then helped her to fold a couple of cheap woollen blankets to serve as improvised sacks, into which the goods were loaded and then carried, one over each shoulder. Sands made one final sortie past the fort's entrances, this time concentrating on the main gatehouse or *Porta Praetoria*.

As Sands approached the monumental entrance, a shocking spectacle met her sight. On the left hand side of the gate stood three wooden stakes; from each of these hung a freshly-killed human carcass. Each was suspended by its feet from supporting ropes and by massive iron pins which had been driven through flesh and bone and deep into the wood behind. The bodies had been stripped bare and the lower halves had been flayed of all skin, leaving a livid display of raw, bloodied sinew, muscle and subcutaneous fat.

Sands' revulsion was too much to bear, and she felt herself starting to retch. She turned to the side of the road, fell to her knees and threw up into a narrow ditch. She'd seen dismembered corpses before when on duty in different parts of the world, and she'd often been appalled by the physical suffering experienced by civilian casualties, especially in areas occupied by her own armed forces, but the overwhelming shock and revulsion she now felt was of a different magnitude. To witness this level of barbarous brutality at first hand, and in such close proximity, was more than she was able to stand.

Sands drew a few deep breaths and tried to restore herself. She was aware that her response had attracted the attention of the auxiliaries on guard duty at the southern gate. She got to her feet, brushed the mud off her knees and glimpsed back at the hanging corpses, unable to contain a sudden fascination with the obscene sight they presented. She felt a desperate sympathy for the suffering of these anonymous Britons who'd probably been flayed while still conscious or, at the very least, still breathing. She tried to imagine what sort of appalling crimes they must have committed to merit such a punishment. There was clearly an element of score-settling involved here. If the Romans had wanted to create an exemplary punishment to cow the local population, then they'd surpassed themselves with this gratuitous demonstration.

Sands spat to remove the foul taste from her mouth. She was aware that two soldiers were now approaching her, so she turned, slung her sacks over her shoulders and started to walk away. She heard laughter behind her and the sound of footsteps quickening as the auxiliaries tracked her down the street. She put her head down and crossed the road, glancing nervously over her shoulder. The faster she walked, the more the distance shrank between herself and her pursuers It was clear that they were toying with her, enjoying her distress at having to flee in fear. She could hear the insulting cat-calls and whistles that they directed at her back and she braced herself for the moment that the play-acting would end and her interrogation would begin. She didn't have long to wait.

At the next intersection the two auxiliaries pounced. They

grabbed Sands by the shoulders and pushed her up against the shop front where she had previously bought her provisions. Sands resisted her sudden arrest, shrugging the men's hands off her body and staring them in the face.

"What do you want?" she demanded in Latin. "I have done nothing wrong."

"Who are you, girl?"

"My name is Galla Placidia."

"And where are you from?"

"My family is from Eboracum."

"That is a long way hence. What are you doing in Aballava?"

"My brother is a trader. He sells grain to the Roman garrison along the *Vallum Aelium*."

"And where is your brother?"

"I don't know. I have come to find him. He must return home. My father has died."

One of the auxiliaries turned to the merchant, who was listening to the conversation and who had sold some items to Sands earlier. "Do you know this woman or her brother?"

He shrugged his shoulders. "I don't know either of them. I keep myself to myself."

The soldier turned his gaze back to Sands. "In that case, we are under orders to arrest you. Strangers must be taken into custody to be questioned by a senior officer."

"I only wanted to buy some food. What do I do with these?" Sands gestured to her sacks.

"Leave your goods here." They pointed to the merchant. "He'll keep them safe till you return. Won't you, old man?"

Sands was bundled down the road, and, despite her frequent protests, she was dealt regular painful whips to the back of her thighs. One soldier in particular, the senior of the pair, appeared to take particular pleasure in tormenting her.

"Come on Galla Placidia. Let's see if we can find your brother," he taunted.

Sands protected herself as best she could, gritted her teeth and responded to every blow by addressing her tormentors in English. "Rome is finished. You're history, you bastards."

Once they entered the fort, the guards adopted a more soldierly manner and the physical abuse ceased. It was replaced, however, by a chorus of wolf-whistles from auxiliaries who were standing outside the half-timbered and thatch-roofed barrack blocks situated on either side of the Via Praetoria, the main access road leading into the heart of the military compound. Sands paid close attention to the lay-out of the fort as she was accompanied through the heart of it. She counted two double-rows of barracks, each about forty to fifty metres long. She knew that a Roman century was comprised of eighty soldiers. She was already beginning to estimate the overall strength of the garrison at less than five hundred foot soldiers.

Once past the barracks, they passed in between two low buildings. The right-hand one was a stable and the other housed a series of workshops, including a smithy and carpentry shop. As far as she could see, this configuration seemed to be mirrored on the northern side of the compound.

Beyond the stable and workshop blocks, they approached a wide street that ran unobstructed between the east and west gates. This was the *Via Principalis*. As they paused, waiting to cross, Sands was able to absorb the scene in some detail and it all seemed rather familiar to her. Everything was neat, ordered and well presented with soldiers going about their duties in practiced routine, some cleaning kit, some undertaking guard detail, some doing training exercises, much as they would do in any typical British Army camp in Afghanistan, Iraq or Germany.

This felt like very familiar terrain to Sands and despite the obvious hostility being displayed to her, she was now in her element. She felt respect for these ordinary men going about the daily duties in such a single-minded manner. They were doing a difficult job in a hostile, strange land, many hundreds of miles from their homes and families. They represented a tradition of progress and order that would survive thousands of years and find echoes in many aspects of advanced Western institutions. These people were her forebears in a meaningful sense, intellectually, philosophically, culturally. Their pragmatic embrace of discipline, organisation and ingenuity spoke to her twenty-first century mind, unlike the disorganised tribes camped on the doorstep, preoccupied with their kinship groups, clans and petty rivalries and disputes. She resented the fact that the merchant had refused to speak up for her when he'd had the chance. His self-interest had won out over any sense of solidarity with a young fellow-Briton in jeopardy.

To the right of where the two guards had halted, there was an impressive-looking small villa with an inner courtyard. This was the *Praetorium*, the garrison commander's house. Occupying the same position to the left, were two large granaries built on raised, pillared floors with ventilation channels beneath and loading platforms in front. Sands knew that there was likely to be enough grain stored in there to sustain the entire garrison for a year or more.

It was clear that the detainee was being taken to the camp headquarters, the *Principia*, the administrative and religious focus of the fort, an imposing stone building which faced the *Via Principalis*. After crossing the street, they entered into a heavily guarded inner paved courtyard, the circumference of which was composed of a columned portico that provided a series of walkways to offer protection from the elements. Sands was told to halt; one of her guards advanced towards the hall which lay at the far side of the courtyard across from the entrance. He exchanged a few words with an unseen interrogator, walked back to where Sands stood and ushered her forward.

"Ok, this is it," Sands said to herself. "Keep it together."

ELEVEN

"Yes? What is it?"

The camp commander and his cohort tribune were deep in discussion and didn't want to be disturbed. They stood at the back of a large room that was lit by oil lamps and seemed to serve as an administrative centre but was also populated with legionary insignia, decorated animal hides and religious effigies, including what looked like a large altar on which sat a number of small sculptures.

The senior guard spoke up with a confident voice. "I beg to report, Commander. We came upon this woman in the vicus. She's a stranger and she's openly wearing military insignia." He pointed to the brooch which clasped the edges of her cape together. Sands winced at her carelessness.

The two men glanced up from what they were studying and then turned their backs to her once more. The younger of the two commanders responded in a distracted manner.

"You've done well, Corporal. We will deal with her shortly."

Sands now had the opportunity to take in her immediate surroundings. Although she was shaking with trepidation, she felt so displaced from events that she could scarcely claim ownership of her fear. She felt sufficiently separated from reality to be nurturing a dangerous and ill-placed bravado.

Her attention was drawn to an altar stone at the rear of the room, and its recently carved inscription:

I O M ET NVMINIBVS AVGGG N MAVRORVM
AVR VALERIANI GALLIENIQ
CAELVIBIANVS TRIB COH P P N S S
INSTANTE IVL RVFINO PRINCIPE

As she waited she started to decipher its meaning.

"For Jupiter Best and Greatest and the Divine Spirits of the three Augusti, the Numerus Maurorum Aurelianorum, for Valerian and the Gallieni, Caeluibianus, tribune of the Cohort, Praepositus of the Company, fulfilled this undertaking in the presence of the commander-in-chief Julius Rufinus."

So she had been right. Those dark-skinned troops were Moors, "Numerus Maurorum", raised by Aurelian in North Africa. And now, after racking her memory, she had a date; the reference to the joint emperors Valerian and his son Galienus placed the time frame at around 255-260 AD. And it was possible that either of these two men in front of her could be the tribune, Caeluibianus, or the commander-in chief, Julius Rufinus. I O M, she knew, was shorthand for Jupiter Optimus Maximus, Jupiter being spelt with the letter I in place of the J, which was missing in the Latin alphabet.

Her attention then focused on the animal hides and their painted surface decorations. As well as displaying examples of complex patterning, the hides were also covered with hand-painted script and Roman numerals, dates perhaps. She stared with fascination, trying to make sense of the symbols displayed on the surface of the hides. She tilted her head slightly to decipher the Roman numerals which at first glance looked like MMV MMVI MMX. Confused, she checked the numerals once more, certain that she must have misread them. But no, those were definitely the numbers and they gave her an uncomfortable feeling, linking her, as they did, to her twenty-first century self.

A horrible realisation started to infect her. The script above the numbers was damaged slightly but it was still legible, especially to an English reader. Slowly the shapes, symbols and digits began to coalesce into a coherent picture, similar to the process through which photosensitive paper begins to reveal an image when submerged in a developing agent. "Oh my God", she thought "it's a tattoo, a human tattoo. Those aren't animal hides, they're human skins!" And then as soon as this appalling recognition dawned, reality started to collapse in on her as all the tattoos became immediately recognisable: Chelsea FC Champions 2005 2006 2010.

The banality of the words and dates resonated like a bell inside her skull. These were human skins, belonging to those poor crucified creatures hanging on their gibbets outside, and had been flayed from their bodies while the men were probably still alive. And those men weren't ancient Britons, they were her fellow countrymen, her comrades in arms, the men of Charlie fireteam.

The reality was too horrifying for her to contemplate but the evidence of her own eyes could not be denied. Despite an overwhelming sense of nausea, all she thought about now was the practical task of identifying these individual men, and she studied each detail of every tattoo with forensic care.

She would honour these men by re-humanising them through maintaining a professional detachment. It's what her colleagues back at the camp would want; information about exactly who had died and, just as importantly, who was therefore still unaccounted for. The tattoos were the only form of identification available to them.

As she stared at the skins in obvious concentration, the two officers nudged each other and began to take an interest in her for the first time. Unnoticed, one of the men moved towards her, out of her immediate line of vision.

"I see you wear an eagle crest crowned with regal insignia." The sudden approach of this younger of the two officers startled her. He spoke in an assertive, declamatory manner, very Roman and grandiloquent. "Does your family have noble connections?" he asked, as he ran his fingers over the surface of the brooch.

Sands fought to retain her composure and to contrive a suitable response. "No, sir, the eagle is the symbol of Roman imperial power."

"It is the symbol of the Roman legion," he corrected. He pulled aside the edges of the cape to inspect her nearly naked body. "An eagle doesn't catch flies. Why do you choose to adorn yourself with such insignia?"

"I love Rome and its citizens. From different peoples you have made one native land. As Rome falls, so falls the whole world."

"But love can be rich with both honey and venom."

Sands would not be drawn. "I possess venom only for the enemies of Rome," she replied, her eyes staring straight ahead, and her body rigid.

"For men such as these?" The commander half-turned and gestured with disdain towards the human hides stretched out on their frames.

"Betrayal is its own reward. Yet I pity the enemy who is treated with such vengeance."

The commander observed her reaction closely as he probed her words for their full meaning. "He threatens the innocent who spares the guilty. No man is above the law."

Sands fought to control her feelings and looked down at the floor. She was determined not to be cowed. "All things are presumed to be lawfully done, until it is shown to be the reverse."

"You condemn that which you do not understand," said the commander with a note of menace. "The welfare of the people is to be the highest law. The law does not concern itself with the smallest things."

"But it's a good shepherd's job to shear his flock, not to flay them." Sands pointed at the skins. "One shouldn't make evil in order that good should be made of it."

"In men's affairs, as in nature, the end justifies the means."

"But nature teaches us many things." For the first time she turned to look her interrogator full in the face. "A water drop hollows a stone, not by force but by falling often. You may drive out Nature with a pitchfork but she'll still hurry back!"

"You favour speaking in epigrams, I see. In that case a word of advice, girl; abundant caution does no one any harm. To quote the great Publius Virgilius Maro, "The only hope for the conquered is the hope for no safety". You'd be well-advised to be more circumspect in what you say."

Sands had been too outspoken already, but her combative

nature would not let her withdraw. "But in the *Aeneid,* Publius Virgilius Maro also wrote "Fortune sides with him who dares". Am I to be condemned for preferring liberty with danger to peace with slavery?"

As soon as she'd spoken, she realised her foolhardiness.

"You ask me if you are to be condemned?" The officer paused to allow the full theatrical effect to be felt by his opponent.

"Certainly, you are, but only for expressing such a preference in front of a Roman commander who is charged with stamping out rebellious sentiments. Do not depend on your sex, bearing and education to win you continued preferment."

The older officer drew his superior aside for a conspiratorial chat which they conducted in an audible whisper. "Commander, do you suspect her of being allied to the four men we captured yesterday? Her appearance and manner gives grounds for suspicion."

"No," said the superior officer. "She's educated, although she speaks an unusual Latin dialect. Those others were raiders from over the sea, from Ireland probably. They were totally illiterate and spoke a strange tongue with not one word of Latin between them. I checked and her body has no sign of the blue body markings of the others."

"But the other prisoner doesn't have markings either."

"And neither do you, Caeluibianus. Would you prefer that I should suspect you too?"

The commander returned his attention to Sands. "You are hereby dismissed. Get back to your family where you belong," he said, his blood-lust clearly sated for the day.

"Return her to where you found her," he said to the guard. "And she is not to be molested – do I make myself clear?"

As Sands turned to leave the room, the commander called out to her, "And girl." He picked up an apple and tossed it to her, amused at his own impetuous generosity. "Go in peace."

Sands glowered back. She stole a final glance at the remains of the dead soldiers, took a bite out of the fruit and returned his valediction under her breath. "Go in peace?" she queried in her native tongue. The two Romans looked at her in surprise. She answered her own question with defiance, her response echoing around the hall. "In your sick fucking dreams."

Seconds later, Sands was ejected back into the bright sunlight and found herself retracing her earlier path towards the main gate. At one point, as she was passing the workshop block on her right, she heard the clear reverberations of an anguished voice crying out in pain. This was followed by the sound of a muffled oath delivered in colloquial English.

She glanced at the guard to her right to gauge his reaction. "Ignore it," he said. "Just an enemy of Rome; he won't be worrying you at all."

Sands' hopes soared. "So that must be the fourth soldier that the commander referred to just now. He's alive still – if only for the time being."

Now she had to get back to the others as quickly as she could. The life of a British soldier was hanging in the balance. And they had to devise a plan to rescue him before he suffered the same fate as his three platoon members.

TWELVE

Sterland Morris and Robert Jamieson are standing outside the main entrance to St Michael's Church in Burgh by Sands. It's mid-afternoon and they've just driven up from Carlisle, which lies half a dozen miles to the south-east, after a long, conversational lunch. The sun-dappled journey, taken at a leisurely pace, has helped to relax the pair of them, following a fraught and fruitless morning in which they'd been stonewalled by the official liaison officers assigned to brief the relatives of those on board the missing Lynx. During lunch, to help raise their spirits, Jamieson had offered to drive them over to inspect the site of the Burgh by Sands hoard and to try and catch a glimpse of the nearby search operation being conducted over the Solway Firth. The two men, although very different in background and manner, have struck up an easy rapport and are now casually enjoying their first sight of this small late 12th century fortified church.

The morning, by contrast, had proved exceptionally frustrating and dispiriting. A series of meetings and briefings with the police, representatives of the emergency services and army spokesmen had revealed little concrete information about the fate of Lieutenant Kal Sands and the other soldiers who were onboard the Lynx helicopter when it went down. The search for survivors was still ongoing, but, as yet, there was no palpable evidence of a crash landing at sea. It was proving very mystifying, and none of the news agencies were able to provide any additional information to help shed light on what was, or wasn't, happening.

The detour to a rural backwater of a village was proving a comforting and timely distraction to the two men.

"So, here we are, Robert. This church sits on the exact site, likely as not, of one of the main structures of the Roman fort of Aballava; maybe the granary or, more likely, the *Principia*, the main administrative quarters."

"Really? I had no idea. I've visited St Michael's on a number of occasions but I never realised the significance of its location. My chief interest has always been in the stained-glass."

The building is positioned in a pleasant spot, surrounded by an ancient, verdant graveyard and reached along a picturesque tree-lined churchyard path. The main rectangular tower has a massive, uncompromising authority, and had clearly been built as a defensive structure, complete with six foot-thick walls, tiny windows and arrow slits.

"You know, when you stand here, on this impossibly beautiful afternoon, in this quintessentially lovely English setting, there are certain things that are impossible to contemplate."

"Such as?"

"Well, how about the fact that, eighteen hundred years ago, around the time that that hoard of gold coins was being buried under a wall near here, the administration of local Roman rule, with all its military pragmatism, would have been conducted from the very spot on which we're now standing?"

"And what else?"

"I beg your pardon?"

"What else? You said that there were *things*, in the plural, that were impossible to contemplate?"

Morris hesitates, taken aback by his own transparency. "You're right, Robert, I was really thinking of Kal. It's impossible to contemplate that I won't see her again."

"I'm sorry, it was thoughtless of me to press you."

"Oh, that's alright, it's time I started facing up to reality. Shall we go inside?"

Morris looks closely at the ancient arched stone doorway as he pushes open the modest front door of the church and ushers Jamieson inside. The interior is bright and plain in appearance, with whitewashed walls supported by warm light-coloured stone columns and arches, above which hangs a dark wooden roof. After circumnavigating the nave, and admiring the stained glass windows featuring various northern saints, they sit down together in the pew nearest the chancel.

"This church dates from the twelfth century, purportedly built with stones taken from Hardrian's Wall," muses Morris. He looks around him, as if to confirm the truth of this supposition.

"It seems a sensible and practical thing to have done, in the circumstances," replies Jamieson. "Do you know who the monarch is, represented in that window, over there?" He points to a long, thin piece of stained glass, clearly not contemporaneous with the ancient fabric of the building itself.

"I could make a wild guess. Is that Braveheart's nemesis?"

"That's right, the 'Hammer of the Scots', Edward the First."

"The man who subjugated Scotland and slew Mel Gibson?"

"Indeed. Seven hundred years ago he was on his way to overcome Scottish resistance when he contracted dysentery near here. His body was brought back to this church and was laid out on this very spot."

"Good God, in the sorry annals of military subjugation, this wee church certainly has some history."

"Oh, but there's more to the story - come and have a look at the West tower."

They walk back down the nave, away from the altar, and at the far end they encounter a massive iron gate, more suited to a prison than a church, which barred the entrance to the square tower. A heavy slide of the bolt unlocks the gate and the two men enter through a thick wall, nearly seven feet wide, into a square tower with a stone, vaulted ceiling.

"Good God, just look at these fortifications, Robert. This was a serious defensive position, and look up there at those arrow-slits high in the wall. This was a place of military as well as religious sanctuary"

"And I think I'm right in saying that the west tower is older than the original church," responds Jamieson. "So, this may be evidence that the Scots were able to turn the tables against their invaders and carry the fight to the local English forces."

"Well, who can blame the Scots?" replies Morris. "It's the

inevitable response to long-term military intervention by a foreign power. It's a point I never stopped making to Kal. I was apoplectic when she decided to join the forces."

Jamieson is taken aback by this unexpected conflation of issues. He detects a cry of anguish in Morris's outburst.

"But why were you so opposed to her enlisting?"

"Partly for the reason I've just outlined. She was a historian, and a bloody good one at that. She had a historical overview that gave her a privileged perspective on current events. She really had no business getting involved in fighting an aggressive, imperialist war in one foreign country, never mind in two, and all by the time she was in her mid-twenties."

"Sterland, I respect everyone's right to their own opinions, and you've clearly got strong ones, but didn't Kal also have a right to do what she thought was best? I mean, she must have thought it through? There are plenty of people - including me, I might add - who think that, sometimes, military interventions produce beneficial results and can be justified on moral and political grounds."

"It may seem irrational to you," replied Morris, "but I just still feel so angry with her. We just don't need people like her fighting wars. Her job was to uncover the truth from the past and, in revealing it to others, to explain the world in a way that sheds light and emancipates people. God knows, there are enough scare-mongers and war-mongers and hate-mongers out there to sink civilisation for good. It's the role of historians like Kal and me to hold the lessons of the past up, like a mirror, to the venal, mendacious politicians who claim to represent our interests."

"Like "Kal and me," you said. Is that how you viewed your relationship? Two noble musketeers off to fight the world? That's a hell of a weight of expectation to place on a young woman who's just graduated."

"I know, I know," says Morris, suddenly chastened.

"In fact, if I was a betting man, I'd wager that it's not her you're really angry with at all. Forgive me if I'm overstepping the mark, Sterland, but is it not more accurate to say you're angry with yourself? Is it possible you're angry for allowing your personal resentments to colour your relationship with Kal over the past few years." He looks closely at his crestfallen colleague and places a comforting hand on his shoulder. "Am I right?"

"Life's not fair."

"Well that's something we can both agree on."

"She has so much to offer and now she may be gone forever. I know I'm clutching at straws but she had such an amazing life-force. She's always been an extraordinary person; I could always sense her presence in a building even when I couldn't see her."

"That sounds like the perfect description of the instinctive bond linking parent and child. I'm very familiar with the feeling."

"But I wasn't her parent, Robert; I was a surrogate, at best, and yet I still feel an extraordinary bond of kinship that seems unbreakable. I mean, I am nowhere near her now, and yet I can sense her physical force in this ancient spot right now as we speak. How does one make sense of that?"

"Love for a child is the most potent force that most of us ever experience. It can destabilise us and soothe in equal measure. But there is a certainty to it that never comes close to being equalled in any other aspects of our existence. And I say that with all due respect to my dear wife, who I'm pretty sure would agree unhesitatingly with me."

"Well that kind of certainty has never existed for me. Every scrap of bonding between the two of us had to be fought for; there was never even the remotest hint of instinctive certitude about the process. We grew to love and respect each other through a battle of attrition. After her parents died, Kal became very much her own person; she was extraordinarily self-possessed and confident in her own skin for a fourteen year old. She simply refused to give up control to anyone else, particularly me, even when it was abundantly clear that it was in her best interests to do so. If she wanted to do something, then she would just go ahead and do it, and no one would be able to dissuade her from her course of action."

"That must have been difficult for you to deal with."

"It was bloody infuriating! I've never had to deal with not getting my own way in life. And now I felt reduced to the role of useless old retainer, out-thought, out-fought and way off the pace. I tell you, she made absolute mincemeat of me, and I'm not ashamed to admit it. Those years of ritual humiliation were the best years of my life – by far."

"It sounds like she knocked you in to shape then, Sterland."

"Certainly did. But she also did a fair amount of bending me out of shape. Do you know why I think she ended up joining the Army Air Corps?"

"To put you in your place, I wouldn't be surprised."

"No, but I did think that might have had something to do with it. No, the reason she joined the Army Air Corps was a deeply personal one, and it really shows you the mark of the woman. She wanted to confront her demons head on, and I'm sure that what was motivating her was the fact that both her parents were killed in a helicopter crash."

"Good God, I didn't know that. That's an appalling coincidence. But you really think that's why she became a helicopter pilot? It seems eminently plausible, given what you've said about her."

"It was a typically up-front statement. At least, that's how I saw it. She was mastering the forces that killed her parents. One could view it as a misplaced, facile gesture, as I chose to do, or, instead, adopt a more generous position and see it as a brave and commemorative act of filial loyalty. I chose to a take a critical position and I regret that now. I was acting out of blatant self-interest."

"But in the light of present circumstances, you could say that you were also acting in her best interests."

"Thanks, Robert, I'm grateful for your efforts, but, no, I've got to face the fact that, in my desperation to wield influence over her, I've failed Kal in many ways over the years. Being up here, in this beautiful church, and talking to you, is helping me face up to a few unpalatable truths about my past behaviour."

"Well, this church has certainly got an atmosphere about it.

If these stones could talk, I wonder what they'd tell us?"

"They've certainly seen a bit of history, that's for sure. And do you know what else I discovered when I did an online search for Burgh by Sands last night? This will give you a good chuckle. The Roman fort of Aballava, later known at Avalana, is seriously touted by some scholars as the site of Avalon, King Arthur's last resting place and the site where Excalibur was forged."

"No, that's pure nonsense."

"Yes, probably, but if we assume for a minute that King Arthur did exist and did die in a place called Avalon, then there's a fighting chance that his body is buried out there somewhere, probably in the fort's old Roman cemetery. Now, all we need to complete the Arthurian puzzle is a lake."

Jamieson chuckles appreciatively and places a consoling hand on his companion's shoulder. "Ok, Sterland, now you're getting me really worried."

"Relax, Robert, even historians are allowed flights of fancy. It helps pay the bills sometimes."

"And did Kal have a particular flight of fancy too? She read History at Cambridge, didn't she?"

"Yes, a joint degree – Ancient History and Classics. She was a brilliant student, actually; did some wonderful research on the development of Roman gaming activities in second and third century Britain. She thought that organised gaming activities were one of the main conduits through which Roman coinage was passed into the wider native communities. She did a lot of her research up here, as you can imagine, but also at the British Museum, too. She'd already taken a great interest in some of the finds to come out of the Burgh by Sands hoard. I was hoping she was going to get down to the BM next week and take a look at some of loaded dice and marked gambling chips we've identified."

"Did she ever make it up here, do you think? To Burgh by Sands, I mean."

"She may well have done. Her surname's a bit of a painful coincidence, if nothing else."

"Of course – Sands! It hadn't occurred to me till now."

"It's silly, but these little coincidences sometimes strike one as meaningful. Emotions overcoming logic, I suppose."

"Who cares? Isn't that what coincidence is, really: the construction of meaning in association with random events? If it has significance for you, then it simply doesn't matter what the external circumstances are."

"And by external circumstances you mean verifiable facts, don't you?"

"Yes, I do. Look, what resonates most with you now: your feelings or the facts? I guess sometimes you just have to trust your emotions, instincts, feelings, call them what you will, to discover meaning in events, rather than relying on a scientific evaluation of cold, objective data."

"And is this the approach you tend to adopt in your Coroners' Court?"

"It may surprise you to hear that, sometimes, it is. When it comes to matters of cause and effect, particularly in relation to premature death, I pay considerable regard to the testimony of close relatives. I often find it contains a kernel of insight - emotional and overwrought, though it may well be - that helps to shed light on the wider evidence."

"Fair enough, then. So, seeing as you're prepared to indulge my current bout of irrationality, what do you make of this? And please don't take what I'm about to say too seriously."

"Go on, then. Let's have it."

"Ok, here we go. Nothing in this present situation has any rational explanation, agreed?"

"I like your style, Sterland, but before I agree with you, I ought, at least, to hear the evidence."

"Alright then, here's a succinct summary. A chopper has disappeared without trace over the sea, probably several miles from land, and probably very near to here." He glances at his watch. "It's now nearly three o'clock; so we can say that forty-five hours after the loss of contact with the helicopter there is still not the slightest shred of evidence about its fate. There is no wreckage, no flotsam, no jetsam, no life-rafts, no bodies, no black box – nothing, not even the remotest hint of proof that this aircraft and its occupants ever existed. What's a Coroners' Court going to make of that, then?"

"Not a lot."

"And would the coroner be interested in hearing testimony from a grieving relative; someone like me, perhaps?"

"Ok, I get your point. Let's hear it then."

"Right, here's my first irrational thought process. When I was doing a bit of digging around online last night, I came across a strange coincidence that pulled me up short. In 1292 the name of Burgh by Sands is recorded as *Burg en le Sandes*, but in the earliest recorded notation, from about one hundred years earlier, it is simply recorded as *Burch*."

"I'm sorry, your point is what exactly?"

"Burch!" Morris repeats. "I know it's mad, but Burch!"

"Burch?" parrots Jamieson in confusion.

"Yes, Burch. It's the name of Kal's co-pilot! Birch! Birch and Sands."

"Oh, I see. Ok. Now I see. You're talking about Captain Birch. But where did this all come from? I must be frank – it's not a connection I'd have drawn."

"But then, Robert, you're not a grieving relative thinking with his feelings, rather than his intellect."

"Very true - hoisted by my own petard."

"Yes, Your Honour."

Jamieson shoots Morris an indulgent look. "Sir is the normal mode of address in a Coroner's Court. But in your case I might allow an exception. So what's the conclusion you draw from this?"

"None whatsoever, apart from the fact that Burgh by Sands would be an appropriate final resting place for the pair of them, should my worst fears be confirmed."

"I agree, there does seem to be a certain symmetry to the linkage of the names. And maybe now's a good time to get down to the crash site, before it starts getting too dark?"

"Yes, let's push on. Apart from anything, I'd like to have a look at the rusted finds they dragged up yesterday. If I was given the chance, I wouldn't mind knocking the concretions off those metal remains to see what's lying beneath them."

"You're up to something, aren't you, Sterland? What have you got running around that brain of yours?"

"What's running around my brain? Something you'd approve of, Robert - emotion, pure, undiluted emotion."

THIRTEEN

Sterland Morris and Kal Sands are now separated by a timeframe of almost eighteen centuries. Despite this, they had, for the briefest possible moment that afternoon, shared the exact same physical space as one another, at a similar time of day, and on identical dates in the Julian and Gregorian calendars. Despite the chasm that divided them, they'd both been aware of the other's invisible but tangible presence.

As Sands trudged back from the village to rejoin Birch, she began to wonder how her uncle would have dealt with the problems that she'd been confronted with over the preceding two days. She had always admired his capacity for clear thinking and decisive action. His rigorous rationality had rubbed off on her. Planning and organisation formed the bedrock of not just his intellectual activity, of which she was transparently proud, but of his unbending domestic rituals, too, of which she had been far less enamoured. She knew he would have disapproved of the headstrong manner in which she'd risked confronting and offending the Roman commander. Now she had to redeem herself in his eyes through a cool, clear analysis of the life and death challenge facing the small group under her command. Within twenty minutes, by the time she had met up with Birch, a plan to rescue the surviving prisoner from his Roman captors was already beginning to formulate itself in her mind.

"Jesus, Sands, what the hell happened to you?" demanded Birch, less concern evident in his tone than he had intended. "I saw them take you into the fort and I thought that was the last I was ever going to see of you. What did they do to you?"

"It's a long story, Birch. I haven't got time to tell you now. I'm going back to pick up a few more things and do some more snooping around. I don't think they'll bother me any more – I have a protector in high places."

"You what - what the hell are you talking about? What am I supposed to do in the mean time?"

"Just carry all this stuff back to the camp and hide it well so it can't be uncovered by any passing soldiers or vermin. Tie it up as high off the ground as you can get it. Then head back here and keep a look out for me again."

And with that, Sands turned and headed back along the road that led into the small distant village, leaving Birch standing in her wake.

On arrival, she walked back through the cluster of shops till she reached the tavern at the point of the settlement nearest the entrance to the fort. She hesitated before stooping and entering the premises. Ten minutes later she was retracing her steps in a state of furious concentration, oblivious to the stares of the local inhabitants, some of whom had witnessed her arrest and subsequent release earlier in the day. On reaching the merchant from whom she had bought provisions, she paused for a while, spoke to him in a friendly manner and spent the last of her money buying a few items of food and cloth, including two small amphorae. Before heading back to her rendezvous point with Birch, she stopped, deep in thought, as she continued to devise a plan, and then took a final turn past the bath-house opposite the eastern gate. As she did so, she observed the comings and goings of the soldiers as they entered to perform their ablutions. Satisfied with what she had observed, Sands set off back to find Birch and to re-establish contact with the others.

By late afternoon she'd been joined by the full group at the same camp site that they'd used the day before. The buoyant mood of the other three soldiers, so evident when they came bursting back into camp fresh from a successful recce and seafood forage, was soon deflated by the sombre expressions that greeted them on their arrival. The soldiers' initial apprehension at their subdued welcome was quickly translated into shock as Sands recounted the terrible news of the fate that had befallen the other team.

The men hung on her every word as she gave a detailed account of everything that she had experienced and witnessed in the village and fort and during her encounter with the Roman commander in the *Principia*. She spared them nothing, sensing that they would prefer candour to a more sanitised account intended to appease their outrage. With every word that she spoke, with every recorded detail, whether it concerned the method of execution, the treatment of the bodies, the identification of the flayed skins or the smirking superiority of the Roman guards, there was a palpable sense of humiliation rising in the stomach of each soldier sitting around the camp fire. Anger, yes, there was anger, too, but these soldiers felt humiliated by the manner in which their friends had been mutilated and then publically disrespected. No soldier had the right to impose that on an enemy.

Once Sands had completed her report, the questions came thick and fast. Everyone tried to talk at once. But there were three critical questions that remained unanswered. The first concerned the identity of the fourth member of Charlie fireteam who was currently being held prisoner in the fort. The second related to the identity of the fifth member of the group who was still unaccounted for. And the third unanswered question concerned the possible fate of this fifth individual.

Through a tortuous process of elimination, during which Sands' detailed description of the tattoos on each individual skin proved decisive, it was ascertained that the two members of the team who had not been executed were Sergeant Rattigan and the youngest of the platoon members, nineteen year-old Private George McKay. The final decision on who was and who wasn't still alive, arrived with a finality and functional practicality that surprised them all. Sands and Birch suddenly became very aware of the strength of friendship that had bound together their colleagues, both the living and the newly dead, through many tours of duty. They agreed to take a short, quiet break during which the ingredients for the evening meal could be prepared and the camp laid out.

Sands had already started to build a fire, and she was now

able to boil up a camp-kettle of fresh water for the assorted shellfish which the others were cleaning and preparing. They'd been as good as their word: oysters, cockles, mussels and long, thin razor-fish had been successfully harvested, and a line-caught ten pound salmon was waiting to be gutted and baked in the embers of the camp fire. They were all ravenous and the prospect of a substantial hot meal served to lift their spirits. Earlier in the day Sands had enlisted Birch's help in locating some suitable stones with which to grind a portion of the grain that she had acquired in the village, and they now set about milling a kilo of flour for flat, unleavened bread to be baked in the frying pan.

While Sands milled she also planned ahead. A kilo of bread would provide over 2000 calories, more than two-thirds of the daily requirements for an active soldier. Her men were going to have to keep on the move to stay alive, and to do that they would need to carry their own rations. Relying on foraging was no longer practical. She timed herself as she ground the wheat, counting out every second. At this rate it was going to take an hour to grind the daily ration for five. Each soldier would have to do their own milling; she had no intention of becoming the platoon drudge.

Later that evening, after eating, they sat in a circle and discussed what should be done next

Corporal Crawley posed the matter in the starkest terms. "So, what are we going to do about getting that poor bastard out of their clutches?"

"We have to devise a strategy to get him out – one way or another," agreed Birch.

"Anyone got any bright ideas?" asked Stogdon.

"How about you, Kal, got any suggestions? Is there a weak spot anywhere in the fort that you think we could exploit?" asked Ojokwu.

"No, I hate to admit it but, in all truth, I don't think there is. Look, we're talking about breaking into a heavily guarded military fort containing over five hundred battle-hardened troops. I don't think we stand a chance as things stand."

"Come on, we can't just leave him in there," urged Stogdon.

"I did say "as things stand," Stog," she repeated.

"And what does that mean, exactly?"

"It means we have to equalise the odds if we are going to stand any chance of getting our guy out."

"Equalise the odds? What've you got in mind?"

"Well, look at it this way: if we're going to walk into that fort, then we're going to have to disrupt the enemy's organisation by softening them up first, right?"

"Yeah, but we've got no weapons to speak of, and we don't even have the advantage of local knowledge or support from the native population," responded Birch.

"Oh, but we do have the weapons. And we do have the local knowledge necessary to acquire them."

"What weapons?"

"Biological weapons."

"What are you talking about?"

"Look around you. We possess the means to poison the enemy troops, at least to the point where we can degrade their effectiveness as a fighting force, particularly when it comes to guarding their fort against a group of determined intruders."

"Death cap mushrooms," said Ojokwu suddenly as he caught the drift of what Sands was saying. "There's a proper ass-load of them round here; man, they're all over the place."

"Exactly, and the toxins that exist in bad oysters are also quite capable of laying low a restaurant full of guests."

Crawley leant forward and picked up some unopened shells. "Well, I kept back a couple here that I thought was proper dodgy," he said. "With a bit of assistance they could become infected with all sorts of nasty bacteria."

"Ok, so, can you, Ojo and Stog put your heads together and come up with a concentrated liquidized poison?"

"That would be a genuine pleasure. The good news is that the toxicity in the Death Cap fungus isn't going to be lessened by cooking, so we should be able to reduce it down to a concentrated form over the fire."

"And once we've done that, how are we going to get this

poison into the Roman fort?" asked Stogdon.

"That's going to be more problematic," replied Sands. "The soldiers are more likely to drink local beer and imported wine than water, and any attempt to poison the fort's water supply would mean diluting the impact of the bacteria to ineffective levels. I think we'll have to deliver the toxins in concentrated form directly into the food chain. The problem we've got is that there's no central army cook house in a Roman fort. Each individual soldier is going to have his own rations and will be responsible for preparing his own food. And, anyway, getting into the fort is going to prove well-nigh impossible."

"So what's the alternative?" asked Ojo.

"We need to administer the poison outside of the fort, and then let the soldiers carry the bacteria back in with them."

"How are we going to do that?"

"Right," said Sands, picking up a stick and drawing a plan view of the fort and village in the dirt, "here's my idea."

The four soldiers, now hooked, stood up and moved next to Sands so they could see the detail of her plan as it unfolded on the ground in front of them.

She pointed to three shapes drawn in the dust. "Apart from the fort here, there are two external locations where the Roman soldiers gather in large numbers. The first one's over here, about a hundred metres to the right of the East gate. This building is the military bathhouse, a five or six-roomed stone-built structure. Nearly every auxiliary is going to pass through this place in a twenty-four hour period, and they won't just come in to wash. This is the nearest thing to a NAAFI or American PX that the ordinary Roman soldier's got. They'd come here to relax, drink, play dice and eat. To the right of the bathhouse there's a midden that's strewn with thousands of discarded oyster and mussel shells. These guys are seriously into their shellfish after taking a hot soak."

"I see what you're saying," said Birch, "but how do we go about contaminating the shellfish?"

"We simply let the Romans do our dirty work for us. Look, I've got some things to show you."

She bent down to uncover one of the folded blankets which had been lying by the fire and carefully extracted two twelve inch-high amphorae.

"These clay containers hold a substance very dear to the heart of a Roman soldier. It's the one ingredient that made his bland cuisine edible; he added it as flavouring to his porridge in the morning and to his steamed mussels in the evening when he visited the …."

She paused to allow her colleagues to add the missing word.

"Bathhouse!" the four men echoed in unison, delight written across the faces.

"Correct! But not only the bathhouse; they also spent an equal amount of time, in their off-duty moments, drinking, gambling and whoring in the local taverns, gambling dens and brothels. Now, as luck would have it, there is one large establishment located in the village, just here," she said, pointing at a rectangular shape which appeared to be located on the road just south of the main gate. "It seems to successfully combine all three vices under one roof. But, more importantly, the place also serves fresh shellfish, on top of which the condiment that's contained in vessels like these is liberally applied - in much the same way that we might pour vinegar on our chips."

"Brilliant!" shouted Stogdon. "Fucking brilliant! We'll really shake them toga-wearing bastards up. I swear they won't know what's hit them!"

"So, all we've got to do is successfully contaminate whatever's in those jars, and then swap them for the existing ones in the tavern and the bathhouse."

"That's it, then we retreat and let nature take its course."

"Stand well back, I'd say," said Stogdon with a whoop.

The others grinned. They were suddenly energised by the prospect of taking the fight to an enemy who'd abused their comrades with such barbarity.

"So what's in these jars then?" asked Ojokwu.

"It's a fish sauce, called *garum*, fermented and liquefied from decayed anchovy and mackerel intestines."

"Mmm, sounds irresistible," said Birch, as he removed the top of one of the jars. "You certainly know how to sell a product." He dipped his index finger in to the liquid and sniffed it before licking it with obvious distaste.

"Worcester Sauce," he announced.

"No way!"

"Just like Worcester Sauce," Birch repeated, "which is, I may add, fermented from anchovies."

Ojokwu responded by dipping his own finger into the jar. "He ain't wrong, you know, but the smell's pretty ripe for my taste. It should disguise the addition of the poison, though."

"It's not exactly a subtle flavour, but that's what makes it perfect for the job," added Sands. Pliny described *garum* as 'the liquor of putrefaction'."

"It's hardly a ringing endorsement from old Pliny, is it?" muttered Birch to general merriment. "No surprise they didn't copyright the slogan. I really can't see it working as an advertising strap line."

"But can you see it working as a means of poisoning the enemy?"

"It should disguise anything we put in it," agreed Birch.

"Good. Well, in that case, we simply need to work out a method for getting the jars into the tavern and into the bathhouse. I've already checked out the tavern and that should pose us fewer access problems than the bathhouse. Women are allowed in, so I'm happy to take Birch with me as my foil if he's okay with that?"

"Count me in, but you'll have to do the talking."

"So how do we get into the bathhouse? I assume it's guarded?" asked Ojokwu.

"Yes, but much less formally than the fort, itself. And one of us in particular is going to be able to march in there without so much as a second glance."

"What?" asked Ojokwu. "Who do you mean?"

"You," replied Sands, pointing at him with an amused look on her face. "One man who is not going to attract a hint of suspicion is Titus Ojokwu of the First Cohort, one of

Aurelian's Moors, a black man looking for a wash at his latest posting in this god-forsaken northern outpost of the Roman Empire. One thing they are not going to confuse you for is a Briton. Trust me, they won't suspect you for a moment."

Ojokwu hesitated for a second. "Do I get some kind of money-back written guarantee with that promise? Is this the bonus ticket of being a black man in Britain that I been waiting all my life for?"

"Hey, Titus, you people are finally in the saddle. Don't complain, man."

"Stop chatting shit, Stogdon. That ain't even funny."

"I was only having a laugh, man. You know me."

"Yeah, but you always get it fucking wrong."

"Like what?"

"Like understanding that there is a bond of trust between us black people, yeah? It's a trust based on hundreds of years of oppression at the hands of racist white people. And, you know what? It's a trust you don't break easily - especially when you got a right ignorant twat like you winding you up."

"Ok, man, just calm down. I didn't mean nothing by it."

"Yeah, yeah, do us a favour, Stog. How many times have I heard you say that?"

"Ojo, I'm sorry," interjected Sands. "I had no right to talk like that. I shouldn't have made those glib comments."

"Too true, you shouldn't. But you shouldn't also assume I ain't as committed as any other man here."

"But do you get my point?"

"Of course I get your point. But do you get mine? I'm looking at a future where I'm the only black man in Britain trying to assimilate into native Briton communities. The fact is the only place where I got any hope of acceptance in the future is in that fort with them guys, my African ancestors. I know it sounds mad to you lot but in the long run that's going to be where my future lies. What happens when you guys aren't around? When I go into that bathhouse I'm risking a lot more than any of you. I'm burning my bridges for good."

"So are we, Ojo."

"No, you ain't. You ain't got nothing to lose. You already see yourselves as the insurgents and them as the bad guys. You talk about bacterial warfare – this is a terrorist outrage you're planning, so don't try dressing it up as nothing heroic. And what about them innocent civilians caught up in this? There're bound to be fatalities and they won't all be legit targets."

"Come on, Ojo, what other options we got?" asked Crawley.

"My point is, whatever the options, you've all got more options than what I have."

"But we're not asking you to take any risks that we wouldn't, if we were in your situation."

"Yeah, but you're asking me to exploit my one advantage. my skin colour, to my long-term disadvantage. I don't see none of you lot having to do that."

"Ok, I accept that," said Sands "and I do understand the point you're making. But, look at it this way, this isn't Iraq and we're not Al-Qaeda. Like Mal said, what other options have we got if we want to get our man out of there? Whether he's Rattigan or McKay we can't just leave him there."

"Let's just think about what we're planning to do," replied Ojokwu, "that's all I'm saying. I'm not afraid of having to survive in a hostile environment. That's what black people have had to do for generations in the West – I'm used to it. But are we really sure them Romans are the bad guys? Once we go for them then there ain't no turning back, right?"

"Yeah," said Crawley, "but you walk in there trying to be friends and they'll hang you up by the balls and strip the skin off your back before you can compare birth certificates."

Ojokwu laughed. "Ok, Corp, you've convinced me; I put my hands up. That's the kind of argument I do understand." He sighed and took a deep breath to regain his composure. "I just ain't happy colluding with you lot on the basis of my skin colour – I ain't never done such a thing and I don't plan to start doing it now. You got me?"

"Loud and clear, mate," said Stogdon, putting his arm around Ojokwu's shoulders.

"Ok, Stog," said Ojokwu, "back off, man. I'm warning you. I ain't ready for this "we're all old chums together" routine."

"Ok, man, just chill, alright?"

"Ok, just give me some space, right?"

"Sure, that's cool."

"Ok, let's move on, then, if we've got that sorted," said Sands. "In that case, we'll concentrate on the tavern and see if we can come up with another plan before tomorrow. And I'm thinking winter vomiting virus, not mass murder. Am I being naïve, Mal?"

"Who knows, Kal? If it suits you to think like that, then fine. But let's see what concoction we can come up with first. If we don't have a major body count then it's not worth doing. Are we all agreed?"

Four voices were raised in tentative approval. There was still a lot to do and there was going to be plenty of time for second thoughts and back-tracking. But one thing was crystal clear: if they did nothing, then there would soon be one less member of the platoon left living under Roman rule.

FOURTEEN

The tavern was a ramshackle building, none too well-built, its timbers sagging and in the advanced stages of decay. The entrance, an open frontage framed with wooden shutters, faced directly on to the road. The long axis, composed of various structures, including an inner yard and several storerooms, appeared to stretch back a good hundred feet. A wooden portico provided some shelter to those customers, almost exclusively military, who wished to enter the premises from the street.

Despite its dilapidated condition, the tavern, in common with most of its kind around the world, possessed a singular allure. The warmth and glow of its interior, when glimpsed through the doorway, proved an irresistible temptation to the casual passer-by. The attraction was enhanced by the aroma of wood smoke mingling with the more prosaic smells of human body odour and fermenting barley. The final temptation, the one that expresses itself through raucous bonhomie and the sounds of conviviality and laughter, was sufficient to entice the most misanthropic of customers. And it was into this feverish atmosphere, so familiar, and yet so alien, that Birch and Sands propelled themselves. Taking a last gulp of untainted air before they entered, they dove through the doorway like pearl fishers descending into a murky world of unseen dangers.

Their first few steps took them into a whole new, undiscovered kingdom. It was a domain that seemed familiar, and, yet, as they struggled to acclimatise themselves, it was one that they scarcely recognised. It was a tavern, alright, there was no mistaking that fact, but that was all they could have affirmed with any certainty. The sound of flashing one-arm bandits and blaring music was missing, superseded by the crash of bone dice dashed down onto stone counting boards. The idle chatter of tired office workers was also absent. In its place was a constant litany of Latin curses and crude, raucous laughter accompanied by the banging of drinking cups and clenched fists onto wooden trestle tables.

At first sight, gambling appeared to be the main activity preoccupying the noisiest clientele. As Birch and Sands began to navigate themselves around the edge of the entrance room they were able to appreciate the scale of the tavern. It was an establishment made up of a number of interlinking rooms of varying size, an indication, perhaps, that it had expanded over time to accommodate an ever-burgeoning customer base from the adjacent fort.

Through one open door, leading off the central room, there was a kitchen area from which emitted huge clouds of steam. A couple of young female Britons, aged no more than fourteen or fifteen, were carrying earthenware bowls of steaming mussels through and placing them over a heated stone on a large serving table. Birch and Sands observed as a soldier summoned a girl and ordered a plate of mussels, which she carried over to his gaming table. In her spare hand she carried an amphora of *garum*. The two colleagues watched transfixed as the soldier doused his mussels with the pungent fish sauce and then handed the jar back to the servant girl, along with a few coins and a painful looking pinch to her right buttock. She yelped in discomfort and moved quickly away, her retreating footsteps followed all the way back into the kitchen by his salacious stare and laugh.

The atmosphere of the interior lay like a damp cloud over the revellers. The air was permeated with eye-watering peat and wood smoke – there were open fires in every room – and choking smog pervaded every nook and cranny. The overriding smell was cloying and pungent but it failed to mask an underlying aroma of decay and poor public sanitation. These conditions would have been a far cry from the cultural sophistication of the soldiers' own domestic arrangements back at the fort. A closer inspection of the delights on offer in the tavern, however, made it easy to uncover the reasons for their willingness to suffer such discomfort.

On all four sides of the main entrance room were arranged a series of low-lying wooden benches, covered with palliasses, on which pairs of soldiers slumped as they drank and played dice. In the middle of the room were positioned a number of wooden square tables at which larger groups of men sat in noisy congregations, eating, drinking and wagering on the outcome of various gaming activities. The smaller middle room seemed to act as an ante-chamber where food was assembled and sold, and, beyond which, the kitchen was located. This room contained additional seating for other gambling activities, as well as shelves holding large wooden barrels of locally-brewed beer and earthenware amphorae containing imported wine. Some of the amphorae were marked as *vinum* or vintage wine and others were scratched with crudely written graffiti indicating that the contents were sweet wine or honey-sweetened.

It was evident that the smaller central room also acted as an ante-chamber to the rear of the establishment, which, as Birch quickly surmised, served as the camp brothel. A quick glance revealed that this area contained a rabbit's warren of squalid-looking smaller cubicles, allowing the prostitutes and their clients to transact their business in some privacy.

Birch and Sands had trouble adjusting to the dimness of the lighting, which when combined with the poor visibility caused by the smoke, made it very difficult both to see and to be seen. The external shutters had been closed and only small cracks of evening light penetrated, now that dusk had begun to fall. The main source of illumination came from the open fires. Additionally, a series of terracotta oil lamps with lit cloth wicks were placed on small shelves at regular intervals around the walls. The overall effect was a very gloomy one, creating pools of darkness in certain sections, and it enhanced the threatening atmosphere generated by the raised voices and regular arguments among the men.

As Birch and Sands moved through the tavern they started

to receive some attention from the rowdier elements among the soldiers. Sands found herself subject to whistles and lewd comments, only some of which she understood. Soon, to their relief, they were approached by one of the servers, shown to a bench in the corner of the room and, at Sands' request, served two mugs of *cerevisia*.

"What this stuff?" asked Birch.

"Celtic beer."

"Looks cloudy to me. I wouldn't trust it."

"Come on, Birch, get it down you. We don't want to attract any more attention."

He steeled himself and took a tentative first sip. "Not too bad, actually, what do you think?"

"I've no idea, Birch. I'm not an expert on heritage ales."

"It's not exactly a pint of bitter. I wonder what's in it."

"Can we concentrate on the matter in hand? Keep that amphora out of sight."

"Of course I will."

As he spoke, Birch held his drink up to the light emitting from the oil lamp on the wall behind him. "You know all things considered, it's not a bad beer, that."

"Birch, come on, concentrate. All we're going to have to do is switch your amphora with the one over there on the table, but without anyone spotting you."

"But I don't quite see how we can do it with those servers hanging around that table. We're going to need some sort of diversion to distract them for a few moments. What's your plan?" he asked with exaggerated gusto. The beer was beginning to have its effect.

"Ok, here's what I think. At Cambridge I did a lot of research on Roman gaming activities."

"You're kidding me! My God, Sands, you've been hiding your light under a bushel, haven't you? I love gambling, you know that, right? I mean everyone knows that." He leant forward to engage her with real interest.

Sands was amazed to see the change that had come over him. "You've perked up a bit, all of a sudden. What's got into you? Beer gone to your head?"

"Look, Sands, the Birches are survivors. They always have been, and always will be. And it's not a tradition that I mean to let die with me. I've every intention of getting out of here in one piece, no matter what it takes. And from what I can see, you're my best option at the moment. Is that clear enough for you? As a betting man I've put all my money on you."

"Now you've really got me confused. Am I supposed to find that flattering?"

"It's up to you, Sands. You can take it any way you like."

"God, you're like a chameleon, Birch. What happened to the arrogant arsehole who wouldn't give me the time of day?"

He ignored her taunt. "Oh that? Forget it. You weren't in command then. You'll find that I can be very loyal when it suits me."

"Oh I don't doubt that," she replied with more bitterness than she intended. "I know it was you who grassed me up over that newspaper letter."

"Oh, come on, Sands, grow up. I assume you sent it to the paper with the intention of having it published. If I hadn't ratted on you, someone else would've. It was hardly a state secret, was it?"

Birch was beginning to lose interest in the conversation. Instead he pointed at the gamblers arrayed in front of them. "So, come on, what do you know about what these guys are playing here?"

"Quite a lot, as it happens."

Despite her obvious misgivings, she suddenly found herself warming to her inquisitor. "That pair sitting next to us, and those two guys over there in the back room, are playing an early form of backgammon called *Duodecimo Scripta* or 'Twelve Points'. The board has three rows of twelve points, thirty-six in total, and each player has fifteen counters which he has to move around the board by throwing three dice."

Sands gestured with her thumb at the players sitting to the right of them. "Watch what he does now. He's just thrown two sixes and a two."

A great shout of triumph ensued, along with much raucous table-thumping, as the player who had just shaken the dice proceeded to outmanoeuvre his opponent with a tremendous flourish.

"Imperator!" he yelled, as he leaped to his feet and taunted his disgruntled opponent. He proceeded to complete a conspicuous lap of honour of the room, hopping from foot to foot as he went, slapping his mess mates on the back as he passed them and singing at the top of his voice.

"How to win with dignity," observed Birch. "What about that bunch over in the centre there who look like they're playing chess? What are they up to?"

"Ok, now you're talking. That is the king of board games as far as I'm concerned. It's really a battle game, so not unlike chess in some ways, but the pieces are all restricted to moving like a 'rook'. You know, moving in a straight line horizontally or vertically but can't jump pieces like a 'knight' can. The Latin name is *Ludus Latrunculorum*, roughly translated as 'Robber-soldiers' in English. The board's made up of sixty-four squares on an eight by eight grid. The pieces are called 'dogs' and are of two colours, one for each opponent like chess."

"So it's pretty much like chess, then?" said Birch with feigned intensity.

"Yes, pretty much, Birch. If that helps you to understand the complexities, then, yes, it's pretty much like chess."

"Just checking. Do go on."

"Ok, so, you take an opponents 'dog' by moving your pieces around the 'city' – that's the name for the board – until you enclose them between two 'dogs' of your own. The one who takes the most 'dogs', wins the game."

"Got it, Sands, but I have to say it does look frightfully complicated. Fancy another beer?"

"Screw you, Birch. You want to see how frightfully complicated it is? Just for you, I'll demonstrate its complexities by kicking some Roman arse. If I win, you get the next round in."

"Sod off, Sands, I was only joking. Anyway, I didn't bring my wallet with me."

Right," she said, slowly getting to her feet, "I'm going to challenge that big brute to a match." She gestured at the largest soldier in the tavern, a man who was clearly the worse for drink. Judging by the scars on his face, he was not used to backing down from a challenge, particularly when it was going to be issued in front of ten members of his cohort.

The expression changed on Birch's face. "You have got to be joking, he'll tear you limb from limb, and then I'll be forced to intervene. Sands, don't be an arsehole, we're here to do a job, remember?"

"Tough, Birch, I'm sure you'll cope."

"But I was only winding you up, Sands, you know that."

"And while I'm at it, use the diversion to swap the amphorae."

"Oh, I see," he said, "there's a method to your madness. Well, in that case, you can count on me to get the job done. It's at times like this that I feel the Army Air Corps could do with a regimental motto."

"Military mottos are self-aggrandising bullshit, Birch, as you should well know."

"Spare us the lecture, Sands, you're in a Roman tavern now, not the officers' mess."

"Fuck you."

"And good luck. I'll be nearby if you need me."

"Same to you, Birch. You know what you've got to do. When all eyes are on me, you swap the jars."

He shot her an earnest look. "You can rely on me. I hate to admit it, but you're one hell of a gutsy woman."

Sands smiled and studied his face for a moment.

"You know something, Birch? I think all this is going to be the making of you."

"Don't go and do anything stupid. I'm not sure I trust you."

"Not sure I trust myself, to be honest. I feel like I'm a pawn in some fantasy game."

"And what about me, do you trust me?"

"Not sure, Birch. I haven't quite worked you out yet."

"It didn't stop you coming down the pub with me."

"Yeah, right. If I didn't know you better, I'd say you're trying to be charming. Don't flatter yourself. Get rid of that amphora successfully and you might go up in my estimation a bit. Now, do your job while I sort that Roman bruiser out."

Sands secured the edges of her cape together and made her way through the throng of chairs and drinkers until she'd arrived at the large table in the centre of the room. She felt suddenly conscious of Birch's approving gaze as he followed some distance behind her, and she experienced a disconcerting surge of gratification at the thought of his eyes tracing her every footstep. Her presence had been observed by most people in the room. Now, as she stood there, without an apparent trace of fear, confronting half a dozen worse for wear Roman soldiers, every pair of eyes in the tavern was trained with concentration on this charismatic figure and her shifty-looking companion.

"*Salvete!* Which one of you blockheads is man enough to take on a woman at a game of *Ludus Latrunculorum?*"

When Sands approached their table, the men had looked at her with amusement. Now they stared at her in consternation, unsure as to how to handle this open display of bravado. After a few seconds their gaze transferred to the hulking shape of their brutish comrade, slumped in his chair. He blinked to clear his thoughts, before emitting a loud, contemptuous snort.

"Don't waste our time, whore," he slurred. "What would a common prostitute know about *Ludus Latrunculorum?*"

"Immortal Gods!" Sands exclaimed, raising her hands to heaven, as if dealing with a half-wit unworthy of her challenge. "There's a big difference between a wise man and a fool. Don't ask a shoemaker to judge beyond a sandal."

"What's that supposed to mean?" he asked in bewilderment.

"It means you're unworthy of competing with me in a contest demanding brains and not brawn. But you are too stupid to realise it."

Sands stood in front of him with her hands on his hips,

defying him to take her on.

"How long are you going to abuse our patience? Shut up and go away, you pathetic cow."

"I could lick any of you in a fair contest."

"Why don't you lick my balls instead?" said the young soldier to her right, as he leant back on his chair and made a grab for her backside.

In a flashing instant, before any of the drunken soldiers could react, Sands kicked away the legs of the man's chair and sent him spinning to the floor with a jaw-dropping echo.

"Show some respect in the presence of a woman."

An astonished silence gripped the room, broken only by the sound of a low, appreciative whistle emitting from the lips of Birch, and the groans of her vanquished assaulter gasping for air.

"Jupiter and all the Gods damn you! You're in for a whipping," replied the stricken soldier, as he tried to regain his footing and what remained of his dignity.

The large brute across the table now intervened, impressed by Sands' fighting qualities. "Calm down, Gaius, you asked for that!"

"She'd never do it to my face, the bitch!" he replied, flushed with humiliation.

"I could do without your face, Gaius," she replied, "and without your neck, and your hands, and your limbs, and, to save myself the trouble of mentioning the points in detail, I could do without you altogether."

The room erupted into a roar of laughter and even young Gaius, prompted by his comrades, was forced to admit defeat, raise his hands in submission and sit down with a heavy sigh.

"Remember, Gaius, it's often said that women have fickle temperaments. Maybe next week I'll make you laugh," she said, slapping him across the back of his head.

"And me!" said the big lout across the table, now enjoying himself. "What are you going to do to make me laugh?"

"You, big-mouth, what can I tell about yourself that everyone hasn't already said? Your mother is so fat, that when she goes to Rome it has eight hills!"

The insult provoked the response that Sands had hoped for. The soldier now found himself subject to public ridicule. It was going to be impossible for him to reject a further challenge from her. He was under a heavy obligation to squash her if he intended to regain his accustomed primacy.

As the laughter resounded around the tavern, Sands caught an angry glint in the man's stare; he was intent on exacting his full revenge and this was one challenge that was going to be played out to its climax.

"So, you want to take me on, do you? And what do you propose to wager, to make it worth my while?"

The enquiry took her aback. She was unprepared for this development. "I have no money to wager," she replied.

"Money's not everything. You appear to have a very tempting body under that cape." He emphasised his salacious intentions by making an age-old hand gesture that was very familiar to Sands.

"You disgust me. If Caesar were alive, you'd be chained to an oar. You ask me to bet the very last thing a Roman lady would want to lose in a wager."

"That's right. You're nothing but a common little whore anyway. It should be of little account to you."

"Alright, but on one condition," riposted Sands. "To make this bet entirely fair, what is the last thing in the world a Roman soldier would want to lose in a wager?"

The crowd emitted a hum of appreciation at Sands' tactics.

It was apparent to the onlookers that the drunken lout was now caught on the horns of a dilemma, and they were ones entirely of his own making.

"Unlike you, I do have money…" he started to say, before he was shouted down by the assembled onlookers.

"That's not a fair wager," challenged Sands, "and everyone here agrees with me. I think that the one thing that no self-respecting Roman soldier would want to lose in a wager is his sword, his *gladius*."

Her opponent was as shaken by this proposal as she had been by his. A comrade whispered in his ear and after much wheedling he was obliged to accept the terms of the bet.

Birch, who'd been following developments with growing unease, lent forward and whispered to Sands, "What the hell's going on?"

"If he wins, he has his way with me – and that ain't going to happen; if I win, I get his sword. Now get over there and swap those jars while you've still got a chance."

Birch responded as best he could, a tone of appalled helplessness in his voice. "Look, Sands, I'm a gambling man, and I'm telling you now, these are not good odds. You've gotta back out!"

"We're pawns in a game, Birch, you and me. You know that, right? And this is the move I've chosen to make. Let's see how it all pans out. Just make sure you do your bit. Now get a fucking move on."

He looked at her in desperation. She felt a momentary stab of fear, but then a deep calmness descended on her. All things being equal, she was more than a match for the Neanderthal across the table from her.

But all things weren't equal; and, in truth, they never really have been, not then and not now. And it was at this exact moment, when fortune should have favoured the brave that matters started to take a very unpredictable turn for Birch and Sands.

FIFTEEN

"Galla Placidia!" a voice boomed from across the tavern. Its insistent tone cut through the heavy atmosphere of alcohol and antagonism, those twin killjoys whose effects had descended like a sodden tarpaulin over the revellers.

Sands felt a shudder reverberate down her spinal column. A glance behind her had revealed an unwelcome addition to the growing throng by the entrance. Through the smoke and gloom she detected a face she recognized. "Oh, Christ," she said.

"Who is it, Sands?" whispered Birch. "Do you know this man? Do we need to get out of here while we still can?"

The confidence drained from Sands' face. "Shit, now we've got a problem. Just remember what I told you earlier. Say what I taught you to say."

"But who is he?" repeated Birch, as the subject of Sands stare pushed his way through the crowd.

"He's one of the guys who arrested me yesterday. Let me deal with this." She retreated a pace or two, forcing Birch back as she did so. "Let me do the talking. Don't speak unless you have to."

The crowd parted, allowing the new arrival to approach Sands. He was followed by a small retinue of drinking companions. He stood before her and bowed in mock supplication.

"Salve, Galla Placidia," said the Roman soldier. Sands was right: he was the very man who had arrested and brutalised her the day before. "Well, well," he smirked, "I didn't expect that we'd meet again. I hoped we'd seen the last of you when the commander-in-chief kicked you out yesterday. Gods above, you've neglected learning your lessons, haven't you?"

Now he stood facing her and cocking his head from side to

side, clearly relishing an opportunity to taunt and intimidate his prey once more. Sands stood her ground and refused to budge a further inch backwards. His face was now so close to hers that she could clearly smell his breath when he spoke. She found him repellent.

Sands steeled herself, once again, and prepared herself for a further battle of wills. She took a deep breath before responding to her interrogator. "In matters of taste, Corporal, there is no argument, and I have no taste for you, nor for the way you dispense law and order."

"Is that right, Galla Placidia?" he said, his bogus familiarity masking a tone of menace. "Well, let me tell you something. I loathe you and your barbarian country and every stinking Briton in it," he intoned, thrice jabbing a finger in her face to emphasise his points. "What do you say to that?"

"I'm not in the least bit surprised, Corporal. As I'm sure you are aware, it's human nature to hate a person whom you have injured."

The soldier looked at her in exasperation, nonplussed by her refusal to submit to his physical dominance. "By the Gods, you have a bad habit of compulsive talking. I'm warning you to beware of what you say, when, and to whom. They say that a man is wise when he knows when to hold his tongue, and this adage is even truer in the case of an ignorant woman."

He recoiled from her, as if repulsed by some hidden force beyond his command, and turned his attention instead to the young pilot shifting about behind her. Sands noted the soldier's unwillingness to pursue his argument with her further. Despite his threatening manner, he had not laid a finger on her and appeared uncertain in asserting himself.

The soldier looked beyond Sands to Birch. He sensed the latter's anxious disposition. This individual, he surmised, would represent easier pickings. Meanwhile, the surrounding onlookers, including the soldier with whom Sands had just contracted a wager, followed the events with rapt attention.

"I see you've finally found what you were looking for yesterday. This is your brother, I assume?"

111

"Yes, Corporal," she replied, glancing at Birch.

"His name?" asked the soldier, addressing Sands.

"My name, Corporal," said Birch in uncertain Latin, "is Sextus Placidius."

"Oh, he speaks."

The audience sniggered at the reticent male stranger. Birch was aware that his manner betrayed his fear.

Sands intervened to deflect the attention of the Roman soldier. "His name is Sextus, Corporal. But he usually answers to the name of Sexy."

Despite his lack of familiarity with the language, Birch detected that Sands was mocking her adversary.

"Sexy, you say?" repeated the Roman as he began to circle the pilot.

"Yes, Corporal, Sexy," replied Sands, staring at Birch.

"So, Sexy, where are you from?" asked the Roman with piercing intensity, his face almost touching Birch's.

"I'm from Eboracum, Corporal."

Sands' ingenuity in belittling his interrogator had lifted Birch. She'd performed this absurd subterfuge purely for his benefit, and his morale inflated accordingly.

"And do you come here often, Sexy?"

"He has never been here before, Corporal," interrupted Sands, unable to contain the delight in her voice. "Our father has died and I have come to take him home to Eboracum."

The soldier turned to Sands and shrugged, as if intending to drop the subject. "Fair enough," he conceded, before adding a final unexpected request, inserted deftly like a stiletto between the ribs. "You are free to go, but your brother may want to tell me what he has got so carefully hidden under his cape."

He turned his gaze back upon Birch, who stood rigid as if anticipating the touch of a frozen hand along his spine.

"Well, what do you say, Sextus Placidius? Would you like to show the kind Roman soldier what you've got hidden there?"

Birch was unsure how to respond to a request that he didn't fully comprehend.

"He who is silent, thereby gives consent," the corporal

pronounced. He nodded to two fellow soldiers standing behind Birch and, before he could respond, they'd pinned his arms behind his back and pulled the front of his cape open.

"*Nemo Me Impune Lacessit,*" shouted Birch in defiance, invoking the Latin motto of the Royal Regiment of Scotland.

"No one attacks you with impunity, eh?" challenged the Roman. He struck Birch hard across his mouth. "You may want to reconsider that boast."

Birch's vain attempts to struggle free were of little consequence - the object of the corporal's interest was already in plain view. The assembled crowd pushed forward to get a better look. Sands, for her part, let out an audible groan of dismay, and signalled to Birch to acquiesce.

Birch spat out a goblet of blood and winked at Sands.

"*Quis Seperabit?*" she asked in response, quoting the Latin motto of The Irish Guards Regiment.

Birch smiled at her insouciance.

"Who will separate you?" asked the furious Roman, now searching Birch with gusto. "I will. I'll separate your heads from your effing torsos if you don't shut up."

He grabbed the amphora from Birch's hand. "What's this then?" he said, thrusting it into Birch's face, and opening up a deep cut along his brow.

"*Garum,* Corporal," Birch groaned, blood flowing down the side of his face.

"Taste it, if you don't believe him," said Sands.

The soldier uncorked the amphora, smelt the contents and then drank a small sip of the liquid, groaning with unfeigned pleasure as he did so.

"Well, lads, here's a treat for all of us tonight. The fish sauce is on our friend here, isn't that right, Sextus?" he said, slapping him on the back in mock jocularity. "Here, lads, pass it around. Sexy, here, won't mind."

Birch shrugged his shoulders, unsure of what was happening, but preparing himself for an unpleasant outcome.

"If that's all, Corporal, then we'll be going," said Sands, turning for the door as if their departure was a formality that required no sanction. "We've a long journey tomorrow. Please, all you men, enjoy the *garum* with our compliments."

Sands reached back and grabbed Birch's arm, indicating that her audience with the assembled company was now at an end, and commenced guiding her companion to the doorway and safety. The onlookers reacted with dumb-struck surprise, and, such was her assurance, some even stood back to ease her passage to the exit.

Sands now had her arm around Birch, whose blood-soaked cape trailed a crimson path across the wooden floor. She inched him closer and closer to the door.

"Look straight down and keep walking," she cautioned. "Don't make eye contact. I'm getting you out of here."

Just when it looked as if they might escape from this bear-pit of a tavern, a deep roar of anger erupted from somewhere behind their backs. The crowd awoke from its supine state and, freshly empowered, hemmed the pair in once more to block their passage. As the mob pinned them in, a huge man pushed his way towards them from the rear.

"You've contracted a wager with me, and you'll not leave here till you've settled it!"

The man stood there, looking unsteady, shaking a couple of gaming pieces at Sands. It was as if he was offering a choice from a pair of duelling pistols.

"Oh hell, I'd forgotten about that idiot. I'm going to have to deal with him."

"Out of the smoke, into the flame," laughed one of the Romans nearby.

The crowd, once more ignited with anticipation, had misinterpreted Sands' expression as an indication of dread.

She turned to face down her challenger once more. "Look, friend, to quarrel with a drunk is to wrong a man who is not even there. Take a bit of advice from an ignorant woman: save yourself the humiliation of losing to me and go back to drinking yourself into a stupor. It seems to be what you're best qualified for."

There was a momentary silence during which the full force

of Sands' insult had a chance to take effect. It swept around the room with dizzying force, disabling those who'd absorbed its meaning but were unable to fathom its consequences. Surely, no native woman had ever had the temerity to speak in such derogatory terms to a Roman soldier in a public arena.

All faces turned towards the huge Roman in an effort to gauge his response. He seemed devoid of balance, unable to respond and physically inert; he swayed from foot to foot. His face, however, revealed a different story. He was flushed, the veins on his temples pulsed mechanically, sweat beading his brow and upper lip, and a slight tremor, at first almost imperceptible but now growing in intensity, started to displace his flaccid features. If left to his own devices, it seemed certain that he would erupt, with fearful consequences for his nearest neighbours, and, more importantly, for the young woman who was standing in his line of vision and within an unsteady arm's reach.

Sensing danger in relinquishing the initiative, Sands followed her opening assault by denying the enemy a chance to regroup. She grabbed the Roman soldier by the arms and to his astonishment twisted him around and started to frog-march him back to the gaming table, complaining in English as she did so. "Come on, come on, let's get on with it then. I haven't got all night."

The huge soldier made his way through the crowd of onlookers, cajoled and directed by Sands, and was deposited with a flourish back in the same chair from which he had earlier dominated the room. Once seated, his expression of resentful compliance mirrored that of an unruly infant who'd been strapped into a high chair.

"What colour, black or white?" demanded Sands, now in full command mode.

The Roman gestured to a white piece, while she set up the board. "Let's get a move on. You start," said Sands. "But before we begin," she added, pointing at Birch, "my brother, here, must be free to leave."

"To hell with him. Get him out of here before we all drown

in his blood," replied her opponent. He was trying hard to focus on the challenge in hand.

"Birch, get going!" she shouted in English. "Wait for me outside the village, somewhere where you can't be seen."

He was half-tempted by the offer. "But what about you? You can't stay here."

"I have no choice," she replied. "I know I can save myself, but I can't vouch for what they'll do to you when I win."

"If you win," he corrected. "Don't be mad, Sands.

"I'll be fine. I've got a get-out-of jail card, you haven't."

"What the hell are you talking about?"

"Never mind, Birch. It's for your own good."

Sands turned to the Roman corporal with whom she had clashed earlier, and addressed him in Latin. "Corporal, I respectfully request that you get my brother out of here now, or I will not fulfil my wager with this ridiculous opponent, drunk though he is."

"My pleasure, throw him out lads," said the corporal, delighted, at last, to be accorded some mark of recognition.

Before he could react to what was happening, a dozen pairs of hands had engulfed Birch, lifted him off his feet, rotated him at shoulder height, and then jettisoned him head-first through the entrance to the tavern and on to the street outside. His removal was accompanied by gales of laughter, which rang through his head in dizzying confusion as he lay spread-eagled on the wet ground, stunned and bleeding.

After the side-show had run its course, the mood inside the tavern became dark and intense. Once again, the two gamblers became the focal point of all interest. The Roman, still pouring with sweat, seemed nervous and unable to concentrate clearly. The young woman, although frail in contrast, had an imposing presence that appeared to unnerve her opponent. She knew that if she was to win she would have to exploit the opposition's weakness. This moment would define her.

As she prepared for mental combat, she reflected on the game she was about to play. How appropriate, she thought, that this was a battle contest. She had studied its history and tactics with interest as a student. The title 'Robber-soldiers' had seemed incidental then: the name a clumsy English translation, perhaps, of little real significance. But now a simple game of *Ludus Latrinculorum*, as the Romans termed it, held a meaning for her that threw a light on whole swathes of human conflict and conquest.

She thought of her uncle, of his passionate, predictable and, frankly, often ludicrous opposition to all manifestations of imperialism, territorial invasion and military intervention. His presence began to feel almost physical. What would he make of all this, she wondered?

Sands was struck by a sudden recognition that she had always disavowed: her Uncle Sterland's imprimatur lay embedded deeply within her. This sudden epiphany fuelled her growing sense of potency and authorisation. What had his favourite Marxian aphorism been – the one that he had quoted *ad nauseam*? It was something about humans taking responsibility for their own outcomes. And then, with startling clarity, it suddenly came to her. People make their own history but not in circumstances of their own choosing.

"Perfect," she thought, as she confronted her fraught situation, "that'll do me nicely."

But there were other competing forces fighting for influence over Sands' consciousness that evening. Once or twice she'd found herself conflicted in her decision making. And at times, she'd been torn between defending Birch, for whom she felt a strong protective instinct, or confronting her opponents, whose superiority she'd resented, or fleeing the danger that the tavern represented, which, in some ways, seemed the most logical course of action. What confused the picture even further, was the fact that her instinctive tendency to challenge authority was undermined by a sudden inexplicable desire to form unnatural alliances and seek assistance from the bullies who threatened her. These alien instincts had to be suppressed, but, as the evening wore on, they had become more and more of a destabilising influence on Sands' ability to make decisions.

Certain expressions kept recurring in the back of her mind, often indistinctly but sometimes almost audibly, which meant she had to struggle to maintain her control over the multiple challenges facing her. The repeated ordinance to "tend and befriend" echoed like a mantra, unwelcome, unfamiliar and aberrant. This alternated with a separate nagging question about whether to "fight or flight", a persistent turn of phrase with which she was familiar but had no meaningful acquaintance.

Sands fought to clear her mind of distracting instincts. She focused hard to bring her full attention to bear on the immediate challenge facing her, and to eradicate the conflicting messages which were pulsing through her consciousness like Morse code.

Her adversary fixed her with an intimidating stare that she returned without blinking. The Roman's expression reflected his barely concealed anger. Here was a man who planned to exact his full revenge, and to do so while causing the maximum discomfort to his opponent. He dealt in the common currency of all bullies: fear, intimidation and the exploitation of his victims' weaknesses. But like all bullies, he shared a fatal flaw that would undo him, an inevitable tendency to underestimate an opponent's fighting spirit and mental resolve. And in Sands this complacent thug had found his nemesis. His worst nightmares were coalesced in the form of a slightly-built, female freedom fighter dropped in from the early years of the 21st century.

"I'll move first," he said, slamming one of his 'dogs' down hard on the board in front of him.

"Whoa, slow down! What's the rush?" enquired Sands. "You'll be humiliated soon enough. Take your time so you don't make any stupid mistakes."

The Roman's anger was ratcheted up another level by this comment. "May all the Gods damn you. Play, before I gut you like a fish."

"With what do you plan to gut me?" she asked, as she made

her first move. "Your sword, perhaps?"

"Don't tempt me, by Jupiter," he replied, moving his next piece before he'd properly considered his position.

"Because if you carry on playing like this," she riposted, enclosing one of his pieces with two of her own, "you won't have possession of it for much longer."

"May the God's damn you for a dirty, twisted hag," he replied, clearly furious with himself for his elementary error.

"Flatterers are the worst type of enemies," she said, surveying his latest move. "So, by extension, you must be the best type," and here she paused for dramatic effect while enclosing another of his pieces, "as you're clearly the king of morons."

Up to this juncture, the assembled crowd had been watching the proceedings with concentrated neutrality, but now they began to murmur in approval at the successful tactics employed by the young woman, and their partiality added to the agitated state of her adversary. He continued to curse with irritation, his focus now distracted by external events. Sands was stripping him of every vestige of confidence, resilience and concentration.

The game proceeded at a pace she dictated and with an outcome she controlled. The Roman's tactical manoeuvres became predictable and inept, and her own counter-attacks were conducted with an assurance and, most importantly, with a dramatic flourish that went down well with the gallery.

As the game entered its final stages the outcome became inevitable. Sands polished off the final pieces, and, amid the applause, addressed a last contemptuous remark to her opponent who sat seething with frustration at his impotence.

"Be patient and tough, my friend; some day this pain will be useful to you," she said, rising from her seat. "Now I must be going. It's late."

"Wait!" he shouted, leaping with a burst of suppressed energy from his chair. "You've forgotten something, haven't you?" He staggered around the table towards her, a look of undiluted malice disfiguring his features.

"Calm down. You have nothing that I want," she replied,

taking a nervous step backwards.

He pushed his comrades out of the way and positioned himself in front of her in an effort to bar her escape. "Well, I've got something that I want to give you all the same. And you're not leaving here till I've given it to you good and proper." His meaning was unmistakable and drew a chorus of salacious laughter and whistles from the mob of Roman soldiers who now encircled them both closely.

"You said you wanted my sword. Well, now you're going to get more than you bargained for." He grabbed Sands' left wrist and thrust her palm on top of his genitals, holding it there as she struggled to free his brutal grip with her free hand.

In desperation, Sands looked around the room for help. Her appeal was met by an array of malicious and ugly expressions. This mob had developed an untroubled familiarity with the concept of sexual gratification though violence and intimidation.

"Now, you're going to take my sword out of its sheath," he wheezed. He reached out his left hand and attempted to seize her by the hair.

Sands' response was immediate and instinctive. In a split second she knew what she had to do if she was to survive. As the Roman moved to grab her, she had to act to save herself; the moment his left arm moved up to secure a hold on her hair, Sands' self-defence training kicked in.

No one in the room who witnessed it will forget what happened next. It was one thing for this young woman to have kicked a chair from underneath an unsuspecting opponent - that was surprising enough - but it was quite another for her to hurl a standing man, twice her size, over her shoulder in a perfect arc and at blinding speed. The impact on the spectators was electrifying, the effect on her opponent debilitating. As soon as he landed, a huge slow-motion wheeze emitting from his stricken frame, Sands was on to him, his *gladius* in her hand, its pointed tip pressed up against his wind-pipe, and her left foot resting on his convulsing chest.

There was a shocked silence among the audience surrounding the pair. The only sound was that of the stricken Roman gasping for air.

"Nobody move or I'll kill him," yelled Sands, looking around at the startled gazes of those nearest her. The crowd was too stunned to do anything but accede to her command.

"Corporal, where are you?" she shouted. "Show yourself!"

"I'm here, Galla Placidia," said the shocked-looking soldier as he pushed his way into view.

"Good, I've a few questions to ask you, do you understand?"

"Yes, Galla Placidia," he responded obediently.

"Right. Yesterday, did I have an audience with the Commander-in-Chief, Julius Rufinus?"

"Yes, Galla Placidia."

"Good, now we're getting somewhere. And did he issue clear orders to you, personally, that I was not to be molested in any way?"

At this point, the corporal glanced nervously around him, as if looking for moral support.

"Answer the question, Corporal!" she yelled, still pressing the sword against her stricken opponent's throat. "Did you receive a clear instruction to that effect?"

"Answer the question, Corporal, please," entreated her captive, his voice strained by the pressure on his wind-pipe.

"Yes, Galla Placidia, I did," the corporal replied in apprehension, suddenly aware of the full implications of the evening's events.

"In that case," she responded with cold authority, "every man in this tavern is in clear contravention of an explicit order issued by the supreme Roman commander, Julius Rufinus."

The invocation of the commander-in chief's name had a dramatic effect on all those within ear-shot. They'd all disobeyed an order; the corporal had confirmed it himself. The temperature in the room appeared to fall by several degrees. A palpable mood of fear floated down like a burial shroud and swaddled those standing in the body of the tavern.

Sands had them where she wanted them.

"The rest of you stand back," she ordered, and the crowd thinned out immediately, some taking the first opportunity to leave the building and return to camp. "Now you, Corporal, are going to accompany me to the edge of the village to guarantee my safety. What's your name?"

"Bostar, Galla Placidia. My name is Bostar."

"Well, Bostar, I am making you personally responsible for my protection. Is that clear?"

Sands removed the sword from the throat of the Roman lying prostrate at her feet. He groaned with pain but made no effort to lift himself up. The crowd, however, was quick to part once more and allowed her to make her way to the door. Most of the men averted their gaze and some turned away, chastened and shaken by the events that they had witnessed.

This was a night that would remain engraved on the memories of all who were present, and for most of these men it threw up a suspicion that they could never quite quell: that the unprecedented events that they'd witnessed in the tavern were a mere foreshadowing of the disaster that was to overtake them all within the next twenty-four hours.

SIXTEEN

The Greyhound Inn lies half a mile or so from the location of the Roman fort of Aballava. It is a solid, two-storied building, faced with whitewash and ornamental stonework in the manner of an eighteenth-century travellers' tavern. The arched entrance is reached through a pleasant little beer garden, which directly overlooks the Hadrian's Cycleway national route 72. Although there is no visible evidence of Roman remains on this spot, it is reasonable to assume that the *vallum* and wall would have run adjacently to the inn's rear elevation. In many respects it is a contemporary incarnation of the local tavern that Sands and Birch found themselves in eighteen hundred years earlier. These days, it's true, the clientele tends towards the cyclist and walker rather than the soldier, gambling is restricted to the electronic, one-armed variety and any fish on the menu is sourced from the local shop rather than direct from the waters of the Solway. The welcome is warm and friendly and the threat of casual violence is neither implicit nor imminent. In short it is a perfect location for a quiet evening drink after a day spent walking along the shores of the Firth.

And it's in the cosy public bar of The Greyhound Inn, that Sterland Morris and Robert Jamieson sit sipping the locally brewed ale, having just placed an order for their evening meal. They are reflecting on the events of yet another deeply frustrating day. Despite an intensive search over an ever-widening area of water, there is still no sign of the helicopter or of its occupants. They have been prevented from approaching too close to the shoreline, where dredged-up metal ephemera are being stored for scientific analysis. Their questions, on the whole, have been met with polite but insistent stone-walling, a response that's made them feel they're being intentionally mislead. It was almost as if the authorities possessed information that they were shielding from the families and friends of the two pilots.

"Dr Morris," a voice calls from the doorway across the far side of the room.

The two men look up from their drinks in surprise. Morris' shoulders slump in dismay. "Oh, damn it, not him," he mutters to himself.

"Who is he?" mouths Jamieson, sensing his friend's unease.

"Oh, he's just an opinionated journalist who was giving me a hard time yesterday. I'll try and get shot of him."

The interloper moves through the drinkers in the bar and stands at the table opposite the two men.

"I hope you don't mind me joining you for a moment?" he asks, not waiting for a response before settling himself down.

"I don't remember inviting you," responds Morris.

"Don't be like that, Doc. We're all in the dark here; the more we help each other the better it will be for everyone."

"If I want help from a hack then I'm perfectly capable of using my own contacts. Now, I'd be grateful if you'd leave me and my colleague in peace."

The young man ignores the request and ploughs on regardless. "Look, Dr Morris, you don't have to be a genius to see that there's some kind of official cover-up going on here. You know and I know that a bloody great helicopter can't just disappear into thin air."

"Ok, so now's the point where you start digging up a conspiracy theory, is it?"

"Look, just hear me out for two minutes and then I promise I'll leave you in peace."

"Ok, get on with it. Two minutes, and the clock's ticking."

"Have you ever heard of Dundrennan Range?"

"No, should I have?" Morris asks, shooting a long-suffering glance at Jamieson as he replies.

"It's a Ministry of Defence weapons testing range situated across the other side of the Solway Firth. It's located on 5000 acres of farmland but extends out into the Firth itself, so it

124

also covers a three hundred square mile sea danger area."

Morris and Jamieson sit up straighter in their seats.

"And what are they doing that's so dangerous?"

"How much do you know about depleted uranium, Doctor?"

"Not much. The American's used it a lot in Iraq, I think, on shells to pierce armoured plating. It's sometimes mentioned in connection with Gulf War Syndrome."

"That's right; it's the tank-busters weapon of choice. It's twice as dense as lead so when used to coat the tips of shells it has twice the impact on heavy armour. When it hits it burns away in to a vapour rather than mushrooming like tungsten, for example. The big benefit is that the projectile keeps its sharp point so it can penetrate armour effectively and – boom! - create an inferno inside anything it hits. But the big worry concerns its side effects on the health of individuals, civilians as well as soldiers, who come into close contact with the fallout – the depleted uranium dust. That's the bit that we don't know about. And it's not just been used by the Yanks and the Brits in Iraq, you know – it's also been used in Afghanistan and in Kosovo. And the Israeli's have used depleted uranium shells widely in Palestine and Lebanon."

"So, you're suggesting what, exactly? That the missing Lynx is tied up with this depleted uranium, that they were transporting something sensitive that blew them to kingdom come?"

"No, not exactly, but I am suggesting that there may well be a link of some kind. That range has been firing depleted uranium shells into the Solway for years now."

"But for what reason, for heaven's sake?"

"They do it so that they can test their effectiveness. They fire them through soft targets made from canvas and plastic hanging from on-land gantries. The depleted uranium shells then sail on out to sea where they sink and are simply left to corrode on the sea bed."

"Come on, that's a bit far-fetched. Why on earth would they do that? What about the health hazards to the local community – and the effects on the environment?"

"Exactly, this is a very sensitive area for the Ministry of Defence. Occasionally they do get called to task, but you won't be surprised to hear that they're very effective at covering up their activities. There was a well-documented case back in 2002 when a ship called The Cork Sands was damaged by a bomb which apparently exploded on the sea bed. It was involved in helping lay a gas pipeline to Ireland. Now here's the interesting thing: when they sent a bomb disposal squad and divers to the area, the MOD delayed in informing the local coastguard for forty-eight hours. Now, please explain to me why any official government agency would choose to do that? Was it because they needed time to clean their fingerprints off the crime scene first? Short of a charge of basic incompetence, it's got to be the obvious explanation."

"I'm impressed. Your cynicism does you justice. But let's have one piece of objective evidence linking the helicopter to this firing range, just one. If you can't convince me, and I'm a dyed-in-the-wool sceptic, then you've haven't got much of a chance with anyone else."

"Look, don't be a complete twat."

Morris shoots him an offended look. "Okay, that's enough, your time's up."

"No, please, I'm sorry, I take that back. Just hear me out. All you have to do is tie the pieces together and look at the bigger picture. You've got a military helicopter gone inexplicably missing and, apparently, irretrievably lost over an area of sea that is a designated firing range. And it's into this danger area that the MOD have pumped over six thousand highly controversial depleted uranium shells, none of which, by their own admission, they've been able to recover. Now throw in to the mix the significant risk to local people and environment represented by the toxicity of these munitions. It's a matter of public record that the area next to the range has the highest excess of leukaemia risk among young people under the age of twenty-four. And that's the highest risk recorded out of eight hundred and ninety-eight postcodes in Scotland. Coincidence, maybe, inconvenient statistic for the MOD to deal with, certainly, and that's what I think may possibly lie at the heart of this case."

"Ok, whatever else we may think about Britain, it is a mature democracy, or at least it was last time I checked. The fact that you're quoting all these facts and figures at me suggests that there is hardly a veil of secrecy covering the MOD's activities at Dundrennan."

"Now you're just being naïve, Doc. Look, the MOD has a major headache. It's lost one of its helicopters, but while it's searching for metal objects on the sea bed the last thing it wants is to have the world's media reporting on the dredging up of the remains of six thousand depleted uranium shells."

"But why would it be such an issue for the MOD if everyone already knows that testing takes place?"

"Why? Because Britain is incredibly resistant to open disclosure of its data on depleted uranium, particularly its effects in zones of combat, and that is a fact."

"You keep making these definitive statements, but what grounds do you have to support your assertions?"

"It's not me – that's the point. It's the United Nations."

"What's that supposed to mean, "It's the United Nations"?"

"Look, for years the overwhelming membership of the UN has been pushing for greater transparency on the effects of uranium munitions. And what happens? Finally, in October 2010, after years of pushing, the General Assembly First Committee passes a draft resolution calling on members who've used depleted uranium to hand over quantitative and geographical data on their use to states affected by them."

"And Britain was opposed to this resolution?"

"Yeah, it was one of only four countries, out of the entire membership of the world's nations, who voted against the motion. Makes you proud to be British, doesn't it? And can you guess who the other three were?"

"Got to be America?"

"Yes."

"France, maybe?"

"Yep

"And Israel?"

"Bingo!"

Sterland Morris slumps back into his seat, suddenly exhausted by the sordid predictability of it all. "I think I'm beginning to get the picture," he mutters into his beer. "What a miserable bunch of swine."

"But it's not all bad news, Doc. In 2009, Belgium became the first country in the world to ban the use of depleted uranium in ammunition."

"Brilliant, that's a relief; now we can all rest easy in our beds. The prospect of Belgium throwing depleted uranium shells around is more than I could cope with."

"I'm impressed. Your cynicism does you justice. We're a lot alike, you and me."

"Oh God, spare me; don't ruin my day entirely. Now, if I'm not very much mistaken, your two minutes are up."

"Okay, Dr Morris, but give what I've said some thought, won't you? And if it helps, I'm not a journalist – at least, not in the sense that you mean. Here's my card. Get in touch if you want to have a further discussion in the days ahead."

The two men shake hands. Morris glances down at the name on the card. "So Mr Gemmell, who do you represent?"

"CND Scotland. You know, the Campaign for Nuclear Disarmament."

"Yes, Mr Gemmell, I am conversant with the organisation – I was a member myself for over twenty years."

"Yes, I know, Doc, from 1979 to 2000. I may not be much of a journalist, but I can still sniff out a fact or two. Keep in touch now."

"Don't bank on it. While I've got every sympathy for CND's cause, at the moment there are more important things for me to worry about than giving succour to self-serving conspiracy theorists."

"Look, I can understand that, Dr Morris. But remember this: the next time you're being fobbed off by a faceless MOD bureaucrat who refuses to tell you what's happened to your niece, try asking him whether her flight path took her directly over the Dundrennan sea danger area and watch what happens to the pallor of his complexion. And with that thought in mind, I'll be off home. Good evening, gents."

"Bumptious character," Jamieson volunteers, once the other man has left the table.

"Yes, I rather liked him," admits Morris. "I'd forgotten how much I enjoyed being given a hard time by the younger generation."

"So what d'you think of his theory? Is there anything to it?"

"Yes, there might well be. But if you're asking whether it has anything to do with the disappearance of the helicopter, then no, I don't think it does. In fact, I'd go as far as to say that I'm absolutely certain that it doesn't."

"Really, Sterland? Rationality getting the better of you again?"

"No, quite the opposite is true, in fact. You see, I'm beginning to think the unthinkable. You'll probably call it wishful-thinking, turning a blind eye to the inevitable, refusing to face the obvious truth. Feel free to select your preferred cliché."

"As you've probably noticed, Sterland, when it comes to using clichés I rarely need any encouragement. But I would caution you to keep your feet on the ground. There's evidently something going on out there that defies simple explanation, but that's purely because we don't have access to all the facts as yet. I can't accept that there's a conspiracy of silence."

"Neither can I, frankly. I think the truth of what we're dealing with here may be even harder to digest, and impossible to verify."

"What are you driving at now? You're way ahead of me."

"Ok, here's what I think – but I'm warning you, Robert, you're not going to like it." Morris eyes his companion cautiously and takes a steadying drink.

"Listen, Sterland, don't forget I'm a coroner and, consequently, I'm no stranger to conflicting theories. With all due respect to your imaginative powers, I doubt whether you could stretch credulity any further than some of the witnesses I've had in my court over the years. But, please," and with this, Jamieson pauses to pat Morris encouragingly on the knee, "be my guest and give it your best shot."

"I think they've probably found the remains of the helicopter already."

Jamieson lets out an exasperated sigh. "Then why aren't they telling us? You've already rejected thoughts of a conspiracy."

"Because they don't realise what they've found."

"What do you mean?"

"How could they know? Have you any idea how many recorded shipwrecks there are around Britain's shores?"

"Oh, thousands, I should think."

"There's forty-four thousand, to be precise. And that means, even if it's just a tiny share of that total, that there must be hundreds of wrecks sitting on the bottom of the Solway Firth. Every time they drag up something, they think they've dredged up the corroded remains of a first world-war vessel sunk by a mine or a shipwrecked Victorian steamer."

"But what does it matter what they're dragging up if they can't locate the helicopter?"

"Because things aren't always what they seem," answers Morris, digging around in his briefcase. He brings out a bulbous, oblong object about 12 centimetres long and places it on the table in front of Jamieson. "What do you make of that, then?"

"Are those barnacles?" asks Jamieson, rubbing his hand gingerly over the surface of the object.

"They're concretions, strictly speaking, composed of sand, iron oxides, cockles and, yes, barnacles, among other things. I'm not a marine archaeologist so I can't give you the exact chemical composition, but that concrete-like shell on the outside encases a metallic object and is formed, over time, as a result of a chemical reaction between iron and sea water."

"So what do you expect me to make of it?"

"I want you to date the metal object that's hidden inside these concretions."

"I haven't got a clue. How could I have?"

"Just use your best judgement and common sense. Take a

look at it and try and decide how long it's been in the sea."

"Look, Sterland, I really haven't got a clue, but judging by the thick build-up of barnacles, I don't know, I'd guess it's been in the sea for many hundreds of years."

"Exactly," repeats Morris, smiling at his companion "many hundreds of years. And that's what anyone might think."

"So, now you're going to tell me it's thousands of years old. I can feel it coming," says Jamieson, wincing in anticipation.

"Quite the contrary, old chap," replies Morris, scarcely able to disguise the note of triumph in his voice.

He picks up the object and turns it over to reveal the flat cross-section of a pointed metal shape sliced in half and embedded in several centimetres of concretions growing around it.

"Good Lord, Sterland, what is it?"

"It's a 20 mm Mauser cartridge from the Second World war. It was the standard Luftwaffe cannon shell from 1941 onwards."

"Where on earth did you get it? Out of the Solway?

"No, it was recovered from the Wadden Sea in Lower Saxony. But the muddy tidal flats found there are not dissimilar to those of the Solway."

"So what is the point of this little demonstration?"

"The point is to prove that peoples' expectations can sometimes, even with the best of intentions, steer them in the wrong direction. And I think that's exactly what is happening here with the hunt for the helicopter."

"So, what is happening with the hunt for the helicopter?"

"Well, to understand that, you need to have a look at a couple of other things I've got here." He returns once more to his briefcase and carefully draws out a small object wrapped in a soft cloth.

He places the bundle down on the table and slowly unwraps it with great care. Jamieson leans forward in eager anticipation.

"Good God, Sterland. What the hell is that doing here? It's supposed to be under lock and key back at the British Museum, surely?"

Despite his concern at the apparent breach of protocol,

Jamieson studies the metal crest from the Burgh by Sands hoard with meticulous attention.

"Don't worry, Robert, if it's survived for nearly two thousand years then it must be built to last."

"Two thousand years? But you distinctly said that this brooch was composed of aluminium; you assured me that it was made no more than fifty years ago."

"And so it was, Robert. But as we know, people's expectations can sometimes, even with the best of intentions, steer them in the wrong direction."

"Why don't you get to the point? Drop the aphorisms, please. It's either fifty years old or two thousand years old – it can't possibly be both."

"I agree. On the face of it, it is not possible for a single object to exist in two different places at the same time. But, self-evidently, there's nothing to stop the same object from appearing in the same place but at two different times."

"Of course not, but only if the said object is two bloody thousand years old. For God's sake, Sterland, what on earth are you suggesting?"

"I'm suggesting this," replies Morris as he produced a gleaming, modern crest and placed it next to the other one, "that these two badges once looked exactly the same. Our expectations are that they date from different eras. Everything would appear to indicate that. But look closely at the basic design and you can see that really, despite the obvious damage to the older one, they are, or were, identical."

"Right, the older one's had the crown hacked off. This new one is obviously a modern military crest. What regiment?"

"It's the Army Air Corps. I bought it in London from an army surplus store the day before yesterday."

"So what we've got here," says Jamieson, pointing at the older crest "is a battered but modern Army Air Corps badge placed in the Burgh by Sands hoard?"

"Exactly."

"But how the hell did it get there?"

"I think you can guess the answer to that," says Morris with a knowing smile.

"Oh come off it, Sterland. This is madness. There's no way that Kal could have placed it there."

"I know that on the face of it none of this makes any sense. But consider the alternative, that two young pilots and a helicopter have simply disappeared into thin air without a trace. At least this way we have a trail of evidence to follow."

"What evidence? Come on, listen to yourself."

"We have an AAC badge found within a 15 mile radius of where the helicopter was presumed to have disappeared."

"But found weeks beforehand, and could've been there years."

"I accept all that. But I still maintain that our expectations are blinding us to an obvious conclusion. Look at what the crest was buried with."

"Gold coinage, and lots of it."

"Forget the gold. No, I'm talking about the gaming artefacts. The crest was buried along with an incredible range of pieces and objects, obviously collected by someone with a passion for Roman gambling activities. Now that is a link to Kal that you cannot dismiss, no matter how illogical and inconvenient the timeframes may be."

"So, you are seriously suggesting what exactly? That Kal and, one presumes, her co-pilot have mysteriously been relocated back in time to the Roman era? And during which period she has hidden some artifacts, including gambling equipment and her cap badge, which we have subsequently found eighteen hundred years later, but in advance of the pair's disappearance? It's preposterous, and you know it is. And what happened to the helicopter, may I ask?"

"Its remains are still out there in the Solway somewhere, covered in concretions and attracting no serious attention because they're not what the divers are expecting to find. I wouldn't mind betting that one of those rusting remnants, which has been incorrectly identified as a corroded propeller shaft or mast, isn't a rotor blade from our Lynx instead."

"Now that would be some kind of evidence, but I can't see you being allowed down there with a hammer and a chisel."

"No, and, anyway, why would they even bring the stuff to the surface? It doesn't match their expectations, so they'd discount it out of hand. Hence, the apparent total lack of crash debris. But what we do have is this," he continues, tapping his forefinger on the battered old military crest on the table in front of him. "This remains our one bit of evidence about the fate of Kal and her fellow pilot."

"Ok, so if this madcap theory of yours is true – and I do hope you realise that I'm humouring you here - then, strictly speaking, we're not excavating their past, we're excavating their future. And as far as they're concerned, they're much more alive than we are. In fact, our very existence must appear to be purely conjectural."

"Well, it would appear that all our choices are pre-determined by the past, at least to some extent. I'm not sure anyone really entirely buys into the notion of "free will" any more, do they? But when good old Marx maintained that the tradition of all dead generations weighs like a nightmare on the brains of the living, I'm not sure that he ever had the prescience to assess whether the tradition of future generations had a similar effect on the brains of the living."

"And I'm not sure how you'd go about making decisions in their position. But at least they must have a strong sense that if events aren't pre-ordained, which, by now, they must be only too bitterly aware, then the future can't possibly be pre-determined either. You can see the nature of the problem for a simple soul like me - I'm not even sure what grammatical tense I should use to refer to them in: the past, the present or the future?"

"I know what you mean. Let's just stick to the conditional tense, shall we? At least that way we've got the factual, the predictive and the speculative areas covered."

"And, heaven knows, we're going to require all three," responds Jamieson with a resigned laugh.

Morris chuckles gratefully. It's clear that his companion is now prepared to consider his proposition with an open mind.

SEVENTEEN

At night, the Aballava bathhouse took on a daemonic aspect. Steam poured from the multitudinous flues, pulsating and shimmering with volcanic irregularity. Streaks of light illuminated the boiling water vapour as it dissipated high into the pitch-black sky. There it mingled in unholy alliance with the expelled waste products, smoke and noxious gases that lay suspended like an infernal membrane around the skin of the building.

This was the sight that transfixed the three British army personnel, who now lay prone in a ditch fifty meters to the south. They were pondering how one of them, Private Titus Ojokwu, was going to gain access to the interior of the baths.

They'd spent the previous hour watching Roman soldiers passing between the bathhouse and fort. They'd reconnoitred the area around the building, piecing together every detail of its layout, function and structure. To the rear they'd located an aqueduct. It supplied water to a six metre long cistern located in an untended shed near the main furnace room. The cistern was connected to a pumping wheel that provided the baths with the endless flow of water demanded by the furnace boilers. Further investigations revealed a complex network of drains, sluices, water courses and culverts controlling the flow of fresh water and the removal of human waste. On several occasions they'd seen attendants discard garbage on a large midden behind the building. On inspection, this rubbish tip was found to contain quantities of discarded oyster shells and other food waste, a discovery that boded well for that evening's plan of attack.

The bathhouse sat in its own perimeter, one hundred metres to the right of the fort, linked by a path directly from its east gate. The external appearance was mundane, its stonework walls and terracotta-tiled pitched roofs carrying a tired reminder of twentieth-century suburbia. At night, thanks to ingenious floodlighting, the bathhouse was transformed into something monumental and imposing. It was a large building, thirty metres long by twenty metres wide. It appeared to be double-storied and possess high ceilings, and its thick external walls contained a small number of wooden-framed windows, glazed with thick, uneven blocks of glass. There were three external doors. One monumental double door was located underneath a triangular pediment at the lightly-guarded front entrance. The two other doors, one at the rear of the building and one around the corner to the left of the entrance, gave access to the two separate furnaces from where the bathhouse sourced its steam and heat. The building was cruciform in shape with a tall central block running its full length. The two radiating arms comprised of single-storey lean-to structures, the left hand one of which was a latrine block, the other being the smaller of the two furnace rooms.

As Stogdon, Crawley and Ojokwu undertook their reconnaissance they were regularly disturbed by streams of passing locals. Throughout the evening, villagers visited the baths, chatted to the guards and delivered goods and fresh laundry. It was clear that the furnaces were the heart of the operation. The never-ending requirement to keep the temperature constant generated a relentless demand for fuel and labour-power. Men rushed backwards and forwards without pause, delivering timber from the wood pile and buckets of coal from an underground cellar. This back-breaking, remorseless work was slave-labour in its most literal state.

Initially, they'd considered that Ojokwu's safest means of ingress would be through a side window. Their reconnaissance had confirmed this decision. Now they had to discount the various alternatives available. The front of the building was guarded and was out of the question, and both the rear of the building, where the main furnace was located, and the long south side, where the smaller furnace room lay, attracted too much human traffic to be considered. That left the long north side, the one facing Hadrian's Wall, as the best option to gain access.

The wall, itself, was patrolled and any passing guard would have an unobstructed view from a distance of no more than fifty metres. However, patrols were timed to start every fifteen minutes, took less than five minutes to complete and, once finished, offered a comfortable ten minute opportunity for the men to work unobserved.

Now they lay in the ditch waiting for the Roman guard to complete his circuit. Once the sentry had returned to the warmth of the wall turret, five hundred metres to the east, the soldiers sprang up and moved to the side of the bathhouse. In one fluid movement Stogdon and Crawley clasped hands at knee level and projected a vaulting Ojokwu up and on to the edge of the sloping latrine roof. He grasped the metal guttering and with a helping shove from below he shimmied his way on to the top of the roof, lying spread-eagled on the tiles. Stogdon and Crawley withdrew to the relative protection of the shadows to keep watch as their companion worked.

Ojokwu slithered up the sloping tile roof on his stomach, reached the wall to the left of the window and coiled himself into a crouching position so he could peer into the interior without being seen from the inside. He'd removed his boots already and was only clad in vest and underpants. As he levered himself into position he was able to look down into a large, whitewashed changing room, measuring some ten by fifteen metres. Several dozen men were engaged in a range of activities. Some were disrobing or in the process of dressing, others exercising and the largest group were sitting, chatting, eating and drinking. Recessed into the wall facing him he could see seven arched niches which contained an array of statues and objects. This room was too busy to provide a realistic means of access.

Ducking back under the window, Ojokwu crept to his left to examine the interior of the next room. Once he'd made it to the end of the latrine block roof he manoeuvred his way on to the main pitched roof. He clung to the overhang as he lay flat, peering upside-down through the window beneath him. This looked much more like it. To begin with, the window was hinged and could be forced without shattering any glass. More importantly, the room, which contained a large bath, was empty. Ojokwu, noting the lack of condensation on the window glass, and having been briefed by Sands, identified this as being the cold plunge bath room or *frigidarium*. The window appeared to have no lock and was held in place by a snug-fitting frame. Ojokwu assessed that he could prise open the window and he gestured down to the others to hurl up his knife.

"Shh, there's someone coming," came the urgent response. "Get back from the edge."

Ojokwu's heart froze for an instant as he cursed his exposed and defenceless position up on the roof. He attempted to edge his way backwards, but with his feet pointing up towards the pitch of the roof he found it almost impossible to gain sufficient leverage. Now he could make out a dark shape in the shadows moving around the side of the building from the rear. He held his breath but could sense his two companions readying themselves to strike at the intruder if their presence was uncovered.

The shape moved nearer but kept hesitating, clearly nervous of revealing itself. Now they could hear a whispered address. Ojokwu glanced down to see Stogdon and Crawley, survival knives in hand, braced for a sudden deadly attack. But something made them pause. Was that a woman's voice coming from the shadows?

"Psst, is that you, guys?" it whispered. "It's me, Kal."

The three soldiers sighed with relief, before Stogdon launched into a sustained volley of abuse. "What the fuck are you doing here, creeping up on us like that?" he hissed under his breath. "Five more yards and I'd have cut your throat open."

"I know, I'm sorry, but I've got some important news," she whispered. She signalled up to Ojokwu who was still on the roof, chuckling with relief. "Ojo, get down here now. Change of plans!"

"What the hell's going on, Kal?" asked Crawley. "Ojo was just about to go in."

"I can see that. But look, the situation's changed," she whispered as Ojokwu joined then. "We can do this a better way, one that's much safer for everyone, particularly for Ojo."

"What's up? What happened to you and Birch?"

"Everything's fine. We managed to drop the *garum* off. Birch had a bit of a rough time – picked up a few cuts and bruises, but he'll be alright. The important thing is I got talking to this Roman corporal when I left the tavern and he wanted to be friendly, keen to do me a favour."

"Oh, yeah, how'd you manage that then?"

"It's a long story. Let's just say we had a disagreement and he wanted to patch things up. He gave me a couple of these things to keep me sweet."

"What are they - coins?"

"No, they're tokens for the bathhouse."

"You what?" Ojo laughed. "Tokens for the bathhouse? You must be bloody joking. You mean I can just walk right in the front door like a regular punter?"

"Pretty much. It beats breaking in through a window."

"Too bloody right, but how am I going to talk my way past the guards? There ain't no way they'll let me in."

"They will if I'm with you. Take a back seat and I'll do the talking. You'll have to put a shirt on, though."

"And what the bleeding hell are we two supposed to do in the meantime?" asked Stogdon.

"Keep out of sight and wait for us to reappear. We may need your help."

"Thanks a bleeding bunch," spat Stogdon. "What happened to good old teamwork?" he asked Crawley.

"No idea, chum, nothing to do with me. I guess our expertise ain't needed."

"You know what, Corp, I ain't prepared to hang around like a sodding spare part. Not when there's lives at stake."

Stogdon shot a furious look at his two comrades' backs as

they disappeared into the dark.

Sands and Ojokwu ducked low and retraced their steps around the rear of the bathhouse so that they could approach the entrance along the principal path from the south-west. As they walked Sands gave her companion a crash-course in Roman bath etiquette.

On arrival at the entrance the pair generated close interest among the guards when they presented their bathhouse tokens. "He can come in," they said, gesturing at Ojokwu, "but women can only enter the baths in the daytime, not in the evening." For the first time Sands felt she was being addressed in a friendly and respectful fashion.

"I know, but I was told by the corporal, Quintus Drusus Bostar, who is a friend of mine, that you would make an exception in my case. It was he, who gave me the token."

The two soldiers looked at one another. This was an unusual request and one which could have unforeseen consequences if word of it was to get back to their superiors.

Sands, sensing their hesitation, played her trump card. She produced the AAC crest, the one with the eagle surmounted by an imperial crown, and flourished it with the sort of assurance that brooked no opposition. "I have a personal guarantee from the camp commander, Julius Rufinus, witnessed by Quintus Drusus Bostar, that I must be accorded every respect by his troops while I am visiting here. Ask him yourself if you don't believe me."

The guards knew better than to countermand the injunction of a senior officer. This young woman's overwhelming confidence appeared to act as a guarantor of her probity, so they admitted her to the baths with a respectful welcome, and called over an attendant to accompany her inside.

Both Sands and Ojokwu felt a spark of apprehension as they were ushered into the *apodyterium*. This was the large, whitewashed changing room that Ojokwu had spied through the side window from the top of the roof earlier. As they entered, Sands was aware of Ojokwu's arm linked through her own, a gesture that she found reassuring and pleasurable.

The attendant ushered them to one side of the changing room and, on being paid a gratuity, brought them towels, a pair of wooden-soled sandals, a small vessel containing oil and a small curved metal tool.

"We use the oil as soap and then scrape it off with this thing," said Sands, holding up the metal implement. "It's called a *strigil*, and acts a bit like a squeegee. It supposed to scrape everything off – dirt, sweat, dry skin, the works."

"It's a right scary looking thing. Think it'll do the trick?"

"We'll soon find out," replied Sands as she glanced around the room. It was clear that any prospect of preserving her personal modesty was going to have to be jettisoned along with her clothes. "Here, Ojo, don't forget your clogs; the floors next door are going to be scalding."

As they slipped their clothes off, they were aware that they were subject to nods and smiles from their fellow bathers. The temperature in the changing room was fresh and the atmosphere calm and relaxed. A number of men went though stretching and strengthening exercises in the middle of the room, lifting lead weights and doing calisthenics. Others sat around chatting in a fraternal and convivial manner. A few were fully dressed and were enjoying some food and wine before returning to their more spartan quarters at the fort.

"This is a chilled atmosphere. Reminds me a bit of a mosque; there's a good vibe, a sense of fellowship and mutual respect among these guys."

"I didn't know you were a Muslim, Ojo."

"There's a lot you don't know about me, Kal. You have to make a lot of compromises when you join the British Army."

"Yeah, so I discovered."

"Anyway, I was never that serious. I got into it through the Nation of Islam."

"That isn't mainstream Islam is it, not like Sunni or Shi'a?"

"No, it's separatist Black Nationalism with an unorthodox Muslim twist - think Malcolm X and Muhammad Ali. I got to appreciate Islam, but never converted."

Their conversation was interrupted by the attendant who'd

come to collect their clothes and usher them into the baths.

"It seems like it's time to hit the showers," said Sands.

"I'm up for this," said Ojo as they entered through a small vestibule. "This has got to be a once in a lifetime experience."

"I bloody well hope not," Sands replied, gesturing to her comrade's filthy feet. "You know something about the Romans' attitude to bathing? They loved it, unlike us. It's a habit we Brits could do with picking up."

"You try telling Stog the trog."

"Yeah, right. The only reason the Romans insisted on going to the baths once a day - and this was Hadrian's view - was simply because they didn't have time to visit twice daily. And if Roman baths were good enough to warrant a daily visit from Hadrian, then that's all the recommendation I need."

As they stood in the vestibule they caught a tantalising glimpse of adjoining, interconnected rooms to the left, to the right and straight ahead of them.

"Look at that, it's like a labyrinth," muttered Ojokwu.

Sands listened closely to the directions issued her by the attendant and then translated them for her companion's benefit. "Ok, so we've got the *frigidarium*, or cold room to our left. Don't fancy that, yet. We've got the warm room, the *tepidarium*, straight ahead. Beyond that we'll find the *caldarium*, or hot room with a nice hot communal bath."

"That sounds more like it. What's to the right?"

"There's another warm room. That then leads on to the *sudatorium* which is the hottest room, like a sauna. All these rooms seem to be more or less interconnected so people can come and go, I guess."

"Ok, so let's go: warm room, hot room, very hot room, with cold room to finish."

"Suits me, Ojo. Sounds like a strategy Hadrian would've approved of."

And with that, the two soldiers entered the *tepidarium*. At the back of the room, two older dark-skinned men were sitting on stone benches playing backgammon and they acknowledged their presence with a wave, which was returned warmly.

In this relaxed and intimate state, Sands and Ojokwu anointed each other with the perfumed oils that the attendant had provided them with. They applied the unguents to each others bodies with great deliberation and concentration, extracting mutual pleasure as they did so. After a period of relaxation in which they exchanged few words, their bodies began to glow and flush with warmth.

Sands added to the intimacy of the moment by inducting Ojokwu into the mysteries of the *strigil*, the Roman implement used for scraping the surface oil, sweat and dirt from their glistening skins. Pleasure mingled with abrasive discomfort as Sands and Ojokwu attended to each others ablutions, both feeling touched by the unexpected and intense nature of the interaction.

After a while they withdrew into the caldarium and the luxury of the enormous hot bath. They lay naked, up to their necks in the steaming water, unperturbed by the occasional presence of other bathers. The huge barrel-vaulted ceiling, painted with complex geometric patterns, hung like a protective celestial canopy above them. Their conversation, proceeding at a deliciously relaxed pace, was underscored by the gentle sound of splashing water emitting from the circular washing fountain located in a small apse to the side of the bath. It felt like heaven on earth.

A little while later they were joined in the bath by a couple of African soldiers in their mid-twenties. They greeted Ojokwu and Sands and were keen to talk to the two strangers. Ojokwu was interested to find out where they were from and why they had joined the Roman army and come to Britain. Sands acted as an interpreter and struck up an easy rapport.

"They say they are boyhood friends and they both come from a city called Volubilis."

At the mention of this name the two men nodded their heads with enthusiasm, encouraging Sands to share her new-found knowledge with her companion.

"It's located in a Roman province called Mauretania Tingitana, in what would be modern-day Morocco. The city's quite a long way inland from the sea, say mid-way between Casablanca and somewhere like Fez. Anyway, they say it's a spectacular place. It's got eight major gates and a forum, basilica, triumphal arch. Needless to say, it's much more impressive than anywhere they've seen in Britain. They're not very impressed with this country. They find it pretty backward, in comparison with their own."

"I like the sound of this Volubilis. How many people live there?" asked Ojokwu, addressing his question in English directly to the two Africans.

"They say about twenty thousand or so."

"What made them join the Roman Army?" asked Ojokwu.

"It was the prospect of Roman citizenship - that and the grant of land at the end of their service. It seems like everyone wants to be a Roman."

One of the soldiers slapped Ojokwu on the back in a jovial fashion, and addressed a number of remarks to him which he was unable to comprehend.

"He's asking if you've come to join the ranks as a Roman auxiliary at the fort. He's serious. Why else would a black man be in this place?"

"Is that right?" he replied with unfeigned delight.

"He says you're not too old. The food is plentiful and the pay's okay. He could put in a word for you with the recruitment sergeant."

Ojokwu shot them both a grateful smile and shook their hands when they got out of the bath. "Say thanks a lot. It's been proper good to meet them."

Pricked by a sudden flash of intuition, Sands asked "Do you think Stogdon and Crawley are going to be ok?"

"Don't worry, Kal. Make no mistake, them two can take care of themselves. They're both good guys, but when you get right down to it they're professional killers. It's what they do for a living and it's what they really understand. Can't you see they can't wait to get stuck into the Romans?"

"And what about you? Are you the same?"

"Nope, I ain't like them two. I get the bigger picture. And as far as I can see, we're here for keeps and we'll have to make alliances if we want to survive. Burning our boats with the occupying power? To hell with that! No, that ain't a good idea, not at all."

"So you're in favour of collaboration?"

"What, with these brothers? Collaborate with a friendly tribe of Africans and their hot bathtubs? Yeah, for sure - why not?"

"I'm not so sure. I've got too many unanswered questions for my liking right now. I'm finding it difficult to think straight. I mean I'm not convinced that "we're here for keeps" is a suitable way of looking at it."

"I don't get you. We're here, that's a fact; and anything else is just a case of wait and see. We just have to deal with the here and now."

"Yeah, but we're living proof that the here and now is a flexible concept. In our world the "here and now" has become the "there and then". No, no one can explain what's happened to us, least of all me."

"You have a theory though, right? So come on then, man, let's hear it. I ain't in no hurry to go nowhere."

"What about the garum?"

"It can wait."

Sands fixed him with a look of intense concentration as she searched for her words. "Okay, look, just suppose for a moment that time splits backwards and forwards."

"You what?"

"Well, imagine it's capable of forking together like a family tree; that what we are experiencing now is the result of innumerable separate pasts which have merged together to create a unified present."

"I don't get you. Are you saying there might be more than one version of the past?"

"Many versions of the past. And the same could apply to the future. Look, this bathhouse is like a labyrinth, right? You said it, yourself, earlier."

"Yeah, I did, but I didn't mean nothing special by it," he replied with a hint of exasperation.

"Ok, so as you walk around this bathhouse there are multiple different routes you could take to get from A to B, right? So multiple paths exist in the spatial sense, agreed?"

"Yeah, but what does that got to do with time?"

"Imagine if time was like a labyrinth, or like this bathhouse, if it makes things any clearer. Now, imagine if the secret centre of that labyrinth, this hot room, for argument's sake, represented the present moment in time as experienced by every individual. We've already established that there are multiple paths in the labyrinth in the spatial sense, agreed?"

"Yeah, seen, seen."

"Now try visualising the bathhouse in the temporal sense. And then try and imagine that the paths to and from the hot room represent innumerable uncertain routes that an individual can navigate, some pointing towards the future, others leading back towards the past."

"But why does that mean that there are multiple versions of the past? Maybe there's just one past and we've landed back in it, just like we're going to end up back in the changing room in a short while, no matter what route we take."

"Why do I think that there must be more than one version of the past? It's a good question and there's a simple answer. It's all explained by something called the "self-consistency conjecture". There's this basic paradox which lies at the heart of time travel theories – you'll know this from watching science fiction films – and it's this: a time-traveller can't change the past without setting up inconsistencies in the future."

Sands leant forward to emphasise the significance of the point she was about to make.

"In the 1980's a Russian physicist, called Novikov, put together a theory about what would have to apply to rule out these kinds of time paradoxes. Firstly, it dictated that changing the past is impossible, and secondly, it assumed a single timeline. And given that we've clearly changed the past, it logically follows that there must be multiple timelines. It's the only rational answer.

"Hold on, Kal. In what ways have we changed the past?"

"Four of us have died, for a start. That's one hell of an inconsistency for the future."

"Yeah, that's true I grant you," he laughed. "But, you know what? Maybe there's another explanation. You know what I think? I think that there is an obvious way in which we regularly revisit and alter the past and yet we never give it a second thought."

"What d'you mean – in our subconscious?

"No."

"You mean in our fantasies? Or in our dreams?"

"Nope."

"Ojo, stop being a wind-up. What you getting at?"

"No, in popular culture - computer games. Just think about it. Don't get the outcome or score you want? Just go back and do it again, but different, better. Do you get me?"

"Ok, so now you think that this can all be explained because we've wound up in a computer simulation?"

"Or a game? No, I'm just saying, it's a possibility. But, at least, it would explain the deaths in relation to that Russian guy's theory."

"Self-consistency conjecture."

"Yeah, whatever. Go on, admit it, you just don't like the fact that my Del-boy theory's got just as much going for it as your Russian geezer. But let's just face it, we ain't none of us got a faintest clue what's going on. That's one fact we can agree on."

"You're not wrong there, that, and the fact that the Romans knew a fair bit about baths."

"So, what are we going to do, then?" asked Ojokwu.

"Going to do about what?"

"You know, the nasty little surprise for our hosts."

"Why? Are you having second thoughts?" asked Sands.

"Yeah, maybe I am. We could still abort it. The guys outside would be none the wiser."

"Not tonight, they wouldn't, but what about tomorrow? We might pay for it then."

"Yeah, you're probably right, but, do you know what I'm saying?" Ojokwu's voice trailed off.

"What? What's the problem? It's very straightforward. We just simply drop the fish sauce off on the way out. It'll be a piece of cake. Nobody will think anything of it."

"Yeah, but these guys – we've got no beef with them. They all seem real cool. They drew the short straw, just like we have. They're doing a shit job in a crap part of the world, hundreds of miles from home. You can relate to that, right?"

"Of course I can. But like you said, you've got to see the bigger picture. Our objective is to get our men safely out of that fort tomorrow. Don't lose sight of that."

"Ok, Kal. You're right." Ojo gave her an inscrutable smile. "Don't let's lose sight of that, that and the fact that you're the boss."

EIGHTEEN

Suddenly the world seemed a desolate and lonely place to Stogdon and Crawley. They were rudderless and cut adrift from their colleagues. They were stumbling through a world of which they had no knowledge and little understanding. And they were ill-equipped to survive other than though the application of brute force and ruthlessness. Sands, in contrast, appeared to possess the adaptability and sophisticated skills required to flourish in this alien environment. They'd begun to resent her glib confidence and the self-assurance with which she'd been able to thrive and assimilate into a hostile society. It was obvious that she had a personal fondness for Ojokwu, an affection that he had not been slow to reciprocate and exploit for his own purposes. And these weren't the only reservations they harboured about their fellow platoon-member. His loyalty was now in question; did he identify his own future as belonging with them or with the African troops in the fort? And as for Birch, he was a slippery customer; he couldn't be trusted to look beyond his own personal priorities, and, whatever they were, they could hardly mirror their own.

The options open to Stogdon and Crawley had narrowed. Their main preoccupation was to rescue their sergeant from the clutches of the Roman army, an unprincipled enemy for whom they had little respect. It had become clear to them that their continued survival would be determined by their physical prowess and ability to live off the land. This prospect would be made more likely if they could relocate to the wilderness of Galloway, an area with which they were already familiar, and from which they could plan and launch guerrilla raids.

These were the conclusions that they were in the process of reaching when a sudden greeting made Stogdon and Crawley jump. Two Roman soldiers, out walking the perimeter, had glimpsed the shadowy figures lurking by the bathhouse wall and were calling to them to identify themselves. They'd been spotted and it was senseless to run. They decided to face the enemy head on.

"Keep calm and don't allow yourself to be provoked," cautioned Crawley.

The two guards walked forwards with their palms raised in greeting.

"Wait for my signal before doing anything."

The Romans approached them with swords sheathed. Their torsos were covered in armour of overlapping horizontal plates fastened front and back with buckles and leather straps, beneath which they wore short-sleeved red tunics. They were in good humour and informally attired, with their top buckles unfastened and their helmets swinging from their hands as they approached.

They shouted several phrases in Latin to which Stogdon and Crawley responded with big smiles and choruses of *"Salvete"*. As the distance between them closed, the two Roman's became alarmed at the appearance of the two large, strangely-attired men striding towards them.

"What ho, mate!" shouted Crawley in English. "You ain't got a light on you, 'ave you?"

The two Romans stopped and took a step backwards, drawing their swords and shouting instructions to Stogdon and Crawley to stand still.

"Whoa, hang on a minute, sunshine," responded Crawley in mock alarm, "no need to get jumpy. I only want a light."

"Don't think he understands English, Corp," replied Stogdon.

"Well he wouldn't, would he, the foreign bastard," said Crawley, unsmiling now. "He should just fuck off back to his own country." He stared into the eyes of the taller Roman and he saw the fear spread across the man's features. "Now, why don't you just be a good little Roman and give me your sword, eh?"

The frightened soldier glanced at his comrade, exchanged a

few words and jabbed the point of his sword at Crawley to make him back up. The other soldier looked around to see whether the sentry on the wall was within hailing distance. In the split second that his head was turned, Stogdon was on to him and had buried his survival knife to its hilt through the base of the man's skull, thrusting upwards towards his brain. The man lay limply in Stogdon's arms, his medulla oblongata serated, all motor control immediately extinguished, all involuntary functions permanently disabled. It was as instant and perfectly executed a silent kill as Stogdon could have wished for.

The other Roman, meanwhile, was about to anticipate his own murder at the instantaneous moment of its execution. An expression of shock froze on his face as the wide arc described by Crawley's knife made its entry point between the unbuckled segmented plates covering his chest and then came to rest, deeply embedded in his suprasternal notch. The knife was then jerked with terrifying force from side to side, rupturing his aorta and superior vena cava in the process, and ensuring a rapid acceleration of death. The Roman subsided to the grass and lay lifeless alongside his former friend and comrade-in-arms, their limbs intertwined in a grotesque *tableau vivant*, a still-born dance of death.

The victim's mouth lay open. He wore a startled grimace, as if interrupted in mid-conversation. It was the only outward indication that he'd experienced his death in a different time register to that of his executioner. He was the victim of an assassination that he'd observed in funereal *Larghissimo Lacrimo* tempo, rather than the *Prestissimo Furioso* blur of action perpetrated by Crawley, who now stood surveying his bloody handiwork with callous indifference.

The Roman sentry had stood as a silent witness to own his murder, observing the evidence as it piled up in front of him. He'd experienced it in drip-drip, freeze-frame, forensic detail. Every microscopic piece of information was recorded, analysed and filed, every reaction was noted, every emotion was recognised and evaluated, and every sensation was experienced and lived fully, as if for the first time. His responses to the unfolding sequence of events that preceded his final breath were not so consistent, however. What began as cold, scientific detachment finally gave way to an excruciating, helter-skelter of memory, loss and longing, an unbearable emotional g-force, which was too powerful and too painful for any living man to bear. And it was this that killed him, not the intrusion of cold steel into his vital organs.

Crawley had no misgivings. He wiped the blood from his knife as he surveyed the corpses with professional detachment. "Round the corner with them, quick," he whispered. "We'll dump the bodies out of sight, next to the water tank."

The two men worked with speed and focus. They dragged the carcasses by the arms to the shed at the back of the bathhouse and forced open the door. Once inside, they stripped the metal armour from the bodies and sluiced it down with water from the huge cistern. Crawley removed the clothes and personal items from the soldiers' corpses while Stogdon returned to the murder scene to reclaim the dropped helmets and swords. Finally, in an attempt to cover their tracks, and with wanton disrespect, they hurled the naked bodies full-length into the prodigious water tank, creating a tidal wave which inundated the floor of the shed.

"Nice one," said Stogdon, as he collected up the dead soldiers' possessions and closed the door behind them. "Time to make ourselves scarce, me thinks." And with that, they were gone, clutching their booty.

The night they disappeared into was a dark one, with no street illumination, no light pollution and no moonlight to reveal their presence. And even if they had been seen, no one was going to look twice at a couple of young Britons making their way home with some bundled goods. That was the reality of third century Britannia. People and life came and went. No one asked questions – it was as simple and as uncomplicated as that.

But for Sands and Ojokwu, who were still enjoying the

luxury of a scalding bath, matters were about to take a more complicated turn than they could have imagined. Still inured to the hideous violence which had just been enacted outside, they continued to soak up the warmth and camaraderie extended to them by the auxiliaries with whom they shared the *caldarium* plunge bath. After a few minutes the two Africans moved over to the nearby apse so that they could revive themselves with fresh water from its large circular fountain.

Sands surveyed Ojokwu closely. "You guys all seem very relaxed with each other. Is your family from Africa, Ojo?"

"Me? No, I'm a Hackney boy, born and bred."

"What about your folks, then?"

"Same thing, except Dad came from Tottenham. He was born in the mid-sixties, moved to Hackney after the Broadwater Farm riot, got married to my mum, had six kids; and that's about as exciting as it got."

"So what school did you go to?"

"The local school."

"What was it called?"

"Comprehensive School."

"Yeah, but what was its name?"

"Local Comprehensive School."

Sands laughed with exasperation. "You're not giving much away, are you? Did you get kicked out or something?"

"No, it was alright," he replied with a straight face.

But there was something about Ojokwu's response, his total lack of artifice that disarmed Sands. He didn't appear to understand the elementary meaning of her question. It was as if basic data had been excised from his memory bank, and he wasn't even aware of it. Sands looked at him in confusion.

"What's up, Kal?" he asked, unsettled by her questioning gaze.

"Nothing, Ojo, sorry, - it's time we got out, I think."

Ojokwu glanced over at one of the Africans standing by the fountain, laughed and pointed at his face. "Hey, mate, you've got a nose-bleed."

The African looked at him in confusion.

"He's got blood all over his face. Tell him, Kal."

"Sanguis," shouted Kal.

The other auxiliary leant forward to wipe his comrade's discoloured face with a cloth.

The bleeding man bent over the fountain with closed eyes before dousing himself with fresh water. When he turned around his whole body glowed in a wash of glistening red liquid. The effect on his comrade was shocking. He shrieked and started to wipe his friend's body with frantic energy.

"The fountain runs with blood. It's an evil omen. Wipe it away, quickly," he yelled.

"I'm cursed," shouted the other auxiliary in panic. "Help me, wash it from me." He was growing hysterical and his actions more frenzied.

The two Britons looked on in stunned amazement, unsure of what to do. "What the hell? It's the water supply – it's been tampered with," shouted Sands. "Oh my God, look at our bath water."

As Sands and Ojokwu struggled to get out of the bath, the water was already starting to discolour visibly, the main tap pumping out a steady flow of coruscating crimson liquid. They were as stunned as the two Romans by this unnerving turn of events. "Oh, Jesus, this is disgusting. It must be blood. What's the hell's going on?"

The yelling brought a large group running to the *caldarium*. On seeing the red liquid emitting from the fountain, the crowd started to keen with dread and set up an unnerving wail that echoed the length of the bathhouse.

"They think it's an omen from the Gods," Sands gasped, the veins in her temple pulsating.

"I'm not bleeding surprised," replied Ojokwu, trying to sponge the gleaming fluid from his skin. "What would you think? What the hell is happening?"

"We've got to leg it, Ojo. Come on, let's drop off the garum and get the hell out of here."

Sands covered herself and pushed her way through the terrified throng, with Ojokwu following in her wake. They felt destabilised by the group hysteria which was engulfing the bathhouse, and had to fight to keep their fears at bay.

By the time they'd made their way to the *apodyterium*, armed guards were circulating inside the building. Overheard snippets of conversation indicated that the entire water system had been affected and was being investigated. The soldiers were sure they could get to the bottom of the cause. There was to be no panic and, in the meantime, to ensure orderly conduct, the bathhouse would be cleared.

It was against this backdrop that Sands and Ojokwu got dressed. She found herself tearful, but recognized that she was less agitated than Ojokwu. He appeared to be in a state of appalling apprehension. They'd already sensed that the unfolding events had been precipitated, somehow or other, by the intervention of their revenge-hungry comrades. Left to their own devices and answerable only to their own consciences, Stogdon and Crawley had decided to take matters into their own hands in the only way they knew how. But what the hell had gone wrong? Whatever it was, it had left an ominous foreboding hanging like a limpet to their presentiments about the future.

As they readied to leave the bathhouse, first reports were arriving of the ritual slaying of the two guards, of a gruesome double-assassination, of bodies found naked, disfigured and drained of blood. It was a terrifying and mystifying discovery, as shocking to Sands and Ojokwu as it was to the local populace. However, to the Romans and Britons it took on a greater significance still: a forewarning, an omen from the Gods, a portent of terrible events to come. And to Sands and Ojokwu, making their way back to camp, and with the screams of anguish from the fort growing in intensity behind them, it represented something else entirely, the dawning realisation that a world of mayhem and catastrophic disorder was all that they had to look forward to.

NINETEEN

On previous evenings, the wood at night time had served as a place of refuge and security. Now it seemed to hold numberless terrors. As Sands and Ojokwu approached through the dark, they did so with a fearful foreboding. The flickering shadows thrown up by the camp fire seemed ominous, threatening almost. The whispered voices they heard through the branches sounded sinister and scheming, no longer welcoming and reassuring, and hinted at an undercurrent of subterfuge and deceit. Soon the Roman soldiers would come, driven by an urge for retribution and the settling of scores. Danger would lurk at every turning for as long they remained alive and within reach of their enemies.

When they entered the clearing by the camp fire, there was no sign of their three comrades, just evidence of a hasty recent evacuation. The fire was lit, uncooked food was lying out in a mess tin and a steaming pot of water lay nearby.

"Where the hell are they?" whispered Sands. Ojokwu signalled her to be silent and motioned her to move back into the shadows. She could feel her heart thumping out of control. The voices that they'd heard seconds earlier were now silent. There was someone out there, none the less.

The sound of a twig snapping underfoot made them both jump. "There," whispered Sands, catching a glimpse of armour through the trees, "soldiers."

"*Salvete!*" screamed a voice behind them. They spun around to see a huge Roman standing in the shadows, his features obscured by the darkness and his massive helmet. The point of his sword caught a flash of light from the flames of the fire as he advanced on them quickly. Suddenly something about the way he moved didn't look right to Sands and Ojokwu as they reversed back into the camp clearing.

"Stogdon, you bastard," yelled Ojokwu.

A roar of laughter erupted behind them as Crawley sprang into view, followed by a sheepish Birch.

"Where the hell did you get that armour?"

Stogdon continued to explode with hilarity. "We rubbed out a couple of Romans who didn't have no use for it no more," he replied as he walked past them and posed by the light of the fire. "Bit small, but beggars can't be choosers. What d'you reckon, Kal? Fancy a man in full body armour?"

"You scared the living shit out of us. We've had one hell of an evening, thanks to you two. What was the purpose of that stupid stunt you pulled earlier on this evening? That wasn't part of the plan that we agreed. You could have screwed everything up. You know that they're going to come gunning for us with everything they've got now."

"To hell with them lot, they're welcome to come and have a go. What have we got to lose anyway?"

"Unbelievable. You're un-sodding-believable, you know that, Stogdon?"

"Okay, you got something to say then say it. What's your problem with us killing a few fucking Romans, eh?"

"You're the bloody problem, Stogdon," she screamed at him. "You put our lives at risk back there. Did you think of that? And you, Mal," she continued, suddenly turning on Crawley, "what the hell were you thinking? I mean the goddamn water tank! Have you got no respect?"

"Turn it up," said Crawley. "You're the one that changed the plan, remember? And besides, we had no option. It was them or us. Or did you not stop to think about that when you two was bunked up together in the bathhouse?"

Sands experienced a sudden flush of guilt and her face reddened. Crawley's words carried just enough truth to drain her anger and eloquence at a stroke. Ojokwu sucked his teeth but said nothing. It was left to Birch to break the silence.

"Come on, now, everyone" he urged, "there's no point in fighting among ourselves. We're all tired and hungry. And in case it's escaped your attention, you're not the only ones to

157

have had a bad day."

All eyes were now turned on Birch for the first time. "Bloody hell, look at the state of you," said Ojokwu in surprise. Birch's face was grazed, bruised and covered in dried blood. His forehead was swathed in a crimson coloured bandage, which had unravelled and dripped blood down his chest. He looked worse than he felt, and he wasn't feeling too bright.

"Are you okay, Birch? You look terrible," offered Sands. "Let me help you get cleaned up. Where are the bandages?"

"Here you go," said Crawley, tossing her the first aid kit that was salvaged from the life raft. "We'll get the food ready. Come on, Stog, make yourself useful. Ojo, you get the shelter set up. Birch, you better get down to the stream and get yourself washed; you want to keep those wounds properly cleaned. Kal, you go with him and make sure he's okay. Then you'll have to get your sewing kit out again," he said, pointing at Birch's brow. "He's going to need a few stitches."

Sands was grateful for Crawley's intervention and clear instructions. She felt exhausted and was in no shape for further conflict. She needed a chance to reflect and wanted to talk to Birch alone, without the others overhearing.

As they left the clearing, Sands could hear the disembodied voice of Stodgon shouting after her. "I'm sorry, Kal, okay? I didn't mean to upset you, right?" Sands shook her head, smiled and swore under her breath, but didn't look back.

The two of them continued to make their way between the trees, Sands guiding Birch as they went. When they'd located the stream, they sat down on a fallen tree trunk and Sands began the careful process of patching up her wounded comrade. Birch was subdued but grateful for the care shown by his first-aider. They sat mutely to begin with, while Sands went about her task with great attentiveness. She was pleased to have an undertaking that she could apply herself to with such concentration; it stopped her thinking of the day's horrors. She was gratified to be given a chance to demonstrate care and consideration towards a fellow human being. Her exaggerated concern for Birch's well-being evoked an intimate bond that both soldiers found touching. Birch, in particular, was thrown by his growing attraction to this young woman. She, on the other hand, felt something more uncomplicated as her fingers came into contact with the wounds on his face and body. Sands yearned for the physical contact; as in the bathhouse earlier, she needed to become reacquainted with something she was in danger of forgetting: her common humanity and decency.

"Can you see in this light?" he asked.

"No, not really, but I'm quite enjoying the peace and quiet." She stroked his cheek gently with the back of her hand. "How are you doing? You had a tough time this evening."

"I'm okay, I guess" he replied, deeply aware of her physical proximity. "Been better, of course. How about you? You were an inspiration in the tavern. I was really worried for you in there." He stroked her hair in reciprocation.

Sands looked down, sensing his growing ardour. She reached up for his hand and grasped it in her lap. "Look," she whispered with difficulty, "we have to talk. We don't have long." She looked around to convey her anxiety.

"What is it?" asked Birch. His thoughts were now focused on the young woman whose warm hands held his own with such conviction.

"I not sure I can trust the others."

"What? Why ever not?" he replied in astonishment. He'd not been expecting the conversation to take this turn.

"I can't exactly put my finger on it. Haven't you felt it too?"

"What do you mean? What are you talking about?"

"I can't make them out. There's something about them that's not quite right. I mean, do you trust them?"

"Look, they mutinied against their commanding officer, didn't they? Do I feel inclined to trust them? No, but, by that token, I wouldn't trust you either, would I? But, in case you're in any doubt, I'd rather throw in my lot with you than them."

Sands grimaced in response. "Look, I'm not surprised you're hacked off with me. I would be too, if I was you. But

I'm not sure they can be trusted to work together with us and stick to an agreed plan. What do we know about any of them? Nothing, beyond a few exterior details. When you scratch the surface there's practically nothing there."

"What do you expect? They're squaddies - I doubt they could scrape together a single GCSE between them."

"I'm talking about something else."

"Like what?"

"Like Ojokwu – he's the most reliable of them but he disturbs me. He's a lovely guy, but there's something missing at the heart of him. He appears sympathetic and intuitive but he's like an automaton – sometimes it's as if he's on auto-pilot. It's like he's being pulled in two directions at once."

"Yeah, but aren't we all? Look at you: one minute you don't trust me, now you don't trust them. The situation is bound to breed paranoia and suspicion. Nobody knows what the hell's going on. Do you? I know I don't."

"But don't you feel that there're forces at play here that are completely out of our control?" She was now beginning to reveal her true anxieties.

"Of course, and you said as much earlier. We're pawns in some big cosmic game. But that doesn't mean we can't still come out ahead if we use our heads and work together. And that's what we've been doing so far, largely thanks to you. So we need you to keep on top of things. They can't do it, and I know now that I can't do it. It's down to you to pull us all together. And like I said, you can count on me."

Sands leant forward and pecked him on the cheek. He looked at her in surprise. "Thanks, Birch, I'm not sure I deserve your loyalty."

"Hello, what's going on here, then?"

The voice came from behind them out of the dark, making them both jump. It was Ojokwu. "Everything okay? Come on, you two, grub's up," he chivvied.

"Okay, Ojo, we're coming," Sands replied.

"And we've got to sort things out tonight," he responded with surprising insistence. "There's a bad atmosphere developing; you're going to have to get on top of it."

Sands gave Birch's hand a squeeze before turning to Ojokwu.

"Okay. Come on then, Ojo, let's eat. Then we can talk. We've all got things to deal with. Whatever the outcome, we're going to face one hell of a day tomorrow."

TWENTY

The following evening, the fort of Aballava began to emit an ominous, fetid atmosphere. To the external observer, used to viewing the Roman fort with a mixture of awe and trepidation, there was a curious change to be detected. A foul miasma now hung over the battlements, like an overpowering gaseous awning. The murderous events of the previous evening had depleted morale within the fort, and the prevailing mood had been worsened by a sickness that had transmitted itself through the barracks overnight. Numerous auxiliaries were now hospitalised.

The sinking of the sun heralded the fifth evening to fall since the disappearance of the helicopter. Exactly one hundred hours had elapsed, during which time a small group of British soldiers had been pushed to the limits of their physical and psychological endurance. The previous evening had been witness to a good deal of argument, accusation and soul-searching; but despite the mistrust and disputes that had surfaced between the various factions, both groups had succeeded in forging their own uneasy alliances and strategies.

Earlier in the day, Sterland Morris had returned to London to undertake urgent research at the British Museum. He and Jamieson had parted company with the gratifying understanding that theirs was a friendship that would stand the test of time. And as if to prove the point, Morris was to return to Carlisle again within forty-eight hours, and, subsequently, on many dozens of occasions over the next fifteen years.

But, in the gathering darkness of this particular evening, the opening act, the first in a sequence of dramatic and choreographed set-pieces, was about to unfold. Through the gloom, two figures, one carrying a heavy sack over his

162

shoulder and the other with a flare pistol tucked into his belt, could be seen approaching the Roman wall. Ojokwu and Birch had chosen this route in order to bypass the village that lay a good half- mile to the east and, in the gloom of a misty evening, with wet and uncertain footing, they had not found it the easiest of journeys. By the time they had made visual contact with the wall and were able to confirm their pre-arranged crossing point, the clouds had closed in and blanketed out the moon. Visibility may have been poor, a fact for which they were grateful, but it was not bad enough to obscure the two torch-lit wall turrets that were positioned 500 meters apart, equidistant from their current position. They watched and waited and then lay face-down as two sentries passed along the wall in desultory fashion. The Roman auxiliaries turned at the mid-point between the two turrets and then retraced their steps to return to the warmth and shelter of the watchtower's hearth and pitched roof.

There would be a five minute hiatus before the next patrol set out from the westerly turret to their left. If Ojokwu and Birch were going to cross the wall then this was the moment to attempt it. But the muffled sound of armoured troops somewhere behind them froze them to the soil upon which they lay. Before they could get to their feet, they were spotted by two Roman soldiers approaching out of the mist. As they got closer, they broke into a steady trot.

"They've spotted us!" said Birch. "They're headed this way."

"You're right," replied Ojokwu, jumping to his feet. "Come on, it's now or never."

The pair started to run towards the wall, pursued by the two heavily armoured soldiers. With every stride the gap between them narrowed, until it disappeared altogether. And now the pursuers became the pursued, racing at full tilt as they were followed by Ojokwu and Birch.

"Come on lads, keep up," urged the leading runner.

"We're right behind you, Stog. I'm ready when you are," replied an exultant Ojokwu. He stopped dead in his tracks ten yards from the wall. "Birch, are you ready?"

"Yeah, go for it," he urged.

At a sign from Ojokwu, Stogdon and Crawley turned to press their outstretched hands against the wall. They leaned their heads forward to present arched backs and then bent their elbows and knees to absorb the shock of what was to follow. They heard the sound of Ojokwu pounding up the slope behind them, followed by a great surging grunt and the impact of his heavy frame as he vaulted over their backs and on to the armoured plates protecting their shoulders, his feet scrabbling to gain ascendancy as their knees held firm beneath his weight. Once mounted on their shoulders, Ojokwu pirouetted and leant the full weight of his back against the wall before stretching his arms out to help lever the leaping Birch up into a precarious frontal embrace. The legs of the two soldiers beneath them began to buckle, whispered curses broke the silence, and Ojokwu and Birch swayed in unison before steadying themselves for the final manoeuvre.

"Ok, on the count of three," said Ojokwu, forming a stirrup with his hands into which Birch placed his right foot.

At the given command, Birch pushed off with his left leg and Ojokwu vaulted him upwards into an undignified and painful clamber, kicking and scrambling, the human pyramid swaying and buckling beneath him, expletives and groans rending the damp air. Somehow the foundations held and Birch managed to lever himself upright on to Ojokwu's shoulders. Then, using his comrade's head as a final footstool, he was able to prise his elbows on to the top of the wall and writhe himself up on to the obstacle itself, a good fifteen feet off the ground.

Stogdon and Crawley collapsed to the ground in exhaustion, while Ojokwu located the sack and hurled it up to Birch who was now kneeling on the wall, scouring the scene from side to side.

"Good luck, Birch, we'll see you later," whispered Ojokwu. "Come on you two, time we weren't here," he said, pulling his stricken comrades to their feet and running off down the slope away from the wall.

Birch was now alone. He opened the sack, pulled out a rope

and looped it around the top of the battlement on the northern face of the wall before abseiling down the side and slipping off into the mist of no man's land.

TWENTY-ONE

Kal Sands stood in front of the east gate to the Roman fort of Aballava. While her colleagues had been risking their lives to get Birch over the great wall, she'd taken on a different mission, one involving subterfuge and betrayal.

She had asked to be granted admittance to the fort. She had urgent information for the commander-in-chief, Julius Rufinus; information that would lead him to the killers of the two Roman auxiliaries the previous evening. She was determined to see that justice was done, but she was equally keen to prevent any further murders.

She feared that her powers of persuasion may have deserted her at this critical moment. The guards were agitated, nervous even, and she recognised in them a body language and mindset that she'd witnessed among members of her own company on recent perilous postings at Kandahar airfield in Afghanistan. Suddenly, and despite her best efforts to remain cool and detached, she felt a wave of empathy for these lowly African recruits. Economic necessity had driven them to a damp, mirthless land two thousand miles from their families and olive groves. Twenty-five years of foreign postings was a heavy price to pay for the prospect of Roman citizenship. Sands sensed that a sense of camaraderie and *esprit-de-corps* was lacking among these troops. Soldiering had always been an alienating, unglamorous activity. Fear and tedium seemed to be the constant stock-in-trade of troops across the millennia, no matter where they found themselves. That, at least, was how she was beginning to see it.

However, her trance didn't last long. She was jolted out of her reverie by the sight of her three colleagues standing to one side of the bathhouse.

They had returned, undetected, earlier than expected, and

had clearly seen her standing by the gate. And, almost simultaneously, she found herself being addressed by the adjutant to Caeluibianus, the company second-in-command, the man who had regarded her with such suspicion two days previously. The adjutant shrugged and ushered her inside. She was then shown into one of the guard rooms in the tower flanking the east gate for further questioning.

Once they'd confirmed that Sands had entered the enemy's camp, the three remaining British soldiers jumped into action. There was no time to lose. Ojokwu pulled the flare pistol out of his waist band and marched over to the bathhouse wall. He was hoisted off the ground by his two companions and immediately discharged the flare into the opening that accommodated the main ventilation shaft. The explosion that occurred surprised them all. They leaped back in amazement. Red flames erupted back out like a bomb blast, sending sparks and neon smoke high into the night sky. Within seconds the flare's discharge was being expelled from every flue in the building, the theatrical effect rising to a crescendo as the sea mist mingled with the illuminated smoke.

Ojokwu reloaded the pistol with the last remaining cartridge and hid it once again inside his waist band. While he did so, the three other soldiers emitted artificial roars of alarm, soon echoed by the guards at the front of the bathhouse. As the chaos spread, half-clad bodies came stumbling in fright out of the main entrance. Other men, attendants and slaves working in the two furnaces, exited to witness the commotion. On viewing the coloured smoke sparking heavenward, they shouted in fear and consternation, rushing to and fro in aimless confusion.

Terror and dread spread like a rampant contagion from man to man. As panic took grip, reason and common sense fled the scene. The presence of the three British soldiers went unremarked, two of them being fully clad in Roman armour. Nobody gave a second glance at their comrade, an African soldier, who appeared to be injured with a gash to the head, and who they were accompanying back to the fort in search of medical treatment.

By the time the three of them came stumbling up to the east gate, the doors had been flung open and sentries had been dispatched to the bathhouse.

On passing through the gate, the three soldiers caught a glimpse to their left of Sands arguing with a young Roman officer. They walked on; rescuing Sands was not on their agenda. As they looked ahead they had an uninterrupted view straight down the *Via Principalis* to the west gate. The camp was well lit and there was plenty of activity taking place for this time of the evening. They kept walking with their heads down and turned right into the *Via Sagularis*, the main perimeter street running along the edge of the fort's rampart.

The interior of the fort was exactly as Sands has described it, and they gained their orientation immediately. To their left ran the east wall of the *Praetorium*, the garrison commander's house, an imposing building reflecting the status of its principal occupant, and to their right ran the fort's eastern rampart. The drama unfolding at the bathhouse ensured that all attention was diverted outside the camp. The sentries on the ramparts were distracted by the external clamour. The three British soldiers made progress through the fort with speed and impunity. As Roman auxiliaries crossed their paths, the existence of the intruders went unnoticed.

On reaching the back of the *Praetorium*, the three soldiers paused before turning into the *Via Quintana*, the other main street running parallel to the *Via Principalis*. Now they could make out their final destination. Half way down the street on the left hand side they could identify the rear elevation of the *Principia*, the headquarters building where Sands had been interrogated by Julius Rufinus several days earlier. Immediately opposite, on their right, ran a long block of stables, behind which lay two barrack blocks. This configuration of buildings was mirrored on the western side of the *Principia*. The men crept along the front of the stables until they reached the *Principia*, which lay in the exact centre of the camp. This was the most important building in Aballava, the administrative headquarters. It contained an assembly hall, behind which sat a row of five rooms, including a strongroom and a small chapel containing the regimental standards and emblems.

"You search for Rattigan north of the *Principia*," Crawley whispered to Ojokwu. "We'll head south to the workshops. Kal said he was being held somewhere down here on the right. Meet back here shortly– hide in the stables if you must."

Stogdon and Crawley turned left and walked along the eastern wall of the *Principia*. They kept their heads down and skipped across the *Via Principalis*, which brought them to two long rows of workshops on either side of the street facing them. Following Sands' instructions, they concentrated on the block to their right, working their way past each workshop, peering into each doorway and window opening as they proceeded. Most of the doors were ajar, the spaces functioning as artisans' workshops, but some were firmly bolted and contained barred windows through which it was possible to examine the interior.

The only clue as to Rattigan's possible presence lay in the first locked workshop they came to. The interior was now empty but it looked as if it may have been used as a temporary jail. It emitted a foul smell and there were chains attached to the rear wall. It was impossible to inspect as it lay opposite the entrance to the *Principia*, outside of which were posted two Roman guards. But if this had been the place where the sergeant was imprisoned, and it fitted with Sands' description as to its likely location, then there was a good chance that he was now dead.

As they worked their way back along the *Via Principalis*, they were startled to see Sands walking towards them. She was accompanied by three Roman soldiers, one of whom was an officer. Sands stared straight ahead as she walked, but at the very last moment she made a discreet gesture with her eyes towards the large headquarters building opposite. Stogdon and Ojokwu kept walking and as they turned left they caught a glimpse of Sands and her guard detail as they stopped in front of the entrance to the *Principia*.

Ojokwu, meanwhile, had been combing the area at the rear of the same building. He'd discounted the possibility of the stables being a makeshift jail and had turned his attention instead to the solid building facing them. In the north east corner of the *Principia* was a barred window that was too high up for him to see into. He grabbed the bars, pulled himself up and peered into the darkened interior. His eyes took a moment to adjust. Slowly in the gloom he began to identify the shape of a filthy and dishevelled human. He wore shackles on his wrists and feet. Ojokwu's heart pounded in excitement. It was a prisoner, but it wasn't the one he was looking for. It wasn't Sergeant Rattigan. But who the hell was it? And where was Rattigan? He pulled himself up again. He scoured the cell, and as he was doing so, he heard a familiar cough, coming from inside.

"Sarge," he whispered. "Are you there? Is that you?"

The shackled prisoner looked up at him in surprise, his white eyes wide-open. As he stared at Ojokwu, he kicked at something on the ground. Ojokwu could now see that there was someone else in the cell too, someone lying on the floor, out of sight.

"Sarge," Ojokwu repeated, "are you in there?"

There was another cough, this one designed to clear a dry throat. Then an unmistakable, shambling figure, initially hidden beneath a sack, started to pull itself up off the floor. "It's me. You gotta get me out of here. Who's there?"

"Shh, keep your voice down, Sarge. It's me, Ojokwu. We're going to get you out."

This was a time for action and bold, heroic gestures, no matter how futile.

Ojokwu pulled out his survival knife. "Here, hide this somewhere," he said, lobbing it on to the sack in front of Rattigan.

The knife hit the ground with a soft thud. Ojokwu watched as Rattigan manoeuvred it across the cell floor with his shackled feet. Slowly he manipulated the knife so that it was hidden out of sight, underneath the sack.

"Don't worry, Sarge," whispered Ojokwu, "I'll be back soon."

"Just get me out of this shit-hole," Rattigan groaned.

Ojokwu released his hold on the bars and sank to the ground. As he did so, Stogdon and Crawley turned the corner. Ojokwu saw them first; they'd stopped to look back at something for a second – Sands entering the *Principia*, as it transpired – and the two of them seemed despondent.

He urged them to hurry over. "I've found him. In the back of this building. He ain't in great shape."

They sprinted forward to confirm the discovery for themselves. "Right, there's only one way in," confirmed Stogdon, "and Sands has already beaten us to it."

"Let's get on with it, then," added Crawley. "Ojo, you follow us in once we've secured the entrance. Here's my knife; you're going to need it."

Ojokwu shadowed Stogdon and Crawley as they returned to the spot from which they'd last seen Sands standing outside the *Principia*. As they'd anticipated, there was no sign of her now, just the same pair of Roman sentries guarding the entrance.

Stogdon and Crawley glanced up and down the street, weighing up their chances of success; the two guards were veterans, not callow recruits, and were armed with spears and shields. They knew that they'd have the benefit of surprise along with a convincing disguise, but they were also aware that their next move would be rife with danger and unknown hazards. Luck would be a major factor in the success of their mission. Ojokwu, for his part, was committed to following his two comrades step for step, no matter how bloody the outcome might be. And he was expecting it to get very bloody indeed.

Now that their sergeant was confirmed alive, any doubts that they had previously harboured were swept away. All they had to do was think clearly, act decisively and stick together; it all seemed remarkably uncomplicated.

"Ok, let's go," said Crawley.

Stogdon followed him out into the *Via Principalis*. Ojokwu held his breath and watched them go. They pushed their way past a cohort of auxiliaries who were marching down towards the east gate and the bathhouse beyond it. Crawley and Stogdon were both big men by twenty-first century standards, and, despite the fact that they were bareheaded and the auxiliaries helmeted, they towered over the soldiers they passed.

Ojokwu never ceased to be amazed at the speed with which his two comrades could make things happen. The pair of guards at the entrance to the *Principia* were taken by surprise. Denied a chance to react and raise the alarm, they found themselves being bundled through the doorway, overwhelmed by the strength and determination of their assailants. Once out of view of the street, Crawley and Stogdon assassinated the two Romans with brutal efficiency. The bodies were dragged under the roofed walkway and then stuffed behind the columns of the portico that ran around the perimeter of the inner courtyard.

Ojokwu slipped into the *Principia* seconds later, just as Stogdon and Crawley were closing and securing the main door from the inside.

"We'll hold the entrance. You see what Sands is up to," whispered Crawley, indicating with a series of urgent hand gestures which route he should take.

Ojokwu dodged past one of the slumped bodies, stepping in a pool of blood on his way. He moved around the walkway with care. A series of scarlet footprints recorded in cartographic detail his precise route as he dodged from column to column around the courtyard.

When he arrived at the far end of the covered walkway Ojokwu encountered a problem he hadn't anticipated. The only way to access the rear of the building, and the rooms where Rattigan and Sands were located, was through a single arched doorway in the centre of the courtyard's north wall. He paused for a moment and leaned out to catch a glimpse of Stogdon, who was urging him to move faster. He appeared to be indicating that the coast was clear. With his back pressed firmly to the wall, Ojokwu started a nervous final approach to the doorway. He could see a warm light and hear the sound of voices. On reaching the edge of the door he could hear three people in discussion, one of whom was Sands. He looked across the courtyard and gave a thumbs-up to Stogdon who was hiding behind a column no more than thirty metres away.

Ojokwu took a deep breath and started to inch his way to the edge of the doorframe. He stole a brief glance around the door. There were five people standing in a large beamed hall, two of whom were facing his way. Sands was the middle figure of the trio who had their backs to him. She was being interrogated. The two soldiers flanking her were the same guards who should be standing where he was now.

Ojokwu could overhear what was being said but was unable to follow even the most basic of exchanges. There was some sort of dispute, though - that much was clear. Sands seemed to be doing a lot of pleading. The two Roman officers were raising their voices in response. If Ojokwu had been able to understand Latin, he'd have been unpleasantly surprised by what he'd have overheard.

"Trust me, I know who murdered the Roman auxiliaries yesterday evening," Sands was insisting.

"How do you know? Why should we trust you, even as our troops are under threat once again?"

"Look, there are going to be more deaths if the perpetrators aren't caught," she was saying. "What the outlaws want is to free the prisoner who's currently being held, and they won't stop killing until their man is free."

"Who is this prisoner?"

"His name is Rattigan. He's the leader of a band of insurgents planning the overthrow of Roman rule in Britain."

"He won't talk. By the Gods, why should we believe you?"

"Look, I implore you in the name of Jupiter. If you, Julius Rufinus, and you, Caeluibianus, are prepared to trust me, then I promise I can deliver your enemies into your hands."

While Sands spoke the two Roman commanders rained

scorn and insults down on her. They contradicted and interrupted her constantly, and refused to let her continue at various points. But her determination to be heard was so indomitable, her courage so patent, that her pleading started to find a more sympathetic ear. Once again, it was Julius Rufinus whose will started to weaken in the face of her verbal onslaught.

"What is it you want then?" asked the commander.

"The way to get to them is through the prisoner. He's the answer to this riddle."

"We'll get nothing out of him. By the Gods, we've tried."

"And he said nothing?"

"Less than nothing."

"That's because you don't speak his language."

"And you do?"

"Yes I do, fluently. It's a tongue native to these islands, but only known to a small number. Its name is English."

"So you and only a small number of other people speak this tongue. What's the point of speaking a dead language? You speak Latin so there may be some hope for you, at least."

"But can't you see? You need me and my dead language to get to him. Dead languages have their use. Maybe people will say the same thing about Latin one day?"

"Enough nonsense. If you think you can get anything out of him, you're welcome to try."

Julius Rufinus addressed the two guards standing on either side of Sands. "I want her properly searched before she goes anywhere near the prisoner." He then turned to his second in command. "You accompany her, Caeluibianus, and keep a close eye on things. Make sure the prisoner is properly shackled before you enter and keep the jailer with you at all times. And post a guard outside. She may only be a woman but we won't take any chances. If she gives you any problems, you have my instructions to kill her on the spot. Is that clear?"

Julius Rufinus addressed the last remark while looking straight at Sands, aware that she was in earshot. She nodded her head in dumb agreement. She hadn't prepared herself for the fact that Caeluibianus would hold her fate in his hands. She'd come across his kind before. He possessed an ambitious zeal, masking a ruthless streak, that spelt bad news, measured in incremental steps from misfortune to disaster, for anyone unlucky enough to fall under his control.

The Praepositus gave Sands a cold stare. "I understand your orders perfectly, Julius Rufinus. I can assure you that it will give me the greatest pleasure to carry them out to the letter."

While the jailer was called for, Julius Rufinus had another, more discreet word with his second-in-command. "I don't trust this girl. Keep a very close eye on her. If she doesn't come up with anything in the next few minutes, then dispose of her. But do try and keep the noise down. The men are jumpy enough as it is. What the hell is going on out there?"

Sands was bundled out of the hall. On reaching the cell, she was subjected to a humiliating body search, undertaken, with lip-smacking relish, by the guard. He had correctly interpreted the degree of license that would be extended to him by Caeluibianus.

She bore these physical indignities with a look of open defiance, but acceded without complaint. She'd determined on a course of action. She'd pursue it to its conclusion, no matter what cost to herself.

Once the guard had checked that Sands was unarmed, Caeluibianus called for the jailer to unlock the cell door. Sands had been surprised to discover that Rattigan was now being held at the rear of the *Principia*; it was clear to her that he must have been moved since the last time she was in the fort.

The guard was told to remain outside and was issued with strict instructions to lock the door and to only open it when authorised by Caeluibianus. The jailer handed the door keys to the guard, picked up an oil lamp and accompanied Sands and Caeluibianus into the small room.

Once the door was locked from the outside the lamp provided the only source of light in the cell. The flickering illumination lit up a brick-lined room of about four metres square with a single, barred window and one means of exit, the door through which they'd entered.

A pair of piteous, dishevelled figures stirred in the gloom; it was not apparent to Sands which one was Sergeant Rattigan. She possessed only the vaguest memory of his appearance. The desperate physical condition of the two men made her shudder with apprehension. Both of them were covered in filth, dried blood and the evidence of physical maltreatment. Neither of the captives acknowledged Sands, nor the two Romans with her. They stood bowed and intimidated, averting their gazes from the visitors.

The jailer was the first to break the silence. He viciously kicked one of the prisoners. "Stand up straight, you son of a whore. You've got a visitor, so pay her some respect."

The victim of this casual brutality was Sergeant Rattigan. The resigned manner in which he bore the assault suggested that it was not an uncommon punishment.

Sands could see that the jailer was setting down a marker when it came to interrogating prisoners. She would have to surpass his brutality in order to maintain credibility with Caeluibianus.

Sands walked up to Rattigan and looked him straight in the eyes. "You were told to stand up straight, you miserable excuse for a soldier. Now stand up straight," she shouted in English, delivering him a spectacular open-handed slap across the side of his face. He jolted bolt-upright and looked at her in astonishment, his shocked expression a mixture of perplexity and alarm.

The jailer and Caeluibianus exchanged an amused glance. They were intrigued by the sound of this unfamiliar language, especially when it was being employed in the service of prisoner interrogation, and particularly when it came from the mouth of a woman. This encounter had the potential to be more entertaining than they had anticipated.

"Now, you and I are going to have a little chat, Rattigan, and you are going to listen very carefully. Do you understand?" She stood right in front of his face, bristling with aggression.

Caeluibianus decided to intervene. "Stand back, girl. Don't

get so close to him."

"What's your game, Lieutenant?" Rattigan replied. His features were contorted with a mixture of mistrust and fear. "What's happened to the others?"

"The others? You've got a fucking nerve asking about that rabble. They've got it in their heads to try and save you, but I'm not about to let them. And neither are you."

"The hell are you talking about?" roared Rattigan.

"You help us and we'll help you. It's very simple, Rattigan. Your men have murdered Roman soldiers in cold blood and these guys want justice." She motioned towards the two men standing behind her. "There's no future for Stogdon, Crawley and Ojokwu now. Help us reel them in and you'll have a chance of survival."

Rattigan looked at Sands in disbelief. She could feel the whiteness of his eyes pinning her to the spot. "You filthy little traitor," he roared. He followed his expletives with an explosion of spittle which caught her full in the face. Despair and fear had given way to outrage and anger.

Sands was shocked. She grabbed him by the shoulders and shook him "Get real, Rattigan. You can't fight these people. Give up, and help yourself while you've still got a chance."

Both Caeluibianus and the jailer were unprepared for this sudden turn of events. After a fleeting hesitation, they pushed in to separate the pair. The jailer kicked Rattigan hard behind his leg, sending him to his knees in pain. As he fell he displaced the sack on the floor in front of him. Sands caught the look on Rattigan's face as he glimpsed the hidden knife, which lay partially revealed in the lamp light. Luck was now on her side. She fell to her knees, gasping and in apparent distress.

"That's it," said Caeluibianus. "I've had had enough of this farce." He grabbed Sands by the hair and pulled her to her feet. She'd tried his patience to its limit. Now he was going to take pleasure in meting out some vengeance of his own. As she rose, her right hand gripped the handle of a British Army survival knife. She swore loudly and cursed at Caeluibianus in

Latin. He laughed and pulled her hair harder, forcing her on to her tiptoes and tilting her head back at an unbearable angle.

"Do you have one last thought before I kill you?" he asked, his right hand already starting to tighten around her neck.

"Yes," she gasped, scarcely able to breath.

"Oh, good – you're determined to fight till your last breath. What's on your mind, then?" He applied greater pressure to her throat. "Speak up, girl, I can't hear you"

"Just this," she wheezed, her voice scarcely audible.

He tilted his head forward as if readying himself to administer the last rites.

"Speak up. Let me hear your dying words."

With her last vestige of strength she pushed the knife hard up underneath the Roman's jaw, forcing his head back and knocking him off-balance.

Sands gasped for breath, desperate to exploit her chance. She clung like a limpet to the astonished Caeluibianus. He stumbled back across the cell, her knife point affixed to his bleeding throat, his grip loosening on her neck.

"Let go of my hair," she panted. He relented, releasing her from his clutches as if to confirm that she was now safe in his hands. The jailer hovered, his sword drawn, but lacking the will to act.

"Free the prisoner or I'll kill him!" she barked at the jailer.

"Don't listen to her," countermanded Caeluibianus. "Come on, man, dispatch the bitch. That's an order."

The jailer cut a pathetic figure. Terrified by the options facing him, he was unable to act. His sweating face, contorted by fear and indecision, betrayed the spiritual corruption common to all men who torture for a living. "Sir, I dare not" he whimpered in supplication. "Please, sir, she'll kill you."

Outside the cell, the guard, alarmed by the sounds within, was banging on the door. "Tell him to stay where he is," Sands ordered Caeluibianus.

The Roman commander realised the odds were turning in his favour and he seized his opportunity.

"Come in now, soldier. Help me!" he shouted, a note of

triumph in his voice. He then looked down at his adversary. "Make the most of your last few seconds on earth," he whispered to Sands, as the lock started to turn.

All eyes turned to the door, which was pushed open to reveal the Roman soldier, spear in hand. His face wore a look of wild disorientation.

"Quick, man, call for help," called Caeluibianus.

But the guard did not appear to share his commander's sense of urgency; quite the opposite, in fact. He seemed to be permeated with an overwhelming lassitude, an inertia so profound that he could scarcely support his own body weight. He opened his mouth, but no words were forthcoming, only the sound of blood bubbling in his larynx. His body reverberated like a crustacean suspended in boiling water, the monstrous pressure causing its carapace to whistle and rattle. His mouth gaped and he lurched forward on to his face. He was dead.

"Ojo," exclaimed Sands, "thank God."

Ojokwu now stood in the same spot that his victim had occupied moments earlier. He held a knife in his right hand and his tunic was soaked with blood. His face wore a desperate, bewildered look that Sands did not recognise.

The jailer, assuming that he was going to receive the same treatment as the guard, threw down his weapon and held his hands up in cringing submission. He implored Ojokwu to show him mercy.

Sands felt Caeluibianus' body stiffen with fear. The Roman wouldn't flinch at dying on a battlefield, but it was unlikely that he'd relish the prospect of being skewered to death in a dark and squalid prison cell. This was not the noble end that Caeluibianus had envisaged for himself.

The next few seconds seemed to pass in a choreographed blur of whirling limbs and angry shouts. It culminated in the cold-blooded murder of the jailer, speared through the heart by Rattigan and his fellow prisoner. The two accomplices had exacted their revenge as soon as they were freed from their shackles by Ojokwu. Sands was appalled by the retribution meted out, especially at the hands of the other, unnamed prisoner. Her appeals for self-control went unheeded. Ojokwu made no effort to intervene, even when it was clear that the victim was long-since dead and the attack was reaching its frenzied peak.

Caeluibianus seemed even more shocked than Sands by the ferocious violence. The two prisoners would surely turn their lust for vengeance on to him next. But Rattigan and his accomplice were exhausted. They slumped to the floor, gasping for breath, strangely sated by the orgy of revenge they'd perpetrated. A stunned calm reigned for a fleeting moment, only to be interrupted by the sound of a loud bell tolling close by.

Even in her agitated state, Sands jumped at the unexpectedness of it. "Jesus, what's that?"

Ojokwu wiped the blood from his hands. He'd had enough. "Come on," he said, grabbing Caeluibianus, "it's high time we wasn't here."

TWENTY-TWO

The sound that had made Kalahari Sands jump was coming from a large bell situated in the courtyard outside. It was being rung by the second guard in order to to alert the camp to an emergency in the *Principia*.

Several minutes earlier, after being sent back to his post at the entrance to the main hall, the guard had observed that the main door to the *Principia* had been closed. He took this to be a purely precautionary measure in response to some incident outside the walls of the fort. He'd been reassured by the sight of the two sentries standing guard inside the locked gate. But, still, he was anxious.

He could hear some sounds coming from inside the hall and detected that the other sentry was no longer standing guard outside the cell door. As he went to check on his comrade, something caught his eye on the floor of the walkway to his left - footprints, perhaps? His eyesight was weak so he had to squint. He shouted over to the two guards at the main gate but they didn't respond. He left his post to inspect the evidence more closely and, as he did so, he saw Stogdon and Crawley advancing on him quickly with swords drawn.

"Assassins!" he shouted, aware of the mortal danger facing his Commander-in-Chief.

"Kill him," yelled Crawley, "before he alerts the camp."

But it was too late to stop him. He may have been short-sighted, but the Roman guard had twenty years experience of fighting at close quarters with a sword and spear. His *speculum* could be used for thrusting or hurling with a force that could penetrate any shield. Stogdon and Crawley started to receive a first-hand lesson in what made the average Roman soldier such a formidable fighting force.

"Get that bloody spear off him," demanded Crawley as he dodged his opponent's thrusts with growing desperation.

"You get the bloody spear off him," yelled Stogdon. He'd been lightly wounded and was beating an undignified retreat behind the columns supporting the portico.

When he'd manoeuvred his attackers out of the way, the Roman made a sudden dash across the courtyard to the bell, and, before he could be stopped, a loud tolling could be heard across the camp.

"Let's just get the others!" shouted Crawley. "The hell with him, our cover's completely blown."

In desperation, the two men scampered through the doorway into the big hall at the back of the *Principia*, which was now deserted. Their chances of escape were minimal. As they turned right towards the end room where Rattigan was imprisoned, they saw the door open and the figure of a Roman soldier appear. They froze for an instant before seeing a familiar face looming behind him. Ojokwu was holding a knife to the Roman's throat. He'd taken him hostage.

"Ojo, quick, the alarm's been raised!" urged Crawley.

"We're coming out, Corp. Give Rattigan a hand," he gestured, as the rest of the crew stumbled out of the cell. "There's another prisoner, too. I think he's coming with us."

Stogdon and Crawley embraced their sergeant and acknowledged the other prisoner when Rattigan pointed to him. "His name's Talorc. Whatever happens, he's coming with us. He's one of us now, you got that?"

"Come on, guys, there's time for all this later," said Sands, "assuming we ever get out of here." She pushed Caeluibianus forward. "Hold on to him, Ojo. He's all we've got."

"You're all as good as dead," shouted the Roman. He was dragging his feet as they made their way towards the door of the hall.

"Save your breath," replied Sands. "None of them can understand a word you're saying. Now keep moving."

"Wait a minute," shouted Rattigan. He was pointing to the skins displayed behind the main dais at the back of the hall.

"What the hell?" he exclaimed, his eyes and mouth agape. He'd experienced some of the very worst in human cruelty over the previous five days, but nothing could compete with this, the sight of his comrades' flayed skins being stretched out between custom-made wooden frames.

Crawley put a restraining arm around him and tried to move him towards the door. "Come on, Sarge, there's nothing we can do for them."

"Yes, there bloody well is. They're coming with us. No way am I leaving those soldiers behind." He passed the spear he was carrying to Crawley. "Here, Mal, give us your knife. I'm cutting them down."

Sands looked around her in quiet despair. Their position appeared hopeless. She breathed a huge sigh. "The hell with it, Sergeant, you're right. I'll give you a hand."

The small group moved to the back of the hall and the sombre ritual began. No one performed the task with undue haste; what occurred was a display of commitment and solidarity. Roman auxiliaries were already pouring into the main courtyard and approaching the doorway to the hall. The British soldiers took it in turn to cut the skins from their frames, passing the knife from one to another. When they were finished the skins were rolled up and handed to Rattigan.

By now, a sizeable body of Roman soldiers had arrived and fanned out to either side of the space. A semi-circle of spear-wielding auxiliaries now trapped Sands and her platoon against the back wall of the cross-hall. In front of them lay the only exit, now completely cut off. Behind them was the locked door to the *sacellum*, holding a sunken strong room and the garrison's standards and altars.

"Put down your weapons, Galla Placidia, and give yourselves up!" cried a familiar voice. Julius Rufinus pushed his way through the phalanx of auxiliaries and now stood facing the insurgents. He surveyed the situation with a calculating eye.

All attention focused on Sands. She was weighing up the odds. The only thing saving them now was the status of the hostage they were holding. But Julius Rufinus's commitment to saving the life of his second-in-command was questionable. The hostage might only buy them a few minutes at best.

"Tell your men to let us go, or we'll kill Caeluibianus."

"We're not going to let you escape, you know that."

Julius Rufinus' demeanour indicated that he meant business. "Release the Tribune and we two can talk; you may well prove to be of some use to us. Your friends, on the other hand, will die. Accept the things to which fate binds you. Nobody challenges the authority of Rome with impunity."

"What choice do I have, then?"

"You have two options: surrender or die."

"And what about the third option?"

"What third option? There is no third option. Surrender or you all die."

"It's simple, there's always a third option," she countered.

"What is your meaning, girl? Stop playing games with me."

"Even a game of chance can call for a mixed strategy," she said in English, glancing around and addressing the remark to her comrades. They returned her look with bewilderment.

She then addressed Julius Rufinus with a new-found resolve. "Your two options are too obvious."

"Explain yourself. You try my patience to exhaustion."

"Like with Rock, Paper, Scissors, there's always a third option."

The Roman commander wore a look of bemusement.

"Watch, Julius Rufinus, watch closely. Rock, Paper, Scissors," she repeated, miming the hand gestures as she did so.

"Rock, we surrender," and she formed her left hand in a fist.

"Paper, we die," she continued, unclenching her hand and laying her palm out flat.

"And Scissors, scissors is the third option." She formed her index and middle fingers into an unmistakably abusive hand gesture and displayed it to the Roman commander with a defiant flourish.

"I choose Scissors!" she shouted.

And as she yelled, she raised up her right arm to reveal the flare pistol she was holding. Rather than discharging it at the enemy, she rotated through ninety degrees and fired through the open metal grille that formed the upper part of the locked door to the *sacellum*.

The impact on the foe was astounding. The flare exploded in an intense shower of smoke, sparks and flames, filling the hall with a pungent aroma, and combusting the regimental insignia and decorations. The Romans were immobilised with horror at the violence unleashed on their Holy of Holies. This was the spiritual centre of their garrison. It safeguarded their shrines, their objects of worship, their imperial images, altars, standards and emblems. And underneath this smoking inferno, secured inside a locked strongbox, lay the regimental pay chest and the savings of over five hundred Roman auxiliaries and their officers.

But above and beyond the conflagration itself, there was one other impression that became seared into the consciousness of these troops. It was an image that would not be forgotten by those who witnessed it. It was the vision of a dauntless female foe, an implacable warrior queen who could harness the forces of nature and shoot blood-red thunderbolts from her fingertips.

The enemy was reduced to an awe-struck stasis, immobile, frozen and suspended in disbelief. Sands seized the initiative. She turned her flare pistol on to the person of Julius Rufinus. He looked at her in fearful apprehension, raising his hands above his head. As she advanced on him, the troops surrounding him shrank back, terrified lest they be engulfed by another firestorm. She pointed the pistol at his head, spun him around and led him towards the exit. "Right, everyone," she shouted, "stick close to me. We're getting out of here."

"Tell everyone to stand back and let us through," she ordered her hostage. Julius Rufinus complied, too shocked by what he'd witnessed to resist. As the troops in the immediate vicinity obeyed his orders, others started to pour into the courtyard to be met by the sight of their commander and tribune being frog-marched through the building.

In the rear of the *Principia*, some of the braver soldiers were attempting to pull burning objects out of the smoke-filled *sacellum*. Other, more superstitious individuals had succumbed to invoking the gods to protect them.

By the time the hostage party had made its way into the *Via Principalis*, the alarm had been raised across the whole fort and soldiers were pouring through the streets. The Roman troops stood densely packed, three or four deep, creating a human tunnel on the main street leading towards the north gate, watching in deep alarm, as their two senior commanders were marched out under armed escort. The speed with which events unfolded made coherent resistance impossible. Lacking an identifiable authority figure around whom they could rally, the troops resorted to hurling abuse and insults. No one was prepared to precipitate action that might threaten the life of Julius Rufinus and Caeluibianus. The orange smoke rose like an evil omen above the *Principia* and added to the pervading alarm and trepidation among the auxiliaries. It appeared as if a curse had descended upon Aballava.

As fear spread like a virus through the immobilised troops, the hostage party continued to move in a tightly-knit phalanx towards the north gate. Crawley and Stogdon led the way with Rattigan and Talorc at the rear. Squashed in between them, and closely protected, were their two comrades with their captives. A section of heavily armed auxiliaries was all that now stood between them and their means of escape.

"Open up, in the name of Julius Rufinus," yelled Sands, "or I'll call down the fires of hell upon his head." Her threat worked. The Roman commander was too traumatised to resist. He waved to the sentries to open one of the massive double gates.

The first sign of resistance started to emerge. Two of the sentries declined to put up their spears or let the hostage party through. They implored the other troops to arrest the enemy and not to allow shame to descend on the camp. This evoked support among sections of troops but their ill-discipline was stayed by a senior centurion who pushed his way to the front and intervened to prevent any unilateral action.

"Any man who is responsible for putting the commanders' lives at risk will be instantly executed," he shouted. "Wait for orders from a superior officer before taking any action."

He then turned to a fellow centurion and whispered an instruction. "I want a cavalry section readied now. Wherever they try to run, they won't be able to escape us."

TWENTY-THREE

The main door of the north gatehouse swung open to reveal a track across the fort's defensive ditch. In the distance lay a dark wilderness, the only view afforded in the pervading mist, and beyond that, presumably, sat the seashore. The small party of hostage-takers plunged into the night, their ears assaulted by the curses, threats and cries of despair issuing from the battlements

Behind them lay a Roman fort bereft of leadership, overwhelmed by a mystery illness and afflicted by a crisis in morale. Word had already spread of the humiliation and sacrilege inflicted on the *sacellum* and the desecration of their unit standards and emblems. But whatever calamity the Roman army faced, it was used to overcoming insuperable odds when confronting its foes. It was able to call on a noble tradition, which extended over three centuries, of defeating its enemies in the open field. The cavalry officer started to appeal to this ingrained self-belief as their men were saddling up.

Sands and her comrades knew that they would have to ford the Solway if they were to escape. Their attack on the fort had been timed to coincide with low-tide. They were now involved in a race against the incoming waves as well as their Roman pursuers. This was a task made more treacherous in the dark and on unfamiliar terrain, but rendered seemingly impossible when compounded by the threat of unseen river channels and pools of hidden quicksand.

Birch was waiting for them on the northern side of the wall. As soon as they appeared through the gate, he sprang into view, carrying his sack of supplies and provisions. "The ford is this way – straight ahead." he yelled, pointing into the murk;

too vaguely for the liking of most in the group.

As they stumbled towards him, the noise of hoofs could be heard from the gatehouse, a hundred metres behind them. Looking back, Sands could see a large group of soldiers preparing to leave the fort. She yelled a warning to her comrades. They turned in time to witness an intensely orange projectile pass within yards of their heads and collide, at incredible speed, with the leading horse and rider. The horse reared, stunned by the power and velocity of the impact, and fell over backwards in a shower of sparks and burning chemicals, unseating his rider and crushing him as he hit the ground. The other horses reacted with immediate panic and a number succeeded in throwing their riders before disappearing off into the dark. A second flare, following closely on the heels of the first, added to the mayhem and succeeded in routing the remaining cavalry. Those riders who'd somehow remained mounted, managed to steer their horses back into the sanctuary of the fort, where the gate was temporarily closed and secured against further assault.

"It's young McKay!" yelled Rattigan. "He's alive. I knew it," he screamed with delight, waving towards the dark shape running towards them. It was clear that he was already loading another flare into his pistol as he approached.

"Georgie boy!" shouted Stogdon and Crawley. Their youngest platoon member had somehow survived by himself, long after they'd assumed he was dead.

"Aye, I knew it was you," McKay yelled as they came together. "I saw your flare earlier and knew you was up to no good." He looked bedraggled and scrawny, but his cheery optimism had a galvanizing effect on everyone.

"Where are the others?" he shouted, as he scanned the faces of those surrounding him.

"They didn't make it, George," replied Crawley. "The Romans got them."

Sands stepped in. "Quick, McKay," she said, "we've got to get down to the ford." The group was already moving away from the fort at speed, dragging their hostages with them.

"Do you know the way?"

"I tell you what - don't even think about it," he replied. "It's totally crawling wi' Romans down there. They got the whole shoreline staked out wi' torches. We won't stand a chance, I'm telling youse."

Talorc interrupted. He spoke a form of rudimentary Latin that Sands was able to translate with difficulty.

"He says we should follow him. He knows a better way across the sea. What d'you think, shall we do it?"

"If he knows the way, then he's the only one who does," replied Ojokwu.

Without pausing, Talorc ushered them to follow him to the left. As they pushed on through the dark he whispered instructions to Sands that she translated.

"He says there's a ford that the Romans are afraid to use because it's too dangerous. It starts near a fort called Concavata. Don't ask me where the hell it is, but he says it's close by. The crossing is wide and we have to ford two separate channels. We'll probably drown, but, if the Gods are on our side, we may survive."

"Shit," muttered Ojokwu, "I can't swim."

"Start praying. It's too late to learn now."

The group stumbled on for two miles before hitting the shoreline. Everyone was fixated on the same thought: what were they going to do with their two hostages? Crossing the ford was going to be hazardous enough without being slowed down by a couple of prisoners. And, anyway, they'd served their purpose.

Caeluibianus and Julius Rufinus sensed their impending fate. They could tell from the dark looks of their captors what sorts of thoughts were crossing their minds. They implored Sands to show mercy and to not upset the gods further. Sands threatened to sacrifice the two of them in order to assuage their anger.

"Let's kill 'em, now," said Rattigan. "They got it coming."

"I agree with you," replied Sands, "but what's the advantage to us in killing them?"

"Dead men tell no tales. Can't argue with that," said Rattigan.

"Yes, but live men don't become martyrs and a justification for revenge, not like dead men do," answered Birch.

"These guys won't need any excuse to exact revenge, believe me," responded Rattigan. "Look what they did to me. And him," he argued, pointing at Talorc.

"Look, if we can get across the Solway then we're safe," said Ojokwu. "And if we don't kill their commanders then they've no reason to pursue us."

"They'll hunt us down to get these two back," interrupted Stogdon. "I agree with the Sarge, let's kill 'em now and go for broke. This ain't no time for half-measures. It's kill or be killed, you all know that."

Ojokwu stepped in once again. "Just stop and think what you're saying for a second, Stog. Killing hostages ain't what the British Army does."

"To hell with the British Army. Where's the British Army now? I don't see no court martials or rule of law. This is the Wild West, man. There ain't no law out here."

"There's a law of right and wrong. Or does that just go out the window too, along with your conscience and self-respect?"

"If that's what it takes to survive, then, fuck, yeah!"

Crawley spoke up for the first time. "Stog's right. If this is about survival then we go back to first principles. All them other things – rules, laws, procedures and morals – them's the icing on the cake, the luxury add-ons. We can't afford them things right now. Let's do what we got to do and get the fuck out of here."

"Look, it's simple," implored Sands, "we tie them up, gag and blindfold them, and leave them here by the shore. We'll be long-gone by the time they're rescued."

"You don't know that. Why take the risk?" replied Rattigan.

There was sudden silence. Sands had no response to that question. It was the only one which cut right to the point of the argument.

Rattigan noted the lack of response with satisfaction.

"Right," he said, "I'll happily do it meself. There'll be no bloodstains on anyone else's hands."

"Wait! For God's sake, Sergeant, at least let's vote on this. You don't have the authority to take unilateral action."

"Ok, let's see all those in favour of leaving them alive," retorted Rattigan. "Come on, let's get a move on. Put your hands up."

Sands looked around her colleagues. Only Ojokwu and Birch supported her. "Three votes, that's all," confirmed Stogdon.

"Hang on, what about him," asked Birch, pointing at Talorc. He'd been left out of the debate so far.

"He don't get no vote," retorted Rattigan. "This is between us lot. It don't involve Talorc."

"Why doesn't he get a vote?" asked Sands. "He's involved in this too."

"Because he don't understand what's at stake."

"He's not stupid. I can try and explain it to him. At least give me a chance."

"No way, we don't know what the hell you're saying to him," replied Rattigan. "Anyway, democracy's alien to him. Come on, let's stop fannying about. All those in favour of silencing the prisoners permanently, stick your hands up."

Rattigan, Crawley and Stogdon all raised their hands. Three-all, but what about McKay? He hadn't cast a vote. "Come on now, Georgie, it's all down to you, son; support your mates," urged Rattigan.

The young soldier looked at his sergeant but failed to recognise him for the first time. Under normal circumstances he'd have followed his guidance unquestioningly. But things were different now. He looked from face to expectant face. All eyes were turned on him.

"I dinnae ken what tae do. I can see both sides, but it dinnae seem right to kill them in cold blood. I agree wi' the Lieutenant. Let's tie 'em up and leave 'em."

Surprise greeted his decision.

"Well done, Private, that was a brave choice to make, and a correct one. We'll all owe you a debt of gratitude in future," said Sands as she put her arm around his slumped shoulders.

"Fuck that. Okay, four-three it is. No hard feelings, son," replied Rattigan, shaking McKay's hand. "Let's hope the Lieutenant's right, or we're all screwed."

"Come on, Stog, let's get these two properly bound and gagged," said Crawley.

The Romans were trussed up with the same lack of respect accorded fictional characters whose sole purpose is to service the needs of the plot when it suits the author, and who're then casually written out when deemed surplus to requirements.

Talorc, meanwhile, was getting anxious to make a start. He could see that the tide was on the turn, and he yelled at Sands to make haste. Once the two hostages were immobilised, the group ran down through the dunes and began the perilous passage across the Firth.

"If we have to swim for it, then you're going to have to lose the armour, guys," warned Sands. "And you'll have to dump the supplies, Birch. Ojo can't swim. We'll create an air-filled buoy out of the blanket so that that he's got something to keep him afloat."

As they proceeded further out into the Solway mudflats, the sea mist began to thicken and all sight of the shoreline was lost. Talorc's anxiety transmitted itself to every member of the party. He led them at a tortuous pace through an intertidal region of sand-ripples, gullies and weirdly moulded patterns sculpted by the action of sea and wind. Whenever he paused to take a bearing, the disconcerting phenomenon of sand mutating from firm to soft to sloppy could be felt underfoot. All members of the party were trapped ankle-deep on occasion, and were unable to free themselves without urgent intervention. The further they progressed into the heart of the Solway flats, the more terrifying it became. And if Sands had known that the passage through the tides would continue for over three miles, she'd
have willingly tried her luck over the shorter distance to the east and braved the Roman sentries guarding the other ford.

The further they progressed through the mud the more they

became preoccupied with a single thought. With every footstep they fancied that the water lapping around their feet was growing ever deeper - deeper and colder. And they weren't wrong. The first river channel that they crossed, the one that fed from the mouth of the River Eden five miles to the east, was relatively easy going and didn't prove too difficult to ford. However, by the time they'd covered another mile and a half, and reached the second channel, fatigue was beginning to take its toll and conditions were reaching their most dangerous and treacherous. The freezing water now reached above their calves and the sea mist had turned into an impenetrable fog. Memories of their horrifying crash into the waters of the Solway returned to haunt the soldiers, adding a powerful stimulus to the growing sense of panic that afflicted the group. Given the option, each individual would gladly have retraced their steps through the mud and died on the point of a Roman sword. But it was too late now for second chances. They had no choice but to keep going in the dark, and risk being sucked to their doom by a deadly combination of swirling tides and man-engulfing mud.

Talorc continued to lead the way doggedly, followed by a single file of soldiers each holding fast to the clothing of the individual in front of them. They finally disappeared from view, consumed by the stupefying miasma that assailed them on all sides.

Paper, pixel and celluloid began to collide and coalesce into a unified approximation of reality. Ever since their helicopter had been brought down five days earlier, the group's progress had been followed with avid attention by a strange consortium of readers, gamers and viewers. Now, floating pontoons, carrying arc lights and camera crews, bobbed up and down uselessly on the flood tide. Gamers issued redundant instructions via a range of interactive devices. Artists and academics cursed the limitations of virtual research and derided the relevance of artificial historical observation. But it was all to no avail. The fog had erased everything.

TWENTY-FOUR

There are times when an English pub can lack the archetypal qualities so admired by foreign tourists. The central London bar that Sterland Morris and Robert Jamieson have entered is a good case in point. It's a desultory place, boasting an interior that's designed with the flair of a back-street chip shop, a typical drinking hole so devoid of atmosphere and architectural interest that it appears to have been designed to repel rather than attract custom. As they wait to be served they will be obliged to stand behind a bunch of over-opinionated media monkeys who are competing for the attention of the sole barman on duty.

Once served and settled in a corner of the pub, Morris lays out an overview of recent events as he updates Jamieson. It's been several months since the two friends have had a chance to discuss developments in the case. On one level, Morris' summary is a bewildering and complex account, involving the unsolved loss of military aircraft and the unaccountable disappearance of two young pilots, of a fabulous Roman treasure trove, of logic-defying archaeological artefacts, of time-bending coincidences and inconsistencies, of forks in the space-time continuum, of the unfathomable mysteries of the first and second laws of thermodynamics. But on another, more intimate, level, it is a simple story, a record of a middle-aged man's grief at losing his adoptive daughter, and of how he has attempted to come to terms with it.

Jamieson sits and listens without interrupting Morris. He is enraptured, lost in the labyrinth of his friend's story-telling eloquence, mesmerised by the perfect complexity of the conception he is outlining with such conviction. Morris is able to make the co-existence of past, present and future appear as a beguiling, even rational, proposition.

"But how do you explain what's going on?" Jamieson asks, as he tries to piece together this elaborate puzzle. "We only experience time moving in one direction, don't we? That's obvious isn't it?"

"Yes we do - or at least we think we do - but as I get older, I increasingly find myself in sympathy with St Augustine when I'm trying to make sense of the concept of time. He lived in Algeria a hundred years after the events in Aballava, so he was more or less a contemporary of those African auxiliaries serving there. When St Augustine posed the question "What is time?" he said "If no one asks me, I know what it is," but then, paradoxically, he went on to say "However, if I wish to explain it to him who asks, I do not know." And that, I would suggest, is a universal challenge familiar to all of us. It's only when no one asks us what time is that we know with any certainty what it is."

Jamieson nods. "I accept that's true for us mere mortals," he agrees, "but physicists can explain what time is and how it works. Einstein and Hawking and Newton – scientists like them understand it because it's a basic law of nature. It behaves predictably. It's common sense, isn't it?"

"Well, you'd be forgiven for thinking so, but I'm not entirely convinced that even physicists agree that 'sense' has anything to do with it. Einstein, himself, wrote that the distinction between past, present and future is only a stubborn, persistent illusion. There are many contradictions that lie at the heart of physics and our understanding of universal laws. Take the first law of thermodynamics, which makes no distinction between past and future and views time as being symmetrical – in other words able to extend backwards as well as forwards. That view of time is then flatly overwritten by the second law of thermodynamics which supports the notion of time being like an arrow which is uni-directional or asymmetrical."

"You mean that time can only extend in one direction, and that's forward?"

"Yes, that's right: straight forward, in the manner that we always appear to experience it. Scientific contradictions exist in the same way that philosophical views are divided about time. I tend towards the view that the 'here and now' is a purely subjective notion, 'now' simply being determined by where each individual's viewpoint is located in a temporal matrix, in much the same way that 'where' we are is subjectively determined by whether we are 'here' or 'there', which are terms that have no objective meaning in a spatial context."

"So when I say I'm 'here', it's a different 'here' from the one you're experiencing – I understand that. But how can my 'now' be a different 'now' from yours?"

"We can both be in different places at the same time and we can both be in different places at different times – it's all a question of perception. A third person seeing us sitting here together might perceive that we are simply in the same place at the same time, but, as I've just demonstrated, that might completely conflict with our own experience. Maybe we just simply exist in a series of 'nows' with each individual moment existing in its own right."

"So does that explain what's happened to Sands and Birch and their helicopter? And how they ended up in another 'now' as they experienced it, rather than the 'now' as we are experiencing it?"

"It may do," replies Morris. "At least, it begins to offer some kind of possible solution. It opens the door to a many-worlds interpretation of time, one which postulates that all possible alternative histories and futures are real, that reality is a many-branched tree, that everything that could possibly have happened in our past, but didn't, has occurred somewhere else and at some other time."

"But I thought alternative universes weren't supposed to coincide and interact with each other? That's the one thing I have real difficulty reconciling."

Morris nods his head in empathy. "On a theoretical level, I think you're right. And I have exactly the same qualms. It's the one feature of all this that I still can't rationalize."

Jamieson is quick to pick up on this hesitancy. "That and the fact that Sands and Birch must have re-enacted, or repeated, or re-visualised past events as 'now' events. Is that how we should view what's happened here?"

"Possibly."

Jamieson decides to push him further. "So, you think that they relived events from some many-world universe, in which their options were constrained by circumstances over which they had no control?"

"But it is a world of which they must have had a growing awareness. That's an important distinction."

"So, what's the way forward?"

Morris clears his throat and starts to pick up the narrative once more. He stares at the floor as he speaks. "The truth is that I've found it almost impossible to focus on my work at the museum, so I've resigned my post."

"You haven't."

"Several months ago."

"You've given up your job?"

"I was already beginning to follow up other lines of enquiry, and this has turned into something of an obsessive preoccupation."

"Well, that's an upshot I can have some sympathy with."

"To the extent that it has taken over my life? Not to put too fine a point on it, Robert, finding out what's happened to Kal has become my own personal quest; it's probably best that you're under no illusions about this. Multiple official investigations have produced nothing, absolutely no credible explanation as to what had happened to the Lynx and its two pilots. And they never will. I'm absolutely convinced of that."

"So to get back to the historical evidence, can you be sure that Sands and Birch ever got further afield than Aballava?"

There's a moment of complete silence.

"I've tracked them to Galloway," Morris replies.

"You what? Oh, come on, you've got to be pulling my leg."

"They left a calling card in amongst a bunch of other artefacts dug up around Barsalloch fort."

Morris puts his right hand into his jacket pocket and holds up a familiar object for Jamieson to examine. He is not disappointed by the response it evokes in his friend

"Good Lord! It's the crest, the same badge that Sands was wearing. How did it get there? I mean, I thought you said it was found in the Burgh by Sands hoard".

"It was. But this is the second badge, don't you see? They had one each."

"Of course they did! So is this your proof that they may have made it across the Solway to Galloway?"

"Exactly. It suggests they may not have been simply lost in the tidal mudflats or murdered by the Romans. There's evidence here that they made it north."

"So what do we do now?"

"We have to expand the parameters of the area covered by my enquiries. There's no other choice open to us."

"But that means creating a whole new area of investigation, doesn't it? How are you going to manage that, Sterland?"

"I'm told that computer modeling and mapping's the way to go. With the proper application of research, prior knowledge and informed conjecture we could even model the likely outcomes in the form of an interactive computer narrative."

"Good Lord, Sterland. You mean you might explore their possible fate as if they were characters in a computer game?"

"It's conceivable, but it would have to be in the form of a serious historical investigation, not as a sensationalised game. Potentially, this could become a large-scale, long-term academic and commercial project. I've been looking to acquire some sympathetic investors."

Jamieson takes the hint. "I'd be prepared to invest time and effort - but not money, Sterland, if that's what you're after."

"That's kind, Robert, but it's not really hard cash that I require from you."

"I hope you haven't sunk a considerable amount of your own estate in the venture, have you?"

"Just a bit for seed-corn investment. No, the really significant investment to date has been pretty much donated for free.

Some of my ex-colleagues, academics and professionals who were forcibly retired early and thrown on the scrap-heap, they're the ones who're volunteering to contribute meaningful amounts of time to the development work and background research. They're what'll make all the difference to this project, that's indisputable. So far, I've got a team of twenty on board. I've also managed to rope in a couple of retired programmers and they've recruited a games designer and a bunch of enthusiastic young testers to come on board at a later date. But, yes, I simply have to find a way to finance the technical research and development side. To quote the parlance, we need to open up some revenue streams."

"What revenue streams?"

"There's no other way. We have to exploit the economic potential of the controversies surrounding the case."

"But how?"

"I'm thinking about getting a book out first to contextualise the events properly. I'm very keen on emphasising the specific historical hypotheses that have underpinned the case. There's been too much wild speculation and conjecture surrounding the Solway Firth incident to date."

"What kind of book? Do you mean some kind of philosophical or historical treatise?"

"No, Robert, that'll be too dry to sell. I had more in mind a form of documentary novel. I've been thinking of calling it 'Pax Britannica'; that'd give it a sort of post-modern ironic slant. It'd recount as accurately as possible the events of the past year, but in dramatic form, and with added conjectural elements and a compelling narrative thrown up by the computer modeling. We've started to make great strides."

"Hang on, Sterland, just rewind a second," Robert interrupts. He surveys the glowing expression on his friend's face. "The last year? So, do you mean we'll feature in it, then?"

"With your permission, of course."

"Are you serious, Sterland? Are you really intending for us to appear as protagonists in this book?"

"Your contributions will be documented accurately in the

book, yes," Morris confirms, "along with the events that have taken place in a wider context. Things have been moving on apace. But this is a long-term project. I'm thinking ten or fifteen years ahead"

"You mean that even this conversation might feature?"

"In all likelihood, yes. It's all being recorded for posterity."

"Good Lord, I can't believe what I'm hearing. Can *you* believe what you're saying? This is ridiculous. Are you really recording everything? I'd better start watching what I say."

"But I want your involvement to go even further than that in the future," Morris continues. He senses his colleague's growing absorption in the narrative he's been developing. He will have to keep the momentum going before Jamieson has time to reconsider his proposal.

"Like what?

"I'd like you to join the team for the next phase of the research development. You've proved that you've got an instinctive grasp for the nuances of Sands' and Birch's motivations. You possess an experience and insight that's unique. It's something that I'm desperately lacking."

"That's because you don't suffer fools gladly," Jamieson retorts. "You said it yourself."

"You see what I'm saying, don't you? You could make a really significant input in the future. With you on board, we'd have a fighting chance of exposing the real fate of Birch and Sands to the world."

"So what's the immediate plan, Sterland?" Jamieson asks, unable to disguise his mounting enthusiasm.

"We head north. You interested?"

"Good Lord, yes. What on earth made you think I'd say no? When do we get started?"

"Seven thirty tomorrow morning," Morris replies, without missing a beat. "You're heading home. We're on the first train back to Carlisle from King's Cross. We'll pick up your tickets at the station. So phone your wife, pack some walking boots and don't be late. We've got a lot to do."

TWENTY-FIVE

At dawn, large numbers of Roman auxiliaries started sweeping the southern shoreline of the Solway. It was a brilliant autumn morning, cloudless and cold. The harsh early rays of the sun reflected off the soldiers' polished armour with shattering brilliance. As the men squinted cross the Firth towards the northern shore, lines of miniscule objects could be detected moving in ordered ranks. These were cavalry, pressed into service just before dawn, and ridden hard across the ford that lay a mile and a half below the fort of Aballava. Like their comrades searching along the southern mudflats and dunes across the water, they'd arrived too late to intercept their prey. The mud and tide had already done their job for them; now it was simply a question of waiting for the Firth to uncover and return their enemies' bodies.

Julius Rufinus and Caeluibianus had survived, however. They, at least, had been able to provide a partial account of the barbarians' attempt to evade capture: the plunge into the freezing darkness of the Solway; the mournful cries of distress as the racing tides hurried them to their deaths. All of them, seven men plus one young woman, had been drowned out there, somewhere in the treacherous vastness of the mudflats. It had been a predictable act of group martyrdom, mass suicide, not untypical of enemies who rightly feared the full weight of Roman vengeance. This, at least, was the version promulgated by the two Roman commanders. Any prospect that their captors might have survived and escaped was more than they were prepared to countenance.

While the Roman soldiers conducted this fruitless and desultory manhunt, seven British soldiers were marching to safety and freedom. For the most part, they hugged the shoreline, feeding off shellfish and line-caught salmon. Talorc, their native guide, was a member of the Novantae tribe. He had an incentive in avoiding the local Selgovae clansmen wherever possible. His regional knowledge would be instrumental in delivering his new-found comrades from the hands of the pursuing Romans. His intentions soon became clear: he planned to lead the group back to the security offered by his own village, a fortified settlement built on a promontory overlooking the sea, five days hard walk away.

During the first twenty-four hours, Talorc's ingenuity was critical in helping his group evade the Roman patrols. On the first night, when they'd stumbled ashore, half-dead with fright and cold, he'd helped them construct elaborate seaweed camouflage outfits so that the small group could remain invisible in the harsh morning light.

Towards the end of their second day, under Talorc's guidance, the group made the first of four major river crossings. To do so, they'd had to complete a five mile detour inland along the edge of a long, wide estuary before locating a primitive crossing point. From this point on, progress was made more quickly as the group proceeded overland. The more miles they were able to put between themselves and Roman civilisation, and the closer they could get to Talorc's tribal homeland, the more relaxed and less watchful they could become. And with this decreased need for vigilance would grow a greater awareness and appreciation of the daily wonders that crossed their paths.

At the end of the third day their route brought them past the remains of an old Roman marching camp. It had been deserted a century earlier when the imperial power had finally decided to withdraw behind the safety of Hadrian's Wall. The next morning they were able to take advantage of a ten mile stretch of old Roman military road that seemed to surface out of nowhere. It traversed one major river and brought them right to the banks of another before promptly vanishing as unexpectedly as it had appeared. Unlike his comrades, Talorc was not downcast at the disappearance of the road. For him this moment represented something enormously significant, the demarcation point that separated the tribal territories of the Selgovae and his own people, the Novantae.

From this point on, the journey to Talorc's village assumed the ritualised significance of a latter-day pilgrimage. And the sights that greeted the British soldiers grew ever more stupendous with each passing mile. From neolithic chambered cairns to giant prehistoric standing stones, the landscape was littered with reminders of the ancient history of this territory.

Late on the evening of the fourth day, Talorc made a short detour to pay his respects at a magnificent stone circle, a site of great religious and memorial significance for his people. Lying within a circle of twenty granite boulders, each at least as high as a man, stood three larger stones placed in a line. The site represented the burial place of Galdus, a local chief who had been killed in battle by the Romans ten generations before. The atmosphere of the site was deeply affecting - myth, legend or truth, it scarcely mattered. All those present felt a common bond with this iron-age warrior. Each individual was united in enmity towards the foreign colonisers who had brought death to Talorc's people and threatened the destruction of their ancient traditions and way of life.

The following day brought another magical discovery, and it was one that would have reached across five thousand years. Here they found a series of beautiful rock engravings, countless numbers of perfect concentric rings carved with clear purpose on giant granite boulders by the earliest inhabitants of this dreamlike landscape. These inscriptions couldn't help but send out a powerful message to the troop of modern day soldiers. It was a communication devoid of rational meaning but open to individual translation and divination. Then as now, each person drew their own inspiration from this unassailable proof of mankind's need to communicate on an abstract level. Who were they speaking to, these ancient forbears? Were they addressing the past, the present or the future inhabitants of their universe? Or, did such distinctions not exist in their cosmos?

And then, after a further two hours marching, they approached the penultimate stop on their long journey. By this point, Talorc had succeeded in bringing them to within five miles of their final destination. Now they were standing on the slopes of a hill. Above them stood a large fortified homestead that was surrounded by a ditch, five metres deep, around which huge banks of soil had been piled. Along the inside of the ditch ran a continuous wooden defensive palisade comprised of ten-foot-high, sharpened tree trunks that had been driven deeply into the earthworks.

From the existing archeological evidence it's not hard to picture the backdrop as the group approached this homestead eighteen hundred years ago. Talorc shouted loudly to alert the inhabitants of the soldiers' approach, his warnings duly followed by a flurry of activity inside the camp. The gate was then flung open wide and a number of adults, young children and dogs tumbled out, eager to greet the returning Novantae tribesman. A lengthy and affectionate welcome then ensued, during which time his British companions stood by and observed the reunion with immense gratification. Eventually, Talorc was in a position to effect some ribald introductions, involving what appeared to be the head man of the village and his wife, and the entire party was then ushered in through the main gate in a spirit of genuine hospitality.

The interior of the settlement contained four windowless circular houses. Each was approximately fifteen metres in diameter and possessed a low doorway through which the soldiers had to stoop to enter. All four houses were topped with an impressive conical turfed roof that reached to a height of ten metres at its apex. Around the edge of the enclosure were pens for livestock as well as various pits containing bones, incinerating rubbish and waste, all of which contributed to the overpowering smell of burning wood and animal dung. The site appeared well-ordered and neat.

The British soldiers felt immediately at home in this raucous family environment. To all intents and purposes this would be the first time that most of them had slept under a proper roof for nearly a month, and the only occasion on which they'd experienced a properly cooked, substantial meal. They were all treated with respect and consideration by the inhabitants of the homestead, many of whom were Talorc's relatives. At that moment, it's not difficult to imagine how enticing the prospect of a warm fire, a comfortable bed, a solid roof and as much freshly cooked meat as they could consume, must have felt to them all. And, most importantly of all, they would once again have been reminded of how good it feels to be in a safe and secure environment.

The celebrations were enhanced by the consumption of prodigious amounts of the local barley-based beer. This ale appeared dark and cloudy and possessed an unusually smoky, sour taste, but, without exception, the troops quickly developed an appetite for its intoxicating qualities. They drank until they could drink no more, and then all fell unconscious onto their soft beds and under their rough woollen blankets. And as they slept long into the next day, it's hard to imagine that they didn't all share the same wonderful dreamlike sensation that would have warmed them every bit as much as the peat fires that smouldered nearby. During that endless sleep, they tapped into a distant folk-memory, and it was a singular vision that would recur and sustain them through the trials that were to come. This is how good it feels to be free.

And something else would become clearer with each passing day. Sands and company, despite being thrown back into the deepest recesses of time, were no more the playthings of history than Morris or Jamieson were. Both groups would be forced to exist and operate within the same narrow constraints as each other, but who would exercise the greater influence over whom? As the two older men galloped north, they might have felt that they were laying down the groundwork for the future, but, in reality, they would simply be pursuing the past, and desperately failing to keep pace with it. But follow in their footsteps they would, mile for mile, and step by step. Most of the journey would be covered by car, of course, and would include detours that would have been unknown to Talorc. Principal among these, almost inevitably, would have been a pilgrimage to Dundrennan firing range, located ten miles to the south of the deserted Roman camp where the soldiers had bivouacked on the third night.

Their penultimate stop was Stranraer, a ferry port located in the far west of Galloway on an isthmus on the edge of Loch Ryan. This town held two distinct fascinations for Sterland Morris, fascinations that he would want, most certainly, to share with his companion.

Firstly, an examination of *Ptolemy's Geography*, dating from the second century, would have indicated that Stranraer was the likely location of the old Celtic settlement, Rerigonium.

Morris had to spell out the significance of this fact in case it was lost on Jamieson. "It's not too much of a stretch to imagine the meaning of Rerigonium as being something along the lines of 'The Place of the King'. We know that the ancient name of Loch Ryan is Rerigonius Sinus, or the 'Bay of Rerigonium'. So if the royal seat of the King of the Novantae was here, then it's almost inevitable that Sands and Birch would have had to come here to pay court."

"Assuming that they did make it here, do you think that this could have been the end of the road for them?" Jamieson queried. "There's only the sea going on out there, and it's going on and on for ever and ever. It feels like the end of the world to me. God knows what it felt like to them." Such comments were addressed to no one in particular, and generated no response from his companion, beyond a wistful, thoughtful silence that seemed as endless as the horizon.

In the afternoon, Morris took his colleague to a temporary exhibition at Stranraer Museum. The stand-out exhibit was a small but exquisite bronze statuette of the god Mercury, which normally resided in the National Museum of Scotland in Edinburgh. It was an object of great significance to Morris.

"This was the sign that that led me to the Barsalloch fort. It pointed the way, you might say."

"It's extremely beautiful. Where does it come from? I feel like I've seen it before."

"I very much doubt it, Robert. It's a pretty obscure object. You'd be hard-pressed to find a photograph of it online."

"So, come on, then, where does it come from? It's got to be Roman, obviously."

"It's Roman, but beyond that, I can't tell you where it comes from. I can, however, tell you where it was found. It was discovered in the 1860s, a couple of miles inland from Barsalloch. Do you remember where we saw the Cup and Ring rock carvings this morning?" he asked, referring to the sight which so enchanted Sands and her company. "It was found buried at that same location."

"My word, it's in good condition."

"Yes, it was obviously a highly-prized object. It was well looked after by its owners."

"But what's he supposed to be holding in his left hand? It looks as though there used to be something there."

"Yes, it was probably a *caduceus*. It was a short staff entwined by two serpents, a symbolic object usually carried by Mercury. It was generally thought to represent commerce, trade and negotiation, that sort of association."

"So what happened to this *caduceus*?"

"No idea. It's always puzzled me. It could simply have got lost or destroyed, but that seems unlikely given the excellent condition of the statuette itself. There might well be some significance behind why it's missing, but I'm damned if I can say what it is."

"But why do you think it might be significant?"

"Because of where it was buried. The location's like a 5000 year-old granite notice board. It's a neolithic library. You must have noticed. If you've got something you want to say to future generations, that's where you'd go to deposit your mark. Kal would have realised that, just as you did, I bet."

"Yes, it's an amazing place. But what's the significance of the statue of Mercury?"

"He's the messenger, the messenger of the gods. But in this case, I believe the medium really is the message. I think Kal used him as a pointer to steer us in the right direction. It just happened to take one hundred and fifty years from the moment it was dug up for someone to make the connection."

"So what led you from the statue to the fort?"

"It was through a process of elimination. Mid-Victorian amateur archaeologists were pretty haphazard in their recording procedures. There was no record of the statue's alignment when it was excavated, so I had to look for other clues. The obvious starting point was the nearest iron-age settlement, the one just down the road on Barsalloch promontory. Uniquely among these types of forts, it had never been excavated. I put two and two together."

"So that's where you suspect they ended up. Are we going to get to see this place? I'd love to see it."

The next day, their arrival at Barsalloch Point neatly coincided with that of Sands and her crew. However, by the dawn of the twenty-first century the effects of erosion and modern farming methods guaranteed a very different approach to the fort than would have been made two thousand years earlier.

Morris and Jamieson started at the southern end of a magnificent curving bay that was comprised of boulder fields and a sandy beach sitting below a backdrop of bracken-covered cliffs. They followed the arc of this natural amphitheatre for two miles and were enthralled by the multitude of sounds, smells and sights that assaulted their senses. The combination of brilliant blue sea, high, scudding clouds and ecstatic wind made this a breathtaking hike, and it was one the two men approached with mounting anticipation.

Once they'd arrived at Barsalloch Point, the reasons for this sense of expectancy would soon become clear to Jamieson. Up there, one hundred feet above them, sat the remains of the fort in a spectacularly dramatic location. It was waiting to be approached from the seaward side by a rickety set of wooden steps.

Eighteen hundred years ago, this was the site of Talorc's homestead. And, unlike today, the sea cliffs would not have provided a means of access to the fortified settlement, but, rather, a secure barrier, which would have been both unassailable and unscalable. In those times, due to its unique position on the tip of the headland above Barsalloch Point, defensive ditches and ramparts would only have been required on three sides. And on a fine day, looking out to sea, an individual, then as now, would have been blessed with an uninterrupted view across the water to the hills of Antrim and the Mountains of Mourne in Northern Ireland.

Even in Roman times, this would have been a magnificent landscape for raising cattle and for arable farming. It was one that the British soldiers had instantly taken to their hearts. And, very quickly, they had got the measure of their hosts' economic situation. Easy access to the sea, combined with the lack of serviceable tracks, meant that if cattle were to be traded with the Romans then they would best be transported by boat. And cattle traders were precisely what Talorc and his ancestors had been for many generations. However, it was clear by now that old traditions were going to have to change.

As the days passed in a dream, the soldiers continued their acclimatisation. They contributed their hunting and fishing skills to offset the heavy strain that they placed on their hosts' capacity to feed them. Centuries later, Morris and Jamieson argued about what these days might have been like for Birch and Sands. Often Morris simply refused to engage in idle speculation and was happy to leave such parochial concerns to his colleague. However, shortly after Talorc's return to his homestead, circumstantial evidence pointed to the likelihood of a strange ceremony having been enacted, and it was one of great interest to the ageing historian.

By now, Sands would have been officially recognised as spokesperson for the British soldiers, and, as such, was nominated to take part in any gathering of the tribal elders. On this particular occasion, Talorc had made it clear that important matters were to be discussed that would affect them all. He'd also instructed that only Sands could attend.

On the day in question, Sands was accompanied by Talorc and a group of older men to a nearby fortified settlement. As the elders arrived in small groups, it was growing clear that this was to be a convocation of several dozen members from across the district.

For the first two hours Sands was entertained by the womenfolk. The men, meanwhile, met in privacy in a large circular lodge at the rear of the compound. On being ushered into the meeting, Sands felt overwhelmed by the intensity of the atmosphere that greeted her. The cavernous space was lit by a single light source, the central fire, around which the elders all sat, facing her in a semi-circle. She was motioned to sit in front of them with her back to the door. The silence was broken by an elderly man who Sands assumed was the tribal leader. He spoke indistinctly and at length and in a language that was incomprehensible to the young woman. She looked at him carefully, studying his gestures and intonation to try and divine some meaning from his actions. Occasionally she glanced at other individual members of the council, hoping to find reassurance in a friendly smile or nod. But no such gestures were forthcoming. Everyone was inscrutable, particularly Talorc. Sands had to deal with a hostile and threatening atmosphere.

Suddenly the old man finished speaking, and then motioned to Talorc to translate.

"My people are happy to offer you hospitality. But your arrival in our midst also coincides with a great sadness that some elders feel you share responsibility for. Many have expressed their anger here today."

"Why, Talorc? What have we done?"

"You are to blame for the death of the two boatmen who were captured with me. We were delivering cattle by sea at the same time that you killed the Roman officer on the beach. Your actions visited disaster on us. We paid for your folly with the loss of our two kinsmen."

"We had no choice. They attacked us. We had to defend ourselves."

"Maybe, but it was my clansmen who paid with their lives. Now there are two widows and seven children without fathers to provide for them. The fathers of these two dead men are here today. They seek compensation for their loss."

"What kind of compensation?"

"You must replace the boat that was lost. And you must provide replacements for the two husbands who were killed. Rattigan is like my brother. He will be one. You can choose the other between you."

It was apparent that Talorc spoke with the full authority of the tribal council. "If you do these things, and if our King decrees it, then you will be accepted as members of the Novantae tribe."

"And if we don't?"

"You have no choice. We're doing you a great honour. This is not a request. You have an obligation to my people. When you fulfill it, you will all be free to go wherever you wish. If you prefer to live with us you will become like a sister to me. And in due course we may decide to select a suitable husband for you. But all that lies in the future. A Novantae tribesman may not be prepared to accept you for his wife."

It's not hard to envisage the effect that all this had on Sands. Her head started to swim. The smoke and humidity in the lodge combined to increase her sense of nausea. She knew that she was in no position to make any kind of decision. But she was also aware that she had no option other than to accept the terms on offer. Once agreement was reached, the atmosphere in the room lightened. Smiles and a spirit of fellowship replaced the grim reception accorded to Sands only minutes before. But before the meeting broke up, she was witness to a mystifying ritual. A small bronze statue of a Roman god was produced, various prayers were intoned and a small piece from the object dropped with great deliberation into the fire.

"This is how we mark the death of our two clansmen. Today we have no bodies to bury. By this act we have broken all trading contacts with the Romans who killed them."

Sands recognized the significance of the ceremony. She pulled Talorc to one side and spoke to him about something that was puzzling her. In place of the missing bodies of the murdered Novantae, why could they not bury the statue of the Roman god, Mercury? That would guarantee that there was a permanent reminder in the soil for future generations to mark the loss of these two men.

Talorc listened with care. Despite everything, by now he had developed a deep trust in her judgement. "We have worshipped the gods of the Romans since the death of Galdus, primarily to please the Romans. Most of us want to return to our old gods who we've never forgotten. The gods of Rome have offered us no protection."

"Look, Talorc, one day, when we are long dead, a holy man will travel here from Hibernia with news of the one new god who will soon replace all of the old Roman gods. Once they are gone, nobody will miss them, not even the Romans. And your people will be honoured for being the first converts in your country to this new god."

"How do you know this?"

"Because there is already talk of this new god in Rome. The Roman gods are false. You know that already. It's time to bury them."

How would a man in Talorc's position respond to such inducements? Would he have sat down and pondered deeply for a few minutes? Would he simply usher Sands away? She observed him as he tussled with this new-found revelation, and she quickly realised that she'd found a ready ally in this anguished tribesman. Watching him, it became apparent to her why the souls of Talorc's clansmen would prove such fertile soil for St Ninian and his followers during the subsequent century. It was not a reflection that Sands found altogether uplifting. And she wasn't at all sure why. "Into your hands I entrust my spirit," she found herself saying. Suddenly she became aware that she was facing the prospect of her own mortality head-on for the first time.

She looked at Talorc once again. It occurred to her that she would have exchanged places with him at that moment. Knowing what the future held in store was a curse. And it would only be fair that Talorc should be spared the torment of experiencing it for himself. But if he was to be effectively quarantined, she'd have to remember to be a lot more circumspect in future.

The burial of the statue took place that afternoon. The wind had got up and the weather was closing in for the first time in several days. The chosen location was the same one suggested to Talorc by Sands. It was the obvious place. She was accorded the honour of positioning the object in its shallow grave, and next to it was placed personal objects belonging to the two dead tribesmen. Reflecting on the event, later in life, Sands was able to acknowledge that this ceremony probably held more long-term significance for her than it did for the Novantae elders who'd been huddling alongside her at the graveside.

As she stood there, watching the hole in the ground being filled, she visualised a day, a special day, at some point far in the future, when this bronze statuette would be excavated by an unknown hand, and a part of her would live again through its discovery. She allowed herself the indulgence of picturing her parents staring at the object in some dusty museum, newly in love and long before her conception, and somehow touched by its mysterious allure. She would find great resonance in this prospect, no matter how fanciful or distant it seemed. Time had already demonstrated to her that it contained a reassuringly flexible property, and, after all, even bungee jumpers reach a point when, at the bottom of their fall, gravitational energy converts into elastic energy and they begin to ascend once again.

And finally, apart from her need to leave a mark in the soil for future generations to uncover, there was another, more immediate imperative driving Sands. There was something else that was unsettling her. It was something she couldn't quite define. Maybe it was provoked by a reflex as mundane as the instinct to survive. But she sensed that she'd have to leave this place. She was feeling trapped, suffocated.

It was plain, however, that her impulse to depart was not shared by the majority of her comrades. Stogdon, of all people, might suddenly find the prospect of paternal responsibilities to be to his liking. Sands would not be alone in suspecting that what might really attract him to the role of spouse was the prospect of a hard-working, submissive wife who'd service his every need, both domestic and carnal: "Yeah, I'll chuck my hat in the ring, if no one else fancies it," he'd offer crudely. Rattigan would be a different kettle of fish, however. He felt manipulated by Sands. She'd gone behind his back. Resentful he may be, but he would still be dutiful enough to fulfil his heavy obligation to his friend, Talorc. As far as Sands was concerned, whatever these men chose to do in the future would be up to them. They would be closely bonded and would stick together anyway, come what may. But she felt differently. She would make her own choices. She'd make them alone, if necessary, but, preferably she'd accept the support of those – and, God knows, there may not be any - who were still prepared to offer her fellowship.

Tempus Fugit! Time was fleeing, and with it would go Sands, inevitably and inexorably. She would remain a victim of gravity, like all those who cast their fate to the stars, tumbling and plummeting along an uncertain trajectory, unable to predict or control her ultimate course.

In the same way that the presence of air resistance distorts the shape of a parabola, so Sands' fate would be warped by vagaries in the law that dictates that time is a universal absolute. She would be subject to the same swirling tides as Birch, Morris, Jamieson and the others. They would all find themselves washed up by multiple waves along an endless conceptual shoreline, cascading on top of each other, and finally coming to rest, heaped together like shells, in a single dimensionless pile.

26588341R00125

Printed in Great Britain
by Amazon